ASHES OF THE SEA

Samantha Seestrom

Enjoy the adventure!

– S. Seestrom

1/18

DEDICATION

Taylor. Thank you for being the absolute best sister ever. I'm
sorry I've ruined every single plot twist for you, but I'm so happy
you allow me to spoil everything in order for me to discuss the
voices in my head. You're my bestie for the restie.

Acknowledgments

Mom. You've always supported my life decisions. I can't stress how thankful I am to have a mom like you. Thank you for supporting my writing dreams, paying for classes, and helping me publish my books. I love you.

Dad. I'm so proud of you. I'm so happy to be able to call you my dad. Thank you for all of your support along with financial help…and mermaid jokes. I love you.

Grandma and Grandpa Hozempa. Grandma and Grandpa Seestrom. All of you have shown me such love when it comes to my passion! All of you have invested time…and money (which I'm extremely thankful) into my writing. Each one of you has read my work and given me such amazing feedback. I love all of you so much. Thanks for being the coolest grandparents.

My family. Zach, James, Mike, Jarrod, Jodi, Dede. You've all been huge supporters and I can't thank you all enough! David and Susie—Thank you for making a special trip to Edisto Island just for me along with collecting shells from the beach.

Dylan. Thank you for encouraging me to write so you can play video games. I also love you very much for reading a book about mermaids.

Sophie. Thank you for being my best friend. Thank you for putting up with me for the past seventeen years. Thank you for listening to my many novel ideas and always giving me your opinions. You mean the world to me.

Alicia. You were the first person to read this novel. I'm very thankful for all your feedback! Thank you for being my #1 fan.

Kelsey. You better catch up. I'm on book #2 already. I love you, girl! Thank you for always being so supportive. You're one of the best friends a girl could ask for.

Jennifer. You've always given me unconditional love and support since the day I met you. I'm truly grateful to have another mother like you.

Laura. I love you. Thank you for always being such a great friend and for always being someone I can confide in.

Vicki. HAPPY BIRTHDAY! This is my present to you. When I'm a best-selling author I'll be able to afford something other than a shout-out.

Ali. You've always encouraged me to dream big and I love you for it.

Rathbone. I'm still so completely thrilled you shared my book with your students! I'm so appreciative of all your support. Much love!

Russell. As I sit here writing these acknowledgments and reflect upon my past, I'm still awestruck by the fact I had the confidence to finish a story. Seven years ago I took your class. Seven years ago I was inspired. Continue to motivate your students! Thank you for the support.

My fan club. Rachael, Clayton, Patrick, Aleshia, Shelbi, Tija, Traci, Amy, Mary, Linda, Melissa, Kris, Sharalyn, Amanda, Kristen, Jill, Stephanie, Sarah M., Sarah G., Kimberly, Jennifer B., Shari, Sandy, Alicen, Cortney, Chrissy, Jess, Jamie, Cindy, Reagan, Alli. I want to thank all of you individually for different reasons, but then I'd write another novel. I can't express my unconditional appreciation for each and every one of you. I'm so thankful for all of the support I receive each day.

Shaela. You're the reason my readers can judge my book by its cover. You're phenomenal.

Leigh Anne Lane, Kathy Wheeler, and Christine Husom. Whether it be editing, formatting, or just giving me advice during a time of writer's block, each one of you has been a life saver! Leigh, I honestly can't thank you enough for being my mentor.

YOU. My readers are the most important people to thank. YOU chose to read my book. YOU are the reason I write. YOU inspire me to keep dreaming.

Chapter One

[MARINA]

BLOOD FILLS MY MOUTH. A stinging sensation electrifies my body. My vision is impaired. I blink, but see only flashes of light. The ringing in my ears drowns out everything but the sound of rushing water. I'm pinned in the sand with a heaviness sinking down on me.

Against the threat of being crushed, I force myself to conjure enough power to surround myself with a force field. It's weak, but for now I won't be flattened. The mass weighing me down grows stronger the more I fight back against its power.

I begin to regain my sense of sight and audibility as I'm freed from the invisible wall. The light from the Surface is blinding as my vision clears. I'm so close to the human world. I could swim to the Surface and be free.

Pushing my barrier further out, I gain a bit of room between myself and the sandy bottom.

I'm stronger than this. I've been training for this attack.

Suddenly, the wall holding me down dissipates. With no force field choking me beneath its power, I slowly push myself from the ocean bottom. I know this fight is long from over. I can't determine from which direction it will assault me. I am unprepared.

In an instant I'm thrust backward, slicing through the water, and hitting the reef with such force it causes debris to drift freely. There's a dulling pain at the back of my head. I sink to the ocean floor with my head spinning and blood still dissipating from my inner lip.

I close my eyes momentarily, allowing my body to calm before I heal my battle wounds. Instantly, I feel rejuvenated.

Clearing my mind of everything, I focus on the target in front of me.

Emperor Flotsam Kenryk.

"You must conjure it from deep within your soul," explains my uncle Flotsam, better known as Sam, with an irritated growl.

"I'm trying!" I grumble at him with annoyance.

"Try harder," he demands.

Without warning, Sam thrusts his forces at me. I whip my tail and shoot around them with ease. I laugh at the emperor's attempts to strike me. I'm quick. He should at least acknowledge my swiftness.

Sam extends his arm straight out in front of him with his palm facing me. Around his fingertips grows a dim amber light as he conjures his powers from within his body. Slowly, a golden haze envelopes him. I watch, mesmerized while Sam deliberately pushes out a wall of energy until it has a two-foot perimeter around him.

This is the real test.

Sam wants me to break his force. For weeks, I've been

struggling to fight against his powers, but now... I must overthrow them. He's emperor—the most powerful being in all the oceans. Thanks to my grandfather Zale, I have the same power flowing through my veins. But, unlike Sam, I haven't learned the extent of my abilities yet.

Although I saved Sam one month ago from slavery, allowing him to take his place as Emperor, he still feels the need to force my powers out of their dormancy.

My aunt Cascade trusts my powers will arrive in full the more I practice. Sam has taken her advice to the next level and battles me every day, attempting to force my gifts to appear.

Maybe I'm not ready. Maybe I'll never be as powerful as Sam or my deceased grandfather. Maybe I'm not meant to fight.

I grow tired and feel more like a failure every day that my powers don't arrive.

"Sam, I know you're getting frustrated with me. I can't break through your power," I sadly admit. "You're the *emperor*. I'm only a princess with a small percentage of my abilities."

"Once you hold the control it'll be as easy as flicking your tail," he advises.

"Like my healing power," I chime in. "I know." I roll my eyes because I've only heard it a million times.

With no warning, Sam blasts me hard with a force field. I haven't had time to prepare. Sam has warned me to never let my guard down. I'm hit with such a crushing weight, my vision blurs. The emperor isn't afraid to bruise me up a bit to teach me a lesson. We both know I can handle it.

"Fight it," Sam orders with a growl from behind his force field. My sight is still blurry, but from what I can tell he wears a stern expression on his young face.

I thrust my palms against the quavering field. The energy surges through the field and tingles my fingers. Gathering all my strength, I shove against the emperor's strength. I stop his momentum for a mere few seconds before Sam overpowers me once again.

"You need to focus!" Sam stresses.

The reef behind me grows closer as Sam intensifies the force.

Conjuring up my protective field, I force it out inches from my body to protect against being crushed. My power is strong, but Sam continues to overpower me. My force field drags through the soft ocean bed, kicking up muck, as I'm pushed closer to the reef.

I push against the barrier. My body lights up with an amber glow as I conjure all the power within myself. I feel the energy surging around my hands as I begin to disrupt its exterior. Although I'm breaking through the force, it's still pushing me closer to the reef. When my field is pressed up against the rough coral I know I'm about to fail this test.

I force myself against the wall of power, but I'm still weaker than my uncle. I'm making very little progress and beginning to lose faith in myself.

But, giving up isn't an option. I'm a royal Kenryk. We aren't quitters.

I close my eyes and imagine myself breaking through the

field. Visualizing my hand breaking through the barrier and allowing myself in, I will myself to push harder. I envision myself becoming stronger. I remind myself of who I am.

I am Princess Marina Kenryk. Royal Kenryk blood flows through my veins while Zale's powers flow through my body. I've defeated a force stronger than me in the past and I can defeat a strength tougher than me now.

The tingling of the field crossing over my body is overpowering and makes every inch of my skin itch. I keep pushing until I thrust myself against something solid. I open my eyes to find Sam proudly smirking.

"I told you," he says with confidence. Around me is the force field. I broke through the wall of energy!

"How—" I begin, but am utterly speechless.

When Sam releases the field, the energy crosses over me and snaps back to him. I feel the tickling sensation once more before the amber essence disappears.

"You wouldn't really have crushed me...would you have?" I ask with a bit of uncertainty.

Pressing his lips in a firm line, he shrugs.

Sam faintly smiles. "I want you to try to create one," he informs me.

He wants me to create a force field? Sure, I can push a small barrier out from within me for my protection, but... can I create a large enough force to protect myself and others? No way!

I laugh. "Don't you think I've done enough for one day?"

"Marina, this is serious. These are gifts you need to know

how to use. Cordelia's gone, but there will be plenty more threats to come. That's the way it is when you're a leader."

I cross my arms. "I'm not like you! I'm not a leader," I debate.

"You're a royal. People will always look to you for guidance. Without you, Cordelia wouldn't have been defeated. You're more of a leader than I am."

"You can't mean that," I argue. "I don't know what I'm doing!"

"Do you think I have any idea? Before I was enslaved, I only followed my father's actions. I didn't have time to learn all the guidelines to being emperor. My father was taken too soon from us."

I cringe as I remember the moment Cordelia slit Zale's throat, forcing me to watch my grandfather die in front of me.

"The power is in you, Marina," Sam promises.

"I can't just snap my fingers and make a force field appear," I confess, casting my eyes to the ground.

"Marina Kenryk," he says, "do you know who you are?"

"You literally just said my name, so yeah," I sass.

"I don't think you do." Sam crosses his brawny arms across his vast chest.

I shrug. "What're you talking about?"

"You're the mermaid who broke the rules. You're the mermaid who saved a human from dying. You rebelled against the empress and destroyed her. You, Marina, are a storm to be reckoned with."

I flash a shy smile. "I guess I am pretty badass."

Sam taps my forehead gently. "You have everything you will ever need in here." He grabs my hand and turns it palm side up. "I want you to try something."

"What're you doing?"

"Close your eyes and focus." Resisting the urge to roll my eyes, I obey my emperor. "Imagine yourself guarded. No one can get in. You're in control."

As a royal, we mainly use force fields to protect ourselves and the ones around us. I'm not in danger. I can't visualize myself on lockdown.

Sam continues to speak, "Conjure the power."

My eyes fly open and Sam releases a defeated grunt. "You mean, if I had known about this power, I could've kept Cordelia out of my mind?" I ask with shock.

"Yes. But you couldn't have known," he explains with a sigh. Sam doesn't seem to appreciate his test being interrupted. "Marina, please." I close my eyes once again, attempting to focus. "Now, visualize yourself on lockdown."

The only thing I feel is my healing gift surface. I groan and open my eyes.

"You're not concentrating!" Sam's entire demeanor shifts from hopeful to irritated as he shouts.

I snap my hand away. "It's not as easy as flicking my damn tail, Sam!"

For a moment, Sam is silent. He seems to be attempting to compose himself. "You're excused for the day," he softly says.

Sam turns to swim toward his kingdom. I know he's under a lot of pressure, and I want to be able to help him—I do—but does he not realize I'm stressed out, too? I don't know how to be a royal or act like a princess or conjure powers within my body.

"That's it?" I ask with disbelief. "I give up, so you give up?"

"You need a break," Sam informs me, without turning to face me.

"I'm sorry," I tell him. "It's a lot of pressure—"

Sam whips around to face me, his golden irises burning with intensity. "Marina, I can't make you want this. If something happened to me, you'd be the one leading our society. You're the one with the royal powers. I have to prepare you for that."

"What if that's not what I want?" I ask.

A hint of sadness washes across Sam's face. "It's the life you were born to live."

"No, Sam, it wasn't. I was born into the hierarchy of Zale Kenryk, and then Cordelia stole his throne. I grew up with Empress Cordelia Anahi. I served her for seventeen years, and as pathetic as our relationship was, Cordelia was the only mother I had. I was raised in her realm, not yours."

He nods with a sorrowful glimmer in his amber gaze. "That may be true, but you released me. You live in my kingdom and you will live by my laws."

"I wanted everyone to have freedom. I didn't want to be a princess." With the last word being said, I swim above the emperor and begin my journey home. Sam flanks me for the entirety of the trip, but says nothing. It reminds me of the days when Sam was Cordelia's slave. He was mute and followed me everywhere due to the orders of the former empress.

When the kingdom comes into view, I can't help but gasp in awe of its beauty. It's twice the size of Cordelia's Caverns. Thousands upon thousands of golden lightning orbs drift in and around the kingdom illuminating the golden reefed structure with an amber glow. Reef towers jut from the sandy bottom with hallways and corridors connecting each and every tower. Guards are stationed at every entrance to the kingdom as well as the outside perimeter.

The Council renamed the kingdom residing within Mysteria, City of Zale. Sam wanted to dedicate the new castle of caverns to his father—my grandfather—who made the biggest sacrifice of all. He gave not only his powers but his life for me. I will honor him for as long as I live.

"Your Majesty," greets Jackson, my nineteen-year-old looking father, when we've made our way inside the monstrous castle.

"You really make him address you like that?" I question Sam. I'm bewildered, and honestly, quite bitter. In my opinion, my father has just as much right to the royal title as me.

"It's the proper title," Sam dismissively answers.

"He's my dad. He's family. He doesn't need to address us with any title," I scoff.

The emperor rolls his eyes. The sass in this family runs deep. "Jackson, any updates on my guest?"

"He arrived about an hour ago. Before you meet with him,

Wade Emerson has requested to speak with you. He's patiently waiting in your royal headquarters."

"Marina, I expect you in my caverns in ten minutes," Sam demands. "This is important."

Although I'm upset, I will respect my emperor. I nod before Sam swims off.

"You referred to me as your dad." Jackson looks delighted to be acknowledged as my father.

A smile forms on my lips. "I guess I did."

Jackson is used to the idea of me being his daughter since he served alongside Sam as a head collector for Cordelia for seventeen years. Me—I'm still warming up to the idea of my father being physically the same age as my best friend. Plus, there is the fact that I only found out he was my dad a month ago when I visited the Surface as an air-breather in order to kill a teenager whom I saved from drowning.

The former empress, Cordelia, thought I had betrayed her by saving the boy named Beck, and forced me into his human world. My mission was to kill Beck and collect his soul before the third sunset. I tried many times to end his life, but instead, fell overwhelmingly in love with the boy. There was no way I was capable of killing him, so I decided to sacrifice myself instead. I had accepted I would live my life as a pet in Cordelia's army of slaves, but when it came time for me to return to the ocean, something unexpected happened. Beck transformed instead of me. Cordelia claimed it was our kiss that changed his fate. My love was exchanged, altering the spell. He was claimed to the sea while I was left on land.

Prior to my birth, Cordelia had enslaved my entire family because of a deal my mother had made with her. My mom Oceane Kenryk—better known by her human name, Annie Hudson—wanted to become an air-breather and so Cordelia granted her a human form for three days. But to remain an air-breather, Annie had to charm a human to fall in love with her before the third sunset or she'd become Cordelia's property. My mother failed. Jackson hadn't fallen in love with her.

"You should start calling me that more often," Jackson suggests, breaking through my memories.

"Okay…Dad." Yep, still feels weird.

"How did today's training go?" Jackson asks with a serious curiosity.

I sigh. "I'm making progress, but not enough to satisfy Sam. He expects me to just flick my tail and shoot a force field out of my fins. That's not how it works. I can feel myself growing stronger, but I can't conjure it all at once."

"You'll get there. It just takes time," my dad assures.

"I'll be eighteen in a few months. My powers should be here in full by now."

"You're putting too much pressure on yourself. Sam may be the emperor, but he still loves you. He cares about you. Your uncle is under immense pressure right now and he only wants you by his side. You two are the only ones with the power. He's frustrated, but he understands."

"I'm trying. I really am."

"I believe you. Sam can see you're trying to learn." Jackson hugs me tightly, washing away most of my worries. "You better get to your meeting with Sam," Jackson warns.

"I will." I start to swim off but turn back toward my father. "Would you happen to know where I can find Caspian?"

"He's out on patrol until tomorrow. I'm sure he'd love to see you when he gets back."

I force a smile, but it's weak. "Maybe."

As I make my way to Sam's headquarters I think of the last time I saw Caspian. It was in a Council meeting about a week ago. He barely spoke to me. Our friendship has been rocky since I saved Beck. I miss my best friend.

I enter Sam's cavern quietly as to not disturb him. He and a fellow council member, Wade Emerson, look my way. "You wanted to speak with me?"

"There's someone I want you to meet," declares Wade with a silvery voice.

"Hello," a voice says from behind me. I turn and find a stranger hovering near the window.

I smile toward our guest, wondering which community this man is visiting us from…and how much power he holds.

"This is my beautiful niece, Marina," declares the emperor with a smile.

I'm mesmerized by the absolute perfection of the stranger. He looks to be in his early twenties with ivory skin that appears as though it was crafted from stone with precision. Every curve on his body is effortless. The visitor's abdominal muscles prove his strength. And I thought Caspian was god-like… This man makes my best friend look like a guppy. Dark, blonde hair frames his face. A mahogany tail with glints of gold match his stunning, dark gaze. The hints of gold give him the appearance of a royal. But as far as I know, I share no relation with this stranger.

The stranger closes the space between us, a smile hinting at his plush lips.

"Marina," he says, letting my name roll off his tongue with ease. "I've heard many great things about you." There's something strange about the way he speaks. It's an accent I've only heard once before… from Wade. This stranger is from the Australian Border.

My mouth moves to greet him a hello, but the words come out in a jumble. He laughs before saying, "My name is Aquarius."

I shake my head, attempting to clear my mind. "Um, hi. So nice to meet you," I tell Aquarius, extending my hand to greet him. He stares at my gesture with confusion and Sam lets out a short sigh.

Of course, shaking hands is an air-breather thing. Sam knows this and must be embarrassed by my act of stupidity. I learned the proper human exchange from the Hudson family when I briefly lived as an air-breather.

Before I can pull my hand away, Aquarius hesitantly takes my grip in his strong clasp. I return my hand to my side with a nervous giggle.

Stop acting like a child. I've been around attractive men in the past. I mean, Aquarius isn't that handsome.

"Wade's son is visiting us from the Australian Border," Sam informs me. "Wade has served as king of the Australian Border for many decades, but soon Prince Aquarius will come forward to take his place."

Aquarius is Wade's son? They show no resemblance to one another. I thought maybe they could be cousins, but father and son? Wade looks to be in his early-thirties but that means in water-breather time, I'm assuming, he's about sixty years old. With dark brown hair and blue eyes along with a cobalt scaled tail, this man shares no resemblance with his son. But what does that prove? I look nothing like my birth father. Maybe, like me, Aquarius takes after his mother.

With a shy smile, I admit to Sam, "I didn't know we were having company. Are we having some sort of celebration to honor City of Zale?"

"She doesn't know?" asks Aquarius. He seems stunned.

Wade clears his throat before turning to Sam for an answer.

Know what?

"I haven't quite gotten that far yet," answers Sam. My uncle grabs my hands, gingerly rubbing his thumbs over the backs of my wrists in an attempt to comfort me. "Marina, you have become one of my greatest assets. I've learned over the past weeks that I can't lose you. This is your home. This is where you belong, and I believe you need to start your life." Then Sam proudly smiles at me before saying, "Prince Aquarius has agreed to marry you."

I rip my arms from his grasp, outraged. I want to ask about

Beck, but know I shouldn't mutter his name with company around. I'm furious at the audacity my uncle is displaying. How could he think he could handpick a husband for me? "What? No, I won't marry someone just because it's an order!"

"Aquarius is set to rule the Australian waters. This particular merfolk community, beside the City of Zale, has one of the largest populations."

"Don't bore me with the facts. I don't care who he is," I protest. Sam scowls in response. "And I certainly don't care if he's future leader of the Australian Border."

I will not be treated like a child who can't make my own decisions.

I look to Wade and Aquarius. "I don't mean to be disrespectful. Wade, you were my grandfather's best friend and have kept an eye on me my entire life. I have respect for you, I do."

Wade remains silent at his son's side. Aquarius wears a stern expression across his godly-sculpted face. What is this man thinking?

"Marina, I understand how you may be shocked," Sam attempts to console me.

"Shocked? You've completely blindsided me. I'm a *princess*. I shouldn't be used to strengthen your personal gains."

"My son is a very honorable man," Wade says with a twinge of arrogance. "Many women back home would fight to the death for an opportunity to wed the prince."

Is that really supposed to persuade me?

"Father, enough." Aquarius seems upset. Did he know about this arrangement prior to today's meeting? He doesn't seem surprised.

"The Emerson family has remained loyal to our family throughout Cordelia's reign as Empress," interjects Sam. "They've always been our allies."

I cross my arms, outraged. "They can be allies without a marriage between our families."

"A marriage only strengthens an alliance," Aquarius adds.

Rolling my eyes at my new-found fiancé, I scoff, "That's hardly a reason to wed someone."

Aquarius smiles, causing little wrinkles to form near his eyes. "This may not be an ideal situation for you, but I would be honored to wed you."

I'm not really sure what I'm supposed to say right now. I want to scream. I want to yell at the emperor and refuse the marriage proposal.

Aquarius must notice my distress despite my straight face because he says, "Marina, have you any idea how many people cherish you? Our civilization looks up to you. You'd make a wonderful partner."

"Yes, because that's what I've always dreamt of...a professional partnership," I laugh. Laughter isn't appropriate at the time, but I can't help but giggle. This is ridiculous. "How romantic. You really know how to swoon the ladies, Mr. Oh-So-Handsome-Aquarius."

His eyebrows rise while he wears an arrogant smirk on the

edge of his lips. "But you do find me handsome?"

"No," I unconvincingly lie. Looking to my uncle, I firmly state, "I'm not marrying him."

"Marina, this isn't a democracy." Sam looks fierce; his voice gruff…no longer a mindless slave, easily manipulated. "I am your emperor and you will obey my commands. You will marry Prince Aquarius."

Sam's words slice me deep. "Wow." An aggravated chuckle rises in my throat. "I was almost positive I had killed Cordelia, yet I could've sworn I just heard her serpentine words escape from your mouth."

"You're missing the point. You won't be marrying Prince Aquarius for love. I know that—we all are aware. You'll betroth him and together the two of you will reign over the Australian Border."

"So because *you* want to strengthen the family ties, *I* have to marry Aquarius. No offense to you," I tell the prince. It's not fair to him either. He deserves true love like everyone.

"The emperor and I think it would be in your best interest to follow our plans to betroth my eldest son," Wade says as a suggestion, but there's a hint of authority in his tone.

I wave my hand dismissing his words. Attitude is definitely not something I should display as a princess, but this is outrageous. "Let the Council take a vote."

"This isn't a Council matter," argues Sam.

"My father is on the Council and he sure as hell won't agree to force me into a marriage."

"Marina," Sam grumbles through gritted teeth.

"I saved you. I had your back, Sam." I sound defeated. My uncle says nothing. "May I be excused?"

Sam pinches his lips in a tight line before nodding with assent.

"It was nice to meet you," I tell Aquarius before leaving Sam's cavern in a sullen rush.

I'm stirring with rage when I reach my cavern. How could my own family member treat me as if I'm a piece of property? And after the bravery I've shown them, it's a despicable act. I've done everything for these people. I killed myself and the empress in order for them to live. I gave up my chance to leave with Beck so I could help rebuild our kingdom. I have every intention of leaving, but it doesn't seem as though my uncle understands my plan. He believes I'm going to stay below the Surface and create a life for myself. I won't do it. I'm far more than just an average water-breather. I'm a hybrid...I have the choice between living as a water-breather or an air-breather. Just the same as I have the choice to marry a man I love.

I will never love Prince Aquarius Emerson.

Chapter Two

[BECK]

A HAND REACHES OUT from the dark, pulling me from my slumber and thrusts me against the wall by my throat. I whip open my eyes to find a pair of magenta irises glaring back. Despite the room being pitch black, I make out the outline of someone… But I'm already aware this someone is Cordelia—the murderess sea empress who enslaved me only a month ago.

"You're dead," I sputter, my voice hoarse.

"Yet, I'm here." Her voice is soft, but menacing.

"This isn't real," I whisper to myself. Cordelia laughs and sends me flying through the air. My back slams against the wall, knocking the air from my lungs.

"You can't escape me."

Then she's gone and I'm left in the dark, screaming until I wake myself up from the terror.

"She's dead," I remind myself, shaking my head in an attempt to forget the nightmare. That's what it was… just a dream—a nightmare. Cordelia is dead. So why am I dreaming of her threats? I'm only freaked out. But my dreams haven't failed me in the past. They help me remember. Maybe they're doing that now.

I crawl from bed with a deep ache in my back.

. . .

CROSSING MY ARMS, I press them to the classroom table, lay my head
down, and close my eyes, pretending I won't be stuck in this
miserable school for the next seven hours.

"Hey," a voice says. The disembodied voice sounds close
enough to be speaking to me directly, but it's not likely, so I
remain in my lazy pose. "Beck," the voice says.

I look up to find Ella standing over me.

"Hi," I mumble.

I like Ella. She moved to Monticello about three years ago
when we were freshmen. I befriended her after she accidently
stabbed me with her pen when she tripped over her feet and
caught her fall against my back on her first day of school. She
was mortified, but after a quick trip to the nurse's office, I was as
good as new. But Ella was one of the many friends I pushed away
after Ethan's death.

"Can I sit here?" She tucks a short strand of brunette hair
behind her ear. Ella has always kept her hair shoulder length. I
don't know why I've always noticed that about her.

"I know you like to have your space, but some jerk took my
spot and I'm not about to fight him for it," she adds with a giggle.

I nod and pull the chair out for her. She smiles gratefully and
slides into it.

"I'm getting better," I tell her after a minute of silence.

"What do you mean?" She folds her hands over her lap.

I shrug. "I'm not such a loner anymore. I know I shut everyone out last year."

"Beck, you don't have to explain. You lost your best friend. If anyone has a problem with how you dealt with Ethan's death, they can kiss your ass as far as I'm concerned."

Her comment causes me to laugh. "I don't think I've heard you swear before."

She blushes, but quickly smirks. "You're not the only one who has changed."

I'm about to tell Ella how sorry I am for pushing her away when she was only trying to be a friend when I was grieving, but my English teacher begins to speak instead.

"Good morning, my ever so awake students! I think we'll—" Mr. Reese begins, but is interrupted by a dinging phone. He pinpoints the student and collects her phone for the hour. "What do I always say?" he asks the entire class.

In unison, we join him in repeating, "The mere presence of a cell phone in our peripheral vision affects the connection we feel to those around us."

"Maybe my fellow colleagues can find the benefits in allowing all of you to use your phone during class, but I prefer you to be disconnected for an hour. So please make sure to silence your phones before you walk through my door. As I was saying before, I would like to jump right into our new project. I want all of you to be creative with this one. Present your information in a way that makes me want to learn."

Mr. Reese's voice carries on, but I can't seem to focus on the directions he sputters. We're handed a list of mythical creatures ranging from werewolves and vampires to fairies and elves. My eyes scan the page for merfolk, but find the category of water-breathers is absent. At this moment, studying the world Marina lives in is the only world I'm interested in…even if no one knows of its existence.

The hour drags on. I don't speak with Ella much, making for an awkward work space, but since I'm not doing much work, I suppose it doesn't make a difference.

When the bell rings, Ella stands and says a quick goodbye before she hurries off to her next class. I consider texting her later in order to catch up, but know I won't do it. My number had probably been deleted from her phone long ago anyway.

By the time I stand from my table, everyone has cleared out of the classroom. Mr. Reese is scribbling notes for the next class on the white board.

"Mr. Reese?" He makes a soft grunting sound that indicates he's listening to me. "I know merfolk aren't on the list, but do you think I could do my project on that particular subject?"

He glances at me curiously and then looks back to the board. "You want to research mermaids?"

"Water-breathers." I nod. "Yes."

"That should be fine." He scrunches up his face out of confusion and looks back to me. "What did you just call them?"

"Who?"

"Merfolk."

"Water-breathers…" I shrug. "I heard the term used once."

"Oh." He caps the marker with a loud *click*. "Well, I'm looking forward to grading your project."

As I'm leaving class, suddenly out of the corner of my eye, I see *him*. He sits slouched in his chair while his fingers tap away at the tabletop. His gaze narrows in on me. I've stopped, frozen in my path. It's Ethan. He's staring at me with curious eyes.

"Beck, do you need something else?" Mr. Reese asks.

I'm forced back into reality. When I look back to Ethan, he has disappeared.

"Beck?"

"No," I say, shaking my head of any insane thoughts—like my dead best friend *actually* making an appearance in my first hour class. "I thought I forgot something."

As I move to leave, Mr. Reese blocks my exit. "Beck, is everything okay with you? I know how high school can be... And with the loss of your best friend coming up on its one year anniversary—"

"I'm fine," I assure Mr. Reese, cutting him off. "But I really do need to get to class."

Mr. Reese nods and gives me a pat on the back before stepping away from the door.

I drag my way through the rest of the boring day. I try to distract myself with pointless gossip from fellow classmates and the tedious lectures from teachers, but I can't get Ethan out of my mind. I couldn't have really seen him, right? That's insane.

Ethan's dead.

Then again, is it so unbelievable if he were alive by some

miracle? One month ago I wouldn't have believed in the existence of merfolk.

I wish I could see Marina. The longer I'm away from her, the more I feel like everything that happened over vacation was all a dream. Lately I've been feeling as if I'm crazy.

Brian, Tyler, and Nate didn't die. Perhaps, they only went for a road trip to another island?

I never drowned and was resurrected by a mermaid with gold eyes. I simply could've had a bad dream and was sleep walking.

Marina never visited. Maybe I was merely bored and made her up, so I could tolerate the dreary trip with my family. I was never turned into a merman and nearly killed by a sea witch who resembled a jellyfish. It was all a bad dream.

Maybe none of it was real.

. . .

WHEN I REACH THE FINAL two hours of the day, I begin to feel relieved. Sixth hour is my time to be a teacher assistant. I lucked out and Mr. Reese claimed me first. His prep time is also sixth period, so he is often so buried in lesson plans he hardly takes notice of me beside giving me a list of copies to make, grades to be entered in his computer, and things to be laminated. I busy myself with the tedious work.

Seventh hour is my easiest class of the day, so I usually look forward to Culinary II with Ms. Mulberry. She always greets me with a bright and happy smile. I've been in her classes every year since I started high school. My freshman year I took Outdoor Gear as one of my electives, while my sophomore year I took Culinary 1. Last year, as a junior, I was placed in her Careers class. Not that she would ever admit it, but I'd definitely bet I'm one of her favorite students. I've never given her trouble, unlike most of my fellow peers. I always keep to myself and work hard on my assignments, along with the cooking groups. Ms. Mulberry even requested for me to be her T.A. after Mr. Reese had already assigned me as his teacher assistant for the year.

Cooking has always been something that has come easily to me. When my mom was still alive, she'd sit me on a stool in the kitchen while she would bake cookies or make dinner. I remember watching her, completely mesmerized. After Mom died and my dad married Annie, I would often assist Annie cooking the family dinners. My twin sister, Lily, never seemed to have an interest in cooking, so I still can't seem to wrap my head around why she's in this class with me.

Lily sits at a table in the back laughing with her friends, but when I pass their table, they stop. Am I the plague? Do I smell bad? Discretely, I sniff an armpit and find myself smelling like the Cool Rush deodorant I applied this morning. I shrug it off and take a seat at an empty table.

Thankfully, no one sits by me before class starts.

I catch Lily staring at me a few times. She mouths "Are you okay?" to me, but I ignore her.

As Ms. Mulberry demonstrates how to make Chicken Cordon Bleu, I find myself sketching images of Marina on the ingredient sheet instead of filling in the blanks and taking notes. One of Annie's best dishes is Chicken Cordon Bleu, so I'm feeling confident I could make this dish tomorrow in class with my eyes closed.

When the final bell rings, Ms. Mulberry excuses us with her famous, "Make good choices!"

Lily races off with her friends, not waiting for me, which is fine. I don't mind walking to my locker by myself in the rushing crowd of students eager to get out of this hell hole.

"You ready?" I ask Lily when I reach her at her locker.

"I've been ready to leave since we got here," she replies with sassiness.

I laugh as I enter the combination on my locker.

Since our last names are obviously the same, our lockers have always been next to each other.

"I guess we really are twins."

"Are you okay? I saw you earlier in the hall and you looked pale. You seemed kinda out of it. Are you getting sick?"

Maybe she's referring to earlier when I saw my dead best friend in class. I could never tell her I saw Ethan. It would kill her. Not only because it would pain her to know I'm still suffering from the accident, but because she loved Ethan deeply. Lily doesn't need the reminder of her lost love. My sister comes across as tough, but I know she still thinks of him often. There's been a few times I've caught her crying out his name when she thought no one was home.

"Nah, I'm fine." I brush off her comment. "I've been getting a lot of headaches lately. I think I'm just tired."

"I can drive home if you want to rest." She holds her hand out for the keys.

"You? Drive? No, thanks. I like living."

She huffs a deep breath. "I'm not that bad!"

"We live ten minutes away. I'll survive."

The drive home is quiet. Lily turns on the radio, but I wasn't lying about my headache, so I make her turn it off. Ever since I shifted back into a human, my head has been bothering me. I've thought about seeing a doctor, but how would I explain the cause of my migraines? I choose to take ibuprofen instead, even though it barely dulls the pain.

When Lily and I arrive home, I pop a few pills and chug down a Mountain Dew to go with it. I pick up one of my sci-fi novels from the counter. Little peanut butter fingerprints are smeared across the cover and there's bits of jelly in between the pages.

"Aubrey!" I yell with a gravelly voice.

I love my baby sister more than anything, but she gets on every last of my nerves.

"What!?" I hear a small voice scream from upstairs.

I wipe the book clean of peanut butter, knowing there's not much I can do about the jelly. I grunt out of frustration.

Aubrey is in her room, so I walk upstairs to inform her she'll be buying me a new copy with her piggy bank money.

I find Aubrey in her bed playing with her dolls. Bandit, my black lab, lies next to her watching her play. My boy is content when he's with any member of the family.

"Becky!" she screams with excitement. "Do you wanna play princess with me?"

"No," I firmly state. "Were you looking at my book?" I hold up the damaged book as evidence.

She briefly looks away from her toys and to me. She shrugs. "Yeah, but there's no pictures so it was boring."

"I noticed you didn't wash your hands."

Her play abruptly stops. "I did wash my hands!"

"Clearly, you didn't since you got peanut butter and jelly all over my book."

"I licked them clean!" she argues in her cutest little singsong tone as she twists her blonde hair around her finger.

"That's not even the slightest bit sanitary—" My eyes are drawn to a gold ring on Aubrey's white dresser top. Normally I wouldn't think much of it, but something draws me closer to examine the piece of jewelry. The ring wraps around to create a dolphin, with its head parallel to its gold tail. This is Marina's ring. So much for my whole idea of everything being an illusion.

I remember the night we were walking to the barbeque back in Edisto. Aubrey asked about the ring and Marina had told her it was a gift from her friend Caspian. He was one of the mermen who saved my life.

I pick Marina's ring up with gentle fingers. "Aubrey, where did you get this?"

"Hey! That's mine!" She drops her dolls and runs for the ring, but I raise my hand, keeping it out of her reach. She jumps for the jewelry. "Give it back!" she screams.

"Calm down!" I demand.

"Becky, give it back," she demands as she begins to cry.

"Where did you get it?"

She huffs a deep breath in order to calm down and crosses her arms. "Marina."

I roll my eyes. Obviously. "Yes, but when did she give it to you?"

"I don't know," she says, her chest heaving.

"Marina's going to want this back," I tell her with a stern voice.

"But she gave it to me!" For some reason I think Marina had thought she wouldn't need it any longer. If she was prepared to sacrifice her life for mine, she knew she wouldn't be allowed to keep the piece. But, she's alive and free. I want to give it back to her.

"Marina will be missing this. Don't we want to make her happy when we visit her?" Sure, it's not until next summer, but in all honesty, I wouldn't mind having something of hers. Aubrey doesn't seem to be willing to give it up easily. "I'll give you a dollar," I add in an attempt to persuade my young sister.

She puts her finger to her chin. "I want a million dollars."

"Aubrey, I'm being serious. You know I don't have a million dollars. I'll give you two dollars."

A little smirk forms on her lips. "One-hundred dollars. "I pull out my wallet and skim through my cash. "I have eight dollars and a dime."

"Deal," she says, holding out her palm for her money.

I can tell Lily has taught our sister well.

. . .

AFTER DAD GETS HOME, he comes down to my room in the basement where he finds me working on homework. Bandit has followed him. My dog jumps onto my bed and makes himself comfortable in my mess of blankets.

"How was school today, bud?" Dad asks, clapping his hands on my shoulders.

I set down my pencil and swivel my desk chair around to face him. "It was school." It's not like I saw my dead best friend or anything.

His eyes examine my mess of a room with pop cans and half-eaten chip bags scattered across the floor. "You really need to clean, before that old pizza box grows mold."

I smirk. "I think it adds character to the room."

"I think it attracts ants...but I'll let you worry about that at another time. You want to come shoot some hoops with me for a little while?"

"I would, but I have a project—"

"Oh, come on. You can't take fifteen minutes out of your day to whoop my ass?"

I smile, knowing I can easily beat him.

"There's my son!" shouts my dad.

The evening air is cool and refreshing as the sun begins to set over the horizon. Dad passes me the ball, allowing me to start.

Dad blocks the hoop while I dribble the ball up the driveway. He lurches for me in a predictable move—I know all his tricks, so I expect his block. I pull back, toss the ball between his legs, spin around him, catch the ball, and shoot. It hits the backboard and exits through the hoop.

My victory continues for half an hour—with a few points for my dad—before he stops and walks to the front steps. I follow and join him on the porch.

The expression he wears on his face is somber. "You know, Beck, she's not the only girl out there," he says.

I know he's referring to Marina. "Dad, please don't give me the 'There's plenty of fish in the sea,' speech," I scoff. They say there are plenty of fish in the sea, but I never thought I'd fall for a mermaid.

"I'm not trying to give you a speech… I'm just trying to tell you there will be more girls, and eventually you'll look back at Marina as a great summer fling." My dad shrugs as though Marina is just another memory of my past.

I clear my throat. "We'll meet up again in a year."

"Beck, you're seventeen. You can't commit to that kind of relationship with someone you spent less than a week with."

"Marina's different, okay? I'm telling you, I could love her one day."

He pinches the bridge of his nose, indicating he's becoming frustrated. I know this because I do the same thing when I'm feeling irritated. "One day." He shakes his head with a slight chuckle. How can he find this amusing? As my father, shouldn't he want what's best for me?

"Believe it or not, I was young once, too. I was in love—or what I thought was love. I was around your age. It was great fun...while it lasted. But that's the thing. Young love doesn't last."

"You met Mom when you were in high school."

"Yes, I did. After Miranda." He takes a deep breath. "Your mom was the love of my life, but I would've never realized that unless I had dated Miranda and had fallen in love with her first. With your mom it was easy. I knew exactly how I felt about her."

"So Miranda was a mistake," I say, attempting to understand my father's logic.

"She was a lesson learned," Dad corrects.

"So you're saying Marina is my Miranda."

"I suppose that's what I'm trying to say."

"Well, you're wrong," I rise from the steps to head back to my room.

Marina might be the love of my life.

Chapter Three

[MARINA]

I LOVE MY CAVERN. It's spacious and beautiful. The glow of amber lightning orbs cause the gorgeous gems embedded in the cavern walls to sparkle. The only complaint I have is the windows are too small, an extra precaution to keep unwanted guests out of the castle. The entrance is heavily guarded, which creates one other downfall…the windows are too tiny for me to escape the kingdom.

I'm near my window looking out at City of Zale when Aquarius makes an appearance in my cavern. I haven't seen Aquarius since attempting to refuse his hand in marriage yesterday. He doesn't utter a word as he joins me at the neighboring window.

Thousands of gold lightning orbs light up the kingdom. I watch the guards maintaining the group of people hovering at the border of the kingdom. Sam has a force field dome keeping the unwanted citizens out. Some of them get a little crazy when the guards refuse to let them enter.

"I'm trapped," I finally say. I don't know why I'm admitting this to Aquarius. "I'm a prisoner in the castle. Soon, I'll be a prisoner in a marriage."

The prince looks to me with his hypnotizing dark gaze. It's hard for me to read him. He remains impassive. "Is that really how you feel, love?"

"Don't call me that," I snap.

Aquarius frowns. "Sorry, it's only a term of endearment where I'm from."

"You can't possibly support this." I point between us, disbelief written all over my face.

"Actually, I do."

His father has probably brainwashed him his entire life to do just as he's told by a higher authority. "Have you ever been in love, Aquarius?"

He narrows his gaze. "What kind of question is that?"

"Just answer it," I demand.

He smirks again, flashing his winning smile. I groan out of annoyance. Does this work with all the ladies? He just smiles or winks an eye and they all come flocking to him? I mean, give me a break. He's not *that* perfect. Studying him more closely, his jawline is a tad uneven and... what else? There has to be something else. Aha! His right earlobe is slightly bigger than his left. So there!

"Are you ordering me on behalf of our engagement or because you're the princess?" he asks.

"Maybe a little of both." I cross my arms. "Now answer the question."

"Yes, I've been in love."

"And how did it feel?"

He chuckles. "You're serious?"

I nod.

"Fine." Aquarius presses his lips in a firm line, followed by a heavy sigh. "It feels as though I can't possibly breathe until I'm with her. I need to ensure her safety before mine. I could never possibly feel myself until she's with me," his voice is soft and sincere, "as if she's my anchor. Every day I wake up with her face in my mind. Every day it kills me because I can't be with her. It causes me to grow mad knowing I'm not keeping her warm at night and waking next to her in the morning. I can't possibly make her see how much I'm madly in love with her." Aquarius' gaze is filled with a deep admiration.

It's clear to me by the way he speaks of his love his heart is taken. If he feels this way about someone else, how can he allow his father to force him into marrying me?

"Then you can understand how I can't possibly marry you. I'm in love with another man."

Aquarius is silent.

"There's no way I can promise myself to you—a man I don't know—when all I can think about is someone else."

With a smug smile, Aquarius swims closer to me. I watch him curiously, my heart beating fast beneath my chest. He tenderly tucks my braid behind my back and lets his fingers trail over my shoulder, tracing up my neck to my chin. Beneath his touch, my skin tingles.

Aquarius raises my chin slightly, bringing my gaze to his dark stare. "You know what I believe, love? Soon, you won't do anything but think about me."

Our eyes are locked on one another. Something about this man hypnotizes me like no other. As much as I want to pull away from him, I can't bring myself to do it.

Someone enters my cavern and clears their throat, forcing me from my trance. I look from Aquarius to Caspian, who hovers in my cavern entrance. I nudge Aquarius away and focus my attention on my best friend and my uncle's right hand man. "The emperor would like a word with you," Cas informs me.

"Well, I would *not* like a word with him," I answer in a calm manner. "I *would* like a word with you though."

"That was me being kind with his words. He's waiting for you in the council caverns." Cas doesn't wait for me nor does he acknowledge my comment about wanting to speak with him. He swims out of my cavern as soon as his task is completed.

I miss Cas. I miss my best friend.

"I'll see you at dinner," Aquarius says taking my hand and pressing a kiss to my skin.

Why does he make me tingle?

When Aquarius exits my cavern, I wait a few minutes before leaving, then take my time making my way to the council caverns. I'll make the emperor wait. Swimming through empty corridors, I take a detour around the castle in order to think.

What will I say to my uncle? I'm furious. Who does he think he is setting me up with a man I only just met? How dare he give me an order when he owes me his life? I'm a free woman.

When I make it to the council caverns, I storm in like a raging hurricane. "What about Beck?" I shout.

Sam is waiting, tail coiled beneath him, in his spot at the stone slab. "Beck is a loyal air-breather, but he isn't your future," he responds with a calm, soft voice.

"We made a promise to each other," I argue with rage.

Sam stares me down. Behind his gold eyes, I can see the fight to be patient with me. "Promises break, Marina."

"Don't speak to me as if I'm a child!"

Sam pounds his fists down on the stone slab, his calm demeanor quickly vanishing and morphing into fury. "You are a child!" He hovers above me, causing me to feel as though I'm a kid. "You're in no position to be giving orders. You, Marina, need to learn how to act when around high ranking citizens. You were an embarrassment with our guests earlier."

Embarrassment? He's ashamed of me? Disappointment I can understand, but embarrassment? "This just goes to show I'm not cut out for this life," I dispute, fighting back tears.

Sam settles, drifting back down to my level. "Of course, you are. You only need to learn," Sam reassures.

"How was I supposed to act? You had just informed me I'd be marrying a man I just met when I'm already in love with someone else."

"You're in love with an *air-breather*."

"I have human blood flowing through my veins! That's never going to change, Sam!"

"You're a water-breather like me, Cascade, and your father. This is your life. This is your home."

"I should be free to choose what I want for my life. I have a gift and no one can tell me how I can use it. You're not my father, Sam. You're my uncle."

"I am your emperor," he snaps, his face turning red with rage.

I remain silent, not daring to say a word.

Sam sighs. The harshness disappears from his voice as he calms down. "I know I've been hard on you. This isn't easy for me. I need your help, Marina. I need your cooperation."

"I've been trying for the past month. I chose to stay and help the family, not be forced into marriage when I'm only on the verge of eighteen."

"Women of power get married much younger than eighteen."

"That's not my point." I roll my eyes which is met with Sam's angry glower. "I should've left when I had the chance."

"You didn't though." Sam exhales with a heaviness. His shoulders are weighted with the responsibility of ruling our citizens. "It's more than just a marriage. It's an allegiance. The citizens living within the Australian Border don't trust me. They cherished Zale. They cherish King Wade and Prince Aquarius, but they don't know me. They believe I should be dethroned. I'm the rightful emperor and no one can overthrow me, but I need them to fall in love with our family. I need you to rule the Australian waters so they gain our trust. You're a loveable princess. You marrying Prince Aquarius benefits our family and *our kingdom.*"

"It doesn't benefit me."

"That's enough." Sam rubs his temples. "Listen, I summoned

you here for a reason."

I cross my arms. "I'm listening."

"You are expected to attend dinner this evening. I allowed you to be absent last night because of the circumstances, but I need you to be on your best behavior tonight. I would much appreciate it if we could make a good impression this time around with Aquarius."

"Is that an order?" I scoff.

"If that's the only way you'll behave, then yes."

"While you're ordering people around, do you think you could order Caspian to talk to me?" I'm only slightly joking.

Sam shakes his head with a small laugh. "That one is on you, Princess."

"I had a feeling you wouldn't be able to help me with that one," I tell him before heading back to my cavern. I decide to not seek out Caspian today. I'll see him at dinner.

Cascade arrives in my cavern to visit me an hour after my meeting with Sam. She looks as stunning as ever. Her crown is far more elegant than mine embellished with more clam shells and gems. A gold chain wraps around her right arm, same as mine. The men wear gold cuffs while we women wear a golden armlet that wraps around our right bicep while three chains hang loose to our elbows. The left arm remains bare until marriage.

"I heard about your engagement," she states with a honeyed tone.

"Please, don't call it that." A sour feeling fills the pit of my stomach. "I'm still hoping Sam will change his mind."

"His decision is final. Prince Aquarius comes from a family of power. Power is in our favor at this time."

I remain silent. My life has been decided for me.

"Sometimes arranged marriages end in happiness," advises my aunt. "Look at Zale and Lynn's marriage."

"Your parents seemed to have true feelings for one another."

"Yes, my parents…" Cascade pauses, "my parents were a true example of endless love."

"I don't think I can see myself loving Aquarius," I admit.

"Why not?"

"He's just—" What is my reason for thinking I could never fall in love with Aquarius? So far, he's been nothing but nice to me. Overall, he's been respectful, although arrogant. I can't deny he's handsome. He's a charmer. And his voice… his voice is so soft and soothing.

I could never make it work because my heart belongs to Beck.

"He's just what?" questions Cascade with a smirk. "Irresistible?" She winks.

"No!" I gasp. "I wasn't going to say that."

"Plenty of other mermaids think so."

"Well, I'm not every other mermaid."

"You're far from it, my dear." Cascade presses a kiss to the top of my head.

"Please, Cascade. Can I be alone?"

Cascade nods. "Of course."

Dinner will be served in an hour and I need some space before I have to face my entire family and my new fiancé.

. . .

SNEAKING A GLANCE AT Aquarius at dinner, I catch him looking at me. He seems more amused than embarrassed that I've caught him staring. Aquarius obviously thinks very highly of himself. He's so unlike Beck who is quiet and humble.

Aquarius winks at me and flashes a smile. My heart beats a tad bit faster. And then I realize he's amused because I looked up at him. I made the effort to look his way. Giving him my attention is feeding his ego. Quickly, I look back to my food, an assortment of squid and kelp. How I'd kill for a bowl of cereal right now.

Sam and Cascade speak with Aquarius' father Wade about when my grandfather was emperor. They boast about how he was one of a kind. He truly cared about his people and was gracious to all citizens who pursued his help. The castle sheltered many of his servant's families. Sam is striving to be as generous as his father. Wade encourages Sam to continue to follow Zale's legacy.

Now I know Aquarius is watching me, making it hard to not glance in his direction. Out of the corner of my eye, I can see him chewing his food with a smug smile. What an arrogant serpent. Just because I took notice of him. He's a guest. Am I not supposed to pay attention to our guests?

Next to him sits his father. Wade is still immersed in deep conversation with Sam. They smile and laugh. They've probably planned out the rest of my life. Where Aquarius and I will live once we're married and how many children we'll have together. I am not having his children.

Focus on dinner, I remind myself.

It doesn't matter that Aquarius is gorgeous. It doesn't matter because I have Beck. I'm devoted to him despite the distance separating us. I love him. So what if I'm attracted to another man? Aquarius is an attractive merperson. Anyone can take notice. It's simply a fact.

Caspian joins our dinner late and is forced to take the open spot next to me. This is the closest Caspian and I have been in... I honestly can't remember how long.

"Hi, Cas," I whisper when he settles in and is served his dinner.

"Princess," he scoffs as he digs into his meal.

"Can we talk?"

Caspian takes a break from chewing. "You can talk all you want."

I sigh. "Cas, I'd really like to discuss our friendship—"

"Prince Aquarius," says Sam, interrupting my private conversation with Caspian, "I believe now would be a wonderful time to make your announcement."

Announcement? What announcement? Oh. Please, tell me it's not about our engagement. What a complete joke. I'm not marrying him.

Aquarius clears his throat, sits up straighter, and smiles.

No. No. No.

"As you all know, I'm visiting from the Australian Border." Aquarius' voice is so velvety and beautiful with a twinge of his foreign accent. "My community had a long standing allegiance with Emperor Zale while he ruled. Now that Cordelia has been eliminated and Flotsam is our reigning emperor, we want our kingdoms to be partnering alliances. What better way to do so than to betroth one of the royal princesses."

Caspian stiffens next to me. I can hear him gulp his food down. He undoubtedly had seen Aquarius in my cavern earlier. I can only assume he's pieced together the announcement.

Shut up, Aquarius. Shut up!

Aquarius continues, "I'm honored to announce I've asked for Princess Marina's hand in marriage, and she has accepted."

Asked? I accepted? This is the first I'm hearing of this version.

We're met with silence. Of course, Sam, Cascade, and Wade were the only ones who knew about my engagement to the Australian prince. Caspian's face has fallen with shock while my father looks outraged.

My father, who sits next to me, turns in my direction. "You're engaged?"

I'm struck speechless for a moment. I'm not entirely sure how to respond. "The technical answer would be, yes."

"Why was I not made aware of this?" Jackson directs his question toward Sam.

Sam tenses up. "It didn't concern you."

"It didn't concern me? She's my daughter!" I smile because Jackson is putting up an argument on my behalf. It feels good to have someone fight for my cause.

"Jackson, I can guarantee you Marina will be in safe hands," assures Aquarius.

"Did I ask you?" Jackson snaps.

I stifle a laugh. This isn't Aquarius' fault. I'm sure he's only doing what's best for his community, but to be fair, neither one of us should be forced into a marriage.

"Jackson, I expect you to act appropriately when we have guests. Now, I understand this is a personal matter for you, but it won't be discussed here."

"And when will it be discussed, Your Majesty?" Jackson's skin is a harsh red.

"In private," Sam hisses with gritted teeth. Quickly, he composes himself. "I'm so sorry," he bids to Wade and his son.

"Really, we understand," Aquarius assures the emperor.

"No worries, mate," offers Wade. "It's big news to comprehend in such a short amount of time."

Next to me, Caspian is furiously picking at his food.

I would have told him sooner if he had given me the chance.

Without a word, Caspian shoves his plate away and swims out of the dining cavern. Maybe he's headed to his cavern for the night. I will visit him tonight before I turn in. I have to explain myself. I need to beg him for our friendship. I miss my Caspian.

Aquarius thanks the emperor for his hospitality; Sam leaves with Jackson and Wade for a meeting in the royal headquarters.

I'm left alone with the Australian prince.

"That went well," Aquarius jokes with a light heart.

I'm not amused. "You could've warned me you'd be making

an announcement."

"I was only ripping off the Band-Aid," he teases.

What's a Band-Aid? "I don't know what that means."

"Never mind, love."

"Stop calling me that," I demand. "That's an order from your princess." With nothing more, I leave the dining cavern in search of my best friend.

Guards follow me through the empty corridors as I make my way to Caspian's cavern in the guard's wing of the castle.

When I arrive, I order the two guards who flank me to wait outside the passageway. I'm disappointed to see Caspian lying asleep on his sponge bed. I don't wake him. He must be exhausted from all the missions he's been working lately. So instead, I coil my tail beneath me and sit on the cavern floor, near him.

On the wall, a fisherman's net is displayed. He kept the net from his cavern in Cordelia's castle. This is supposed to be a happier place, but Caspian still insists on torturing himself—reminding himself every day his parents are dead. He blames himself for his father's death, but it wasn't his fault.

Caspian was a curious child and happened to get himself entangled in a fisherman's net. His father came to his rescue only to become entwined himself, then brought above the Surface by humans. He was never seen again. Caspian's mother committed suicide the next day, leaving Caspian orphaned.

What happened to Caspian's parents is horrifying and tragic. As much as I hate to say it, because it's incredibly selfish, I'm thankful Caspian was brought into my life. Without him I wouldn't have been so strong. Cordelia would've eaten me up and spat me back out.

"Cas," I whisper, "I feel so lost."

He doesn't answer with "It's okay," which are the words I long to hear.

But I don't need his words to comfort me. I only need his presence.

Chapter Four

[MARINA]

GENTLE FINGERS COMB THROUGH my hair, rousing me from my sleep. Warm, frothy waves crash at my bare feet when I awake in the sand next to Beck.

"Good morning," he says before kissing me. I pull his body harder to mine and tug lightly at his hair. I'm afraid if I let him go, he'll disappear.

Beck rolls on top of me and I press my hands firmly against his back. He stares at me with his bright emerald gaze. "Don't forget about me," he whispers.

"Never," I reply with a smile. Pressing my lips to his, I kiss him with tenderness. I want to savor him and the moment.

A wave crashes over us and pulls us into the ocean, but it doesn't stunt the rhythm of our kiss. We don't break our bond until my back is pressed into the sandy floor.

I open my eyes to find Beck is replaced by Aquarius. He has a hand under me, pressing into my back as he arches my body against his. Our tails wrap around one another, entangling our bodies. Only a moment ago I was kissing Beck and now Aquarius is above me. I do nothing to stop Aquarius' kisses. I embrace them.

"I can give you more than him," Aquarius tells me before kissing me, hard and deep. I groan as he presses himself harder against me.

"Marina," he mutters as I rake his back.

"Aquarius," I moan into his neck.

"Marina?"

I open my eyes to find Caspian hovering above. I slither away from him with my cheeks burning a deep red. Was I really dreaming about being intimate with Aquarius?

"Have you been here all night?" Caspian asks.

I shake the dream from my mind and straighten myself. "I came to talk to you last night, but you were asleep."

He stretches his arms and his long, silver tail while yawning. "You know you can always wake me."

"No, you've been working so hard. I didn't mind waiting for you."

He rubs his face roughly, still rubbing the sleep from his eyes. "When were you going to tell me about your engagement?"

"I wanted to as soon as I had the chance, but Aquarius beat me to it at dinner... and let's be honest, we've been growing apart."

Caspian shrugs. "Marina, you and I live very different lives. You rank higher than me now."

"That's not true," I argue. "I don't see it that way."

"You may not look at it with the same point of view, but I'm your servant."

"That doesn't mean you can't be my friend."

"So you do think of me as a servant?" Caspian is clearly upset; he glowers.

"I didn't say that," I claim.

"You didn't correct me either."

"Cas, you're still my best friend!" I dispute with no avail.

Caspian shakes his head, blowing off my comment. "So you and the prince are engaged." He rolls his eyes. "What about the human?"

"The human has a name, Cas."

Caspian groans. "Beck. What about Beck?"

"He's still very much in my heart. It wasn't my choice to marry Aquarius. This is Sam and Wade's plan for us."

Caspian crosses his strong arms across his muscled chest. "What are you going to do?" There's the hint of compassion I've been looking for in my friend.

"I don't know what I can do." I sigh. "Guards are always on my tail, watching me."

"Sam has put you in a tough spot."

"Understatement of the year." I cross my arms. "How's it going with your new team?"

Caspian has calmed a bit. "It's an honor to lead the team of guards, but no one can take your place as my partner." He smirks revealing his dimples. His face has returned to his normal shade of light-brown.

"It's a strange thing…us not collecting anymore. Our lives have changed so drastically over the course of one month."

A guard appears in the doorway. "Emperor Flotsam has called

upon you both for a council meeting," he says.

"Regarding what?" I ask.

"The emperor is making an announcement."

I can't handle anymore announcements.

. . .

AT THE HEAD OF THE stone slab is Sam, sitting upon his throne with his hands folded on the stone top. He nods at me when Caspian and I enter, gesturing for us to take a seat. Cascade and Jackson sit next to one another while Caspian takes his spot next to Wade.

Sam clears his throat. "I've spent eighteen years as a slave under the control of a vile monster. Thanks to our princess, I was released from slavery and able to deem my rightful place as emperor. I have the blood of Zale Kenryk flowing through my veins. I am the strongest being in all the oceans, yet our people doubt me."

"Our people are growing anxious," says Wade. His Australian accent is thick with worry. "I watched my best friend and former emperor Zale raise Flotsam into an outstanding merman. I believe Flotsam has all the qualities to make a strong ruler, but our communities are beginning to rebel. They won't tolerate another dictator."

Cascade interjects, "Cordelia's gone, people are rejoicing, and this is the time for our family to rise. We need to show them we've got this under control. I think it's time we host a celebration."

"A celebration?" I inquire.

"Your wedding," Sam responds, with an excited grin.

"No, Sam," argues Jackson. "I'm not allowing my daughter, who is only seventeen years old, to marry a man who's in his twenties. Where I'm from, it's very much frowned upon."

Sam chuckles. "We don't do things the same way as the mindless humans."

"Let's not forget I was once one of those so-called mindless humans."

"And how did that work out for you, Jackson? Please, enlighten me. Oh, wait. I already know. You mated with my sister, turned into one of us, and was enslaved for seventeen years. Does that pretty much cover it?"

Jackson's annoyance is plastered on his face. He sucks his teeth, clearly irritated. "That's not my point."

"Enough," interjects Cascade. "Not only is Marina marrying someone, but I'm promised to the prince of the Northern High Seas. We will hold the celebrations of matrimony here. We will invite all the high ranking leaders and citizens. End of story."

"Marina, you're the most beloved of all of us," Sam says. "The people will look most forward to the ocean's sweethearts marrying one another."

"We're the ocean's sweethearts now?" I ask, wryly.

"My son has always been cherished," adds Wade.

"I'm sure it's for his personality," I scoff as I roll my eyes.

"Marina," scolds Sam, "you will show respect for your fiancé."

I shut my mouth, but am not happy about it.

"Messengers have been sent to the Australian Border," informs King Wade. "My wife and youngest son will be two of the many who will travel here for the extravaganza."

"The messengers were sent?" I question as my heart races. Why were messengers sent so soon? Surely they wouldn't be notified until… until the wedding date was scheduled.

I gasp. No.

"When is the wedding?" I ask, afraid for the answer.

"Preparations are being made," answers Sam. "You'll be married within the next week."

My jaw drops.

"And I have no say in this matter?" questions Jackson.

"It's a royal matter," Sam declares.

"I'm a member of this council." He slams his hand down upon the stone revealing his frustration. "My opinion is valued."

"My friend, when I need a valued opinion, I will ask for it. Until then, I ask for your support and your respect."

Caspian remains silent. He hasn't said a word. He only listens.

"When will people be arriving from the Australian Border?" I ask, changing the subject, and giving my father a chance to calm down.

"Within the next few days," answers Wade. "My wife and son should arrive in two days."

I'm at a loss. There's no escape. There's no time to formulate a plan and get out of the kingdom. "And what exactly will I have to do?"

"Well, for starters, you and Aquarius can officially state your engagement to the kingdom," Cascade chimes in. "And then, I believe if you can establish a bond with the merfolk we'll have a good chance of gaining their trust. We want the community to believe in us and it's your job to make them. Answer their questions. Hug them. Bless their children. Do what they desire and win them over."

"I'll say what you need me to say and do what I can to make them admire us, but I will not declare my love for a man I've known for ten minutes."

"We talked about this," Sam reminds me.

"You talked about this," I retort.

"Marina, this isn't a negotiation."

I bite my lip, fighting the urge to argue. In the end, I speak my opinion. "Aquarius is a good looking guy. He could have any mermaid...let him choose."

"Marina," Sam rubs his temples. "Aquarius did choose. He chose you."

I stare blankly at my uncle for a moment, almost believing I heard him incorrectly. "What? I thought—" I just assumed Sam and Wade set up this arrangement. I had no inkling Aquarius was the one who chose me. "Didn't you select him for me?"

"No. Aquarius came to me and asked for your hand specifically."

I look to Wade. He nods only confirming what the emperor has told me.

But why? Because I'm the savior of Cordelia's slaves? Because I'm the savior of the seas? Because I'm the princess of City of Zale—the most powerful city to rule the oceans?

"I want you in his territory. I want you to rule your own kingdom. We're no longer discussing it," continues Sam. "You will marry Prince Aquarius."

Chapter Five

[BECK]

THE IMAGE OF MARINA comes easy to my hand as I press the pencil to paper and create her flawless features with lead. The night of the surfing accident replays in my mind as I recreate the scene on paper. In the first box of the story board, four boys are messing around with their surf boards after dark, while waves begin to rage to the shore. The second space holds the image of Tyler drowning and Brian diving for his brother, and in the third box, Nate and I watch anxiously for them to surface. They never do. I draw Nate in the fourth box diving for them while I'm left alone on my surf board. Now, I leisurely draw the scene of my death.

I've already drawn the image of myself—lifeless as I sink to the bottom of the ocean. Marina swims for me with her arms outstretched, desperately trying to reach me.

"Nice images, Beck," praises Mr. Reese. "I do hope you're working on a short paper to go along with your comic strip."

"Story board," I correct him with a smile. "And yes, one-hundred words, right?"

"That's correct," Mr. Reese answers before moving to the next student.

Ella speaks up for the first time today. "What's your story

about?"

"Um… Well, four friends go out one night to surf. They all end up drowning, but one of them happens to be saved by a water-breather."

"And why was that guy saved?" She asks, pointing to the image of me drowning, her brown eyes lighting up with curiosity.

"The mermaid saw something important in him. She couldn't live with herself if she let him die. So, against the laws of her society, she risked her life to protect a human."

"You have quite the imagination," Ella giggles.

I chuckle under my breath. "I suppose I do."

If only Ella knew the truth…

The bell rings, dismissing the class from first hour. I follow the herd out the door and drag myself through the next two classes. Astronomy and calculus. Two classes that involve numbers and thinking. With the lack of sleep I've been getting lately, they haven't been my strongest courses.

. . .

I'M DESCENDING THE STAIRS of the balcony after third hour when I catch a glimpse of Nate sitting at a lone table at the edge of the cafeteria. I stop short, nearly causing a girl behind me to trip. She cusses at me before proceeding around me. I don't bother to apologize because I'm too shocked to move. I know it's him. I only met him once, but he was one of the guys killed by the hands of Marina's friend while I was on vacation in South Carolina. I could never forget his face. Not only am I dreaming of him and his cousins, but now I'm hallucinating about him, too?

From across Main Street—what the school named the large area that serves as a cafeteria and holds several rows of locker bays—Nate watches me. The expression on his face isn't anger, it's malice. This guy hates me. I rush down to the first floor of the school. I have to get to him.

When I get to the ground floor, Nate is lost in the crowd, but I'm determined to find him. I push my way through the masses of students and make my way to the opposite side of the cafeteria. In between people passing in front of me, I catch glimpses— fragments, really—of him. He's sitting with a stack of books piled in front of him. His brooding gaze meets mine and I'm met with an overwhelming feeling of misery. A tingle begins in my toes, rising through my veins, causing me to feel nauseous. I open my mouth to speak—to ask Nate why he's here—when suddenly he rises to stand and abruptly disappears. I search for him in the crowd of my fellow students.

I hear my name being screamed. It echoes through Main Street as loud as an announcement over the speakers. It's clear as day, but no one seems to hear it except me. The screams don't cease as I frantically search the cafeteria. And then I see him. Nate is standing on a table in the middle of the lunchroom. His dark gaze meets mine and he grimaces a menacing smirk.

"You survived," he hisses, his head twisting in an inhumanly way.

Nate disappears again.

How can I be imagining this? Or the better question being: Why am I imagining this?

Then I hear my name yelled once more. This time it comes from behind me. I examine the rest of the lunchroom. Everyone is busy eating and gossiping. Meanwhile I'm going insane seeing a dead guy.

"Beck," Nate's voice taunts. I shudder. My feet are planted firm on the tiled floor. I don't dare move. Slowly, I turn to find Nate standing on a table on the other side of the cafeteria.

"What gives you the right to live?" asks Nate.

I begin to run. I'm rushing through the crowd for him. I'm not sure why. Once I get to his side, I don't know what I'll do—what I'll say to him. My plan hasn't been thought out and doesn't have much logic. Then again, my dead friend showing up at school and provoking me doesn't make much sense either.

I burst through the rest of the crowd, racing to get to Nate, but when I accidentally knock over a younger classmate's lunch tray, my plan is depleted. The girl's mashed potatoes and gravy smash into her chest as her chicken nuggets fly off the tray and land on the floor next to her sandaled feet. Foul language spews from her mouth—for which I can't blame her.

"I—" I look for Nate but can't find him.

"Are you mental?" she hisses. "You're an idiot! I spent sixty dollars on this blouse and now it's stained." Angry tears streak her face as she attempts to wipe the mess from her outfit.

"I'm really sorry."

"Sorry isn't going to buy me another shirt *or* a new lunch."

I'd give her money, but I gave my last bit of cash to Aubrey. "It was an accident."

"Screw you," she says before stomping toward the ladies room.

Classy.

I skip lunch and head straight to the nurse. Faking a headache and a cough, I tell her how sick I feel and ask if I can go home.

"Beck is requesting to go home to rest," the nurse says when my dad picks up the phone. She nods as she listens to my father. I can't hear his words, only his muffled voice. "Would you like to speak with him? He's sitting right next to me." I'm rarely sick, so of course, he's not buying it.

She smiles as she hands me the phone. "Hi, Dad," I say, trying to sound sickly.

"You want to go home?" Dad asks with confusion. "You were fine this morning."

"I know. It just hit me in my last class. My head is pounding and I feel...nauseous. I just think if I could go home and rest, I'd feel a lot better for tomorrow."

"I don't believe you, but we'll talk when I get home," he sighs. I can imagine him shaking his head. "Put the nurse back on."

I give the nurse the phone and soon I'm handed a pass that allows me to leave school.

The drive home as I blast music helps me clear my head. The music helps drown out the thoughts of Nate haunting me and helps me focus on the task of driving. Maybe if I'm able to focus on one thing, my mind won't mess with me and cause me to see things that aren't really there.

When I arrive home, Bandit barks at me with joy, jumping at me and giving me kisses. I get down on my knees and pet him, and naturally he rolls over for a belly rub.

My stepmom, Annie, is in the kitchen bleaching the sink. The overwhelming scent of the disinfectant may actually cause me to develop a headache.

"What are you doing home?" she asks, with surprise in her voice.

"I got sick at school. The nurse called Dad and he said I could come home."

"You got sick?" Annie strips her hands of the rubber gloves, sets them on the edge of the sink, and walks over to me. She places her cold hands on my forehead. "You don't feel warm."

"I just need some sleep." I stride for the stairs, but Annie's voice causes me to stop.

"Beck, are you ever going to talk about it?"

"Talk about what, Annie? The fact that I'm losing my damn mind? The fact that I can't tell anyone what happened to me?" I shake my head, adding a faint smile to cover the hurt in my voice. "There's nothing to talk about."

"Whatever you're going through, I can help. I'm the only one you can talk to about this," she urges.

"No, the only person I can talk to is thousands of feet below the surface of the Bermuda Triangle."

"I'm right here though. I can listen. I can help," she pleads for me to open up.

Pressing my back hard against the wall, I slide to the floor, and hang my head in the palm of my hands. "I can't put my feelings into words. Maybe it's because I'm not sure how I feel exactly. I understand what happened to me and I know I lived it...but it just doesn't seem real to me. Every time I think about it...it's as though I imagined the whole thing. I feel like I'm crazy."

Annie strides over to the stairs and takes a seat on the bottom step, laying a gentle hand on my shoulder. "You're far from crazy."

"Why was I chosen to live? Why did Marina save me?"

Annie pulls me into an embrace. "She was drawn to you. It's hard to explain, but my kind—" She shakes her head and is silent for a moment, undoubtedly reminding herself she is no longer a water-breather. "Merfolk fall in love differently than humans. Their lives are longer than ours, yet they fall faster than us. It's almost a sense. It begins as a lingering feeling you can't shake and before you know it, you're in love." She sighs with a smile. "It's difficult to understand as a human."

"Marina chose me because of a feeling?"

"Yes...much like the feeling I had when I met her father, Jackson...and your father many years later. It's a sensation like no other. I don't think Marina knows what it is exactly. It took me several years to figure it out."

I stumble to make sense of what Annie's saying. "Like fate?"

"Fate would be a good way to describe the feeling. Honey,

life works in mysterious ways. You and I know that better than anyone. Sometimes we just have to let the waves carry us and hope we stay afloat."

I nod with a solemnness. "I'm gonna take a nap."

. . .

I CAN'T FALL ASLEEP. It's not much help when Bandit takes up half of my bed when he sprawls himself out, but as much as I'd like to blame my dog, it's the thoughts constantly racing in my mind keeping me awake. My guilt for Ethan's death, although it wasn't my fault. My knowledge of and remorse for what happened to Tyler, Brian, and Nate, yet I must keep the secret from their families. My fear of Cordelia, although she's dead. My mind is projecting these worries in my everyday life and it's messing me up.

Before I know it, dinner is ready. At the smell of food, Bandit races up the stairs not bothering to wait for me. My stomach grumbles, so I force myself up from bed and follow him upstairs.

"Beck, could you call your sister for dinner, please?" Annie asks when I make it to the kitchen. She pulls the spaghetti hot dish from the oven.

"Lily!" I yell at the top of my lungs. "Dinner!"

Annie lets her shoulders roll forward and huffs out a breath of annoyance. "Well, I could've done that."

"Then why didn't you?" I smirk.

"Don't be a smartass." There is a slight smile at her lips,

indicating she's only joking.

When Lily descends the stairs from her room she's glowering at me. "Because of you I was forced to ride the bus home."

"You have plenty of friends with cars." Scooping up a cheesy glob of the pasta, I slap it on my plate and grab a few pieces of garlic bread before taking a seat next to Aubrey at the dining table. Lily joins me with a plate for herself and a smaller plate for Aubrey. Bandit sits on the floor next to us, begging for food while he drools. I rip off a corner of my bread and feed it to him under the table.

"Are you going to school tomorrow or can I take the car?" Lily asks before shoveling a forkful of pasta in her mouth.

"He's going to school," replies Annie.

Lily's phone dings and she smiles down at the screen.

"Your phone needs to stay in your pocket at dinner," Annie reminds my sister.

"I'm sorry," says Lily as she quickly responds. Her cheeks are red. Is she blushing?

"Zach can wait until after you've eaten."

"I'm not texting Zach," Lily says with a mouth full of food.

Annie looks to be surprised. "You're not?"

Lily swallows. "We broke up."

"You never told me that," insists Annie. "I thought you liked him?"

"I don't want to talk about him, okay?" Lily gets a bit of an edge to her tone. "It's all good."

Lily's phone dings again, but before she can answer, Annie

holds out her hand for the phone. "Well, whomever you're texting needs to wait until after dinner."

"Fine." Lily hands over her phone. Since the family trip in August, Lily has shown Annie more respect. Marina really must've made an impression on my twin sister.

Outside I can hear Dad's car pull into the driveway. As he cuts the engine and I hear the car door shut, I grow nervous. He knows I was faking sick today and he's been asking a lot of questions lately. He's my dad, so I can't be totally shocked he's concerned about my well-being. But, he's noticed I'm different since vacation.

I wipe my palms on my jeans and prepare for his interrogations at dinner, but when he walks through the door, he's ecstatic.

"Hi, Daddy!" Aubrey runs from her spot at the table and jumps in our dad's arms for a hug and kiss.

"I have great news!" he says, with a grin plastered on his face. The rest of us look to him, waiting for his big announcement. "As all of you know, I've been trying to expand my practice. I have many patients and not enough space, but financially, I can't support the costs of another practice or more staff." My dad lights up with excitement and hugs Aubrey a bit tighter. "I have an investor!"

"Are you serious? That's so wonderful!" exclaims Annie as she rushes to give him a kiss.

"New beach house, here we come!" jokes Lily with a dreamy look in her eyes.

"Who's the investor?" I ask.

"Jeff Rathbone."

Jeff Rathbone... father of Dylan Rathbone, my sworn arch nemesis. Was that a bit dramatic? Asshole is a better way to describe him.

I shovel more pasta in my mouth. "I thought he hated us because I beat Dylan bloody in Marina's defense?"

"I guess Dylan forgave you," says my dad.

"What? Why would he do that?" I swallow down the lump of food.

"Maybe Dylan's not that bad," Lily suggests.

If Dylan's dad wants to invest, more power to him. As long as I don't have to see Dylan Rathbone, I don't care.

. . .

LYING ON MY BED, throwing Marina's dolphin ring up in the air, I catch it as it falls. It's one of the only pieces I have left of her.

A knock at the door startles me. I miss the catch and Marina's ring falls, hitting me in the eye.

"Shit," I cuss. That hurt more than I'd expect. I toss the ring in the drawer of my nightstand before telling the knocker to come in.

Dad opens the door and leans against the doorframe. "Are you feeling better?" he asks as he crosses his arms over his chest.

"Yeah," I answer, not in the mood to talk about it.

"Look, I'm not about to lecture you. I skipped school when I was your age, too. Honestly, I'm too happy to even be mad at you for cutting class."

My dad has been working hard for years in an attempt to expand, so for Jeff Rathbone to invest in his practice is amazing. "I'm excited for you, Dad."

"Thank you. Fortunately, this news came to me just in time for the convention next week. Maybe I can pull in more clients with the promise of a bigger office."

"For sure." My tone doesn't match his excitement, but that doesn't mean I'm any less happy for him.

Dad faintly smiles before striding across my room and sits in the desk chair. Examining the items on my desk, he picks up the framed picture of me and Marina at the Rathbone's mansion of a beach home. Lily was taking pictures of Marina, making her feel awkward, so I offered to be in one with her. Lily loved it, so she printed it off and framed it for me. Now, it sits on my desk next to the dolphin paperweight Marina gave me.

"Marina's a very beautiful girl. I can see why you're hung up on her."

"It's more than that," I tell him. I rise from my spot on my bed and take the picture from him, examining it for the thousandth time.

My arm is tucked around her shoulder, pulling her close to me. I remember thinking at that moment how I didn't want to let this girl go.

Our smiles in the frame bring a smile to my face now. "She's like no other girl I've met." When I say this, I'm aware of how corny it sounds. It's true though. How many guys can tell you their girlfriend is a mermaid?

He holds his hands up in surrender. "I'm not going to lecture you on young love anymore." Looking down at the ground before meeting my gaze, he seems unsure of what he's about to ask. "Are you okay?"

I place the picture back in its spot next to the paperweight. "What do you mean?"

"Don't act like I haven't noticed the nightmares. You have bags under your eyes and you've been irritable."

"I just haven't been sleeping well."

"A year is coming up on Ethan's death."

"Don't you think I'm aware? People keep informing me of that...like I could forget."

"Do you think you need to see your doctor again?"

The therapist. "No! Dad, please." I press my lips in a hard line. "I'm fine."

I just need sleep.

It would also be helpful if I could stop seeing dead people.

. . .

"BECKY," WHISPERS A SOFT voice as it drags me from slumber.

I groan in return.

"BECKY," the whisperer becomes more aggressive.

It's Aubrey. "Did you have a nightmare?" I ask with a deep yawn.

"No. It was just a dream," she answers as I feel her small body plop at the end of my bed. Bandit wags his strong tail. He's always loved Aubrey even when she was a toddler who would pull at his ears and tail.

I check my phone for the time. The bright light illuminates the dark room, hurting my eyes. "How can I help you at three in the morning?"

"I miss Marina," she confesses with a sigh.

I flip my bedside lamp on, blinding the two of us. "I do, too," I admit.

"I had a dream about her," Aubrey says bubbling with excitement. She continues, "She was wearing a pretty dress. It was fluffy and white. She looked like a princess!"

White dress. "She was getting married?"

"Yup! I think." Aubrey giggles. "A boy was there."

A boy…friend? "Me?"

"No. You weren't in my dream."

"Who was the groom?"

She shrugs with a long yawn. "I don't know."

Aubrey has been correct in the past. Maybe she can sense things beyond the average person. Aubrey had dreamt of Cordelia before I knew I was in danger. Could she be right about this?"

"It was only a dream," I say, attempting to reassure not only Aubrey but myself.

Chapter Six

[MARINA]

Two days have passed. High ranking leaders and citizens from Northern High Seas, Australian Border, and Antarctic Waters, along with many other notable communities all over the oceans have been arriving to stay in the miraculous castle. I've never seen so many people swimming through the corridors. It's upright chaotic and I hate it.

I can't wander anywhere without someone stopping me to either congratulate me on my engagement or question me about life with our former Empress. Most of our guests are curious to know why I would be wandering without my fiancé, as if I'm supposed to be accompanied when I'm on my way to dinner or a meeting. Some guests inform me of how lucky I am to have caught the ocean's most handsome bachelor.

I'd like nothing more than to hide away in my cavern until this is all over. The problem is all of these people are here for me.

I've been summoned to the royal headquarters by the emperor. There I wait with Aquarius for his family to arrive. They've just reached the front entrance, meaning they'll be here in a few minutes. They've brought a few of their guards to accompany them during their travels.

Wade waits patiently by his son's side. Caspian and Jackson flank behind me. Sam sits on his throne with his tail coiled beneath him, while Cascade is nowhere to be found.

Did Sam summon her? Is she late?

With a gentle nature, Aquarius reaches down and intertwines his fingers with mine. I'm about to meet his family.

"Don't worry about my mum. She'll love you," Aquarius promises me. "My father already loves you, so there's nothing to concern yourself about."

"Laguna," Wade smiles as a beautiful mermaid with the lightest of blonde hair and a bright violet tail swims into his arms.

"I've missed you so much, baby." She kisses him deeply and passionately, not caring about the audience.

"If you were curious, that's my mum," Aquarius says with a laugh.

"I gathered that," I joke.

"First Lady of the Australian Border. Queen to the most handsome man in the oceans," Laguna gushes as she pulls Wade to her and embraces him tightly.

A merman swims in after Laguna. He can't be much younger than Aquarius.

"This is my brother, Bay Emerson," Aquarius informs, introducing us. Bay gives his brother a quick, stiff hug.

Although not nearly as chiseled, Bay shares similar qualities to his older brother. He shares the same dark, blonde hair, although he wears it short, cropped close to his scalp. He has bright blue eyes and a shimmering cobalt-scaled tail like his father.

"Brother, I've never understood your obsession with this Sheila," Bay says examining me as if I'm not hovering two feet in front of him. Sheila? My name is Marina.

"Excuse me?" I ask, my tone matching my obvious annoyance.

"Bay, you will show my fiancé respect," his older brother demands.

Bay examines me up and down with his gawking blue eyes. "She's all right for a princess, I suppose."

Aquarius looks back to me. "Ignore my brother. He's a dill."

In response Bay rolls his eyes and crosses his scrawny arms. "You're bloody wicked with your insults, mate," Bay scoffs at his brother before returning his attention toward me. "Thank you for inviting me into your home." His dull tone doesn't convince me of his words.

"I'm so happy to have you," I mock his monotone voice.

"I'm Caspian Adair, if anyone cares," Caspian chimes in. It must feel good for him to finally say his last name aloud after years of working under Cordelia's commands. When he was taken in, he lost the privilege of his surname, like all of the empress' workers and slaves. This was one more way of Cordelia's dictation.

"Adair?" Bay repeats almost assuring himself he's heard the name correctly.

"Yeah. Caspian Adair. I worked for Cordelia when she was the reigning empress."

"I know who you are," Bay snubs.

Caspian smiles, his ego surely growing. Many people know of us. Cordelia's workers have become very talked about individuals. We're always approached with questions since we were the ones who knew her best.

Aquarius intervenes. "We only wonder because there's a bloke who works for us who shares the same name as you."

"He arrived with us," informs Bay. "I saw him stop to speak with that other sexy princess."

"Cascade?" I ask.

"Cascade Kenryk. That's a real mermaid." Bay winks.

"Maybe you should demand her hand," I add.

"If you ask me, my brother chose the wrong Kenryk."

Aquarius releases my hand in order to shove Bay hard in the chest. "I will banish your tail back home if you can't keep your mouth shut."

Bay throws his hands up in surrender. "Easy, mate."

"Boys!" yells their mother. Laguna swishes her tail through the water and makes her way over to greet me. "You're quite as lovely as they say you are."

I can feel my cheeks blush. "I am?"

"You have the fair skin of a goddess and beautifully long hair." She brings my braid in between her fingers. "You look so much like her… it's uncanny."

Look like who?

Laguna looks as if she'll cry as she sweeps her gaze across my features.

"It's as though I'm staring at my best friend." Laguna chokes on a sob.

I suddenly realize she's speaking of my grandmother Lynn. Laguna and Lynn were best friends just as Zale and Wade were pals.

"Aquarius, she's gorgeous." She pulls us both in for a hug. "Usually I disapprove of Aquarius' choices of women, but you... you're perfect."

She embraces me tightly once again. I don't know what to say, but I do choose to hug her back. "Thank you."

Laguna laughs, attempting to compose herself. "So tell me who this handsome bloke is next to you."

Which one? Caspian or my father?

"I'm Jackson, Marina's father." Jackson grins, surely embracing her compliment.

"Marina's father?" She claps her hands and has a good laugh. "But you're only a fin-biter!"

"I was enslaved by our former empress when I was nineteen. I haven't aged since." Jackson smoothly answers.

"So what's the story regarding Princess Oceane Kenryk?" she asks, prying further into our lives. "She birthed your child, you must know the details."

"Annie?" Jackson clears his throat, visibly uncomfortable with the subject of my mother. And suddenly I realize I have no idea what I'll say about my mother. Sam never prepped me on a cover story. He certainly wouldn't want me to reveal she's been living on land for almost eighteen years.

"Yes, she went by that name also. It was very disrespectful of her to refuse her birth name" Laguna comments. The bitterness in her tone makes me feel as though my mother wasn't her favorite princess. "Her father gave his baby everything."

"Annie was my girlfriend, but our love was threatened when her father was planning to marry her off to a prince in the Antarctic Waters. Annie had heard a rumor Cordelia, the sea witch, could help her escape her life. She had no desire to marry a stranger, so we fled. But, of course, Cordelia's good deed came at an expensive rate. Zale found out and attempted to bail her out, but he ended up losing his throne. Annie and I were set to be executed while the rest of Annie's family was enslaved. It was revealed Annie and I were expecting a baby, so Cordelia instead enslaved me while Annie carried Marina to birth. Once Marina was born Cordelia killed Annie."

Did Sam advise Jackson to tell that story or had Jackson thought of that on a whim? I think I've discovered where I get my ability to lie.

"That's a disturbing story," chokes Laguna, clutching her chest.

Jackson nods his head, agreeing. Even as he speaks about Annie, he seems to remain emotionally distant.

"How were you able to cope with losing the love of your life and being a father to your child after your enslavement?" Laguna continues to pry.

"I—" Jackson struggles to answer. Sam didn't prep him to disclose his feelings. "I was infuriated for many years. My life wasn't my own. My daughter didn't know me."

Jackson hangs his head. Is he reliving the memory?

The cavern becomes awkwardly silent.

I leave Aquarius' side to swim to my father. Embracing him, I reassure him I know him now. He softly smiles before pressing a kiss to my cheek.

"Oh—" Aquarius smiles at a new visitor near the entrance. "Dune, come in, please. Meet Princess Marina Kenryk and our gracious hosts."

The visitor is a handsome man with dark hair and a silver tail.

There's a gasp from behind me. I turn around to find Caspian tense. His face has fallen. His smile turned to a stunned frown. His eyes are filled with curiosity as he tilts his head slightly out of confusion.

"Caspian," the man whispers with delight.

My best friend says nothing. His mouth parts slightly as though he wants to speak but can't force out the words. It seems as if his words are choking him.

Dune doesn't seem as surprised as Caspian. "My son." His voice trembles while he keeps a calm demeanor.

Father? But Caspian's father is dead. He witnessed him taken by humans. And now, here he is in the flesh.

We all hover in silence. I know Aquarius and his family are trying to comprehend the scene playing out in front of them, while Jackson is just as dazed as I am.

"How're you here?" Caspian finally asks.

"I have a lot of explaining to do," says Dune with no hint of an Australian accent. "I'm not sure right now is the best time—"

"How is it *not* the best time? I thought you were dead...for the past *ten* years. I think now is a great time!" Caspian's dark skin is flushed with anger.

"Dune," says Aquarius, "I wasn't aware you knew one of our hosts."

Caspian's father clears his throat. "Quite frankly, I didn't know he'd be here along with the princess."

"You've known this entire time I live here in the capital?" asks Caspian with disbelief. "And you never tried to reach out to me sooner?"

Dune looks apologetic. "Son, please forgive me. I never meant to hurt you."

"Son?" Cas asks still outraged. "You left me!"

Dune looks to the emperor. "If I could have a moment with Caspian, I would love to explain myself."

Sam nods. "Yes, of course. You may use my cavern if you'd like."

I swim to Caspian before he leaves and grab his hand. He stiffens at my touch. I give his hand a squeeze despite the awkwardness between us. "Let him speak," I whisper to my best friend. "Your dad is here. He's alive—that's the only thing that matters. Give him a chance."

Caspian nods before letting go. He then leads his father into the emperor's cavern where they can talk privately.

I'm not going to lie. I'm worried about Caspian. I know how it feels to find out your parents are alive. It's a huge relief. The scary part will be finding out why he was gone from Caspian's life for so many years.

How will Caspian cope? When I discovered my father had been by my side my entire life and my mom was living as a human, I felt as if my whole world had been turned upside down.

Aquarius cups my hands in his and bring them to his chest in a loving manner. "Come with me."

"Where are we going?" I ask.

He smiles. "I have a surprise for you."

"I don't know if I can handle more surprises today."

"Just follow me," he says as he pulls me with him. I swim after him as we race through the busy corridors. We've finally given the people what they've desired. A moment with the ocean's sweethearts hand in hand.

I laugh once we've escaped the border of the kingdom.

"What's so funny?" Aquarius asks. My laughter must be contagious because he begins to laugh too.

"I haven't been outside the castle without Sam for weeks! Sam is always with me for our training. It feels nice to be free."

"You're free with me, Marina. Don't think of this marriage as a prison."

And as quickly as I had a smile, it's now a frown. I don't want to talk about our marriage at the moment, so I change the subject. "Did you know Dune had a son?"

"Yes. But I didn't know his son was Caspian."

"For so many years, we thought he was dead. What happened to Dune?"

"You're full of questions today." Aquarius flips on his back and begins to swim through the water. I swim upward and over him, so we're now face to face. "Dune came to us after he went searching for his wife and son. He had just saved his son from a fishermen and almost died himself."

"How'd he escape?"

"There was a storm. The freight ended up sinking and Dune was able to escape...but it was too late. His family was already gone. Assuming the worst, Dune joined our kingdom. He and my father became fast friends. Dune filled the position as personal guard to Bay and me."

"I can't believe after all these years, Caspian found his father to be alive."

"Your friend is fortunate."

I take notice we're swimming upward toward the Surface.

"Wait." I abruptly stop. Aquarius rounds back to swim in circles around me. "You're taking me to the Surface?"

"I won't tell if you won't tell," he assures me, flashing a bright smile. Why does he have to be so cute when he grins? It's annoying.

Despite my curiosity about the Australian prince, I follow him to the Surface. Aquarius doesn't seem like one to break the rules. Maybe he's full of surprises.

Aquarius and I are smack dab in the middle of Mysteria, otherwise known as the Bermuda Triangle.

Off on the horizon, the sun is setting. An array of deep blue, dark crimson, and vibrant violet dance in the dusk. I've always found evenings in the human world to be breathtaking. While under Cordelia's reign, I made it a priority to visit the Surface as many nights as possible. Many times, I would have to drag Caspian with me. He never understood my fascination with sunsets when I held my own magic. Though I could never create something so beautiful.

"This used to be my favorite place to visit when I was growing up," Aquarius admits.

"You enjoyed visiting the Surface?" I'm honestly surprised. Maybe he's just as rebellious as me.

"I loved it. I know it's forbidden." He shrugs his broad shoulders. "I have a theory."

"And what's that?"

"If no one catches you visiting the Surface, did you really go?" He winks at me.

I flash him a genuine smile. He makes a valid point.

"You're not in love with me," Aquarius bluntly states. "I know that… but maybe we'll get there one day."

He doesn't seem to understand I'm in love with some else. "Aquarius—"

He holds his hand out to me—gesturing for me to stop talking. "You don't have to explain. I understand you don't want to marry me."

"Why'd you choose me? Sam informed me it was you who chose me to be your wife. Did your father force you? Will you lose your place in line for the throne? Did he threaten to give your place to Bay?"

"No." He laughs. "I wanted to choose you."

I'm still confused as to why he'd choose me. "But why not Cascade?"

"Cascade isn't my type," he answers with a very matter-of-fact tone.

"Your type? We practically look the same!" I argue.

"No," he argues. Don't get me wrong, she's a spunk of a Sheila, but—"

"What?" I blurt. "You need to speak English when you're with me."

He's amused. "It is English, love. What I'm trying to say is Cascade is also very beautiful, but I didn't choose you as a wife based off of your looks. You're absolutely stunning, but you're so much more than that. You're brave and selfless. You show compassion for our society and you're a rebel."

Aquarius holds out a gorgeous sapphire that is embedded in a band made from waves of gold. "I've been waiting for the right time to give you a ring fit for a princess." He slips the beauty on my left ring finger. "Does the jewel live up to its purpose?"

I look to the ring. It is quite gorgeous. "I suppose."

"I know it's not our tradition to bind love with a ring, but I felt you needed to have this piece."

Again, I look down at my hand. Despite the dimming daylight, the sapphire sparkles. I can't deny its magnificence

Aquarius swims in closer to me. He slowly pulls me to him and embraces me. He almost seems as if he's testing the water, and ensuring I'm okay with his close touch. I don't pull away.

Beck is always in the back of my mind. A hug won't hurt anyone. It pains me knowing Beck is thousands of miles away from me and I can't see or speak to him. With all the stress I've endured lately it's nice to receive some sort of affection.

Trailing his fingers up my arm, Aquarius leaves me with a tingling sensation. When he leans in closer, I don't push him away.

My mind is racing. I could kiss him. It's what Aquarius wants. How would I feel if I kissed him when I've promised myself to Beck? Why would I kiss Aquarius? It would only confuse him. It would confuse me as well. I'm only craving an affection I can't reach from Beck.

Aquarius closes the space between us. His lips brush against mine, and I linger for a moment. I can feel his soft lips against mine, tempting me, but I don't return his love. Instead, I pull away.

"Too soon?" he asks light-heartedly. I know he wants this to be as easy going as possible, but I can't do it. I won't kiss him. I won't let him believe I agree with this marriage.

We return to my kingdom without a single word said between the two of us. Aquarius tried to kiss me. And that's not the part that scares me. Something about Aquarius allures me. I felt myself *wanting* to return his kisses. Which is absolutely ridiculous because I don't have feelings for him—I hardly know him. Beck and I made a promise to each other.

One year.

We promised.

Chapter Seven

[MARINA]

CASPIAN IS ON MY MIND as I sit in my cavern alone. After the incident with Aquarius, I need space. Caspian is the one person I can talk to about how I'm feeling, but he just discovered his father to be alive, so I'll keep my feelings to myself for now.

An hour passes before I decide to seek out Cas. I want to know how he's doing.

I find Caspian and Dune in the council cavern. "I'm not interrupting am I?"

"No, sweetheart. Please, come in," says Dune. Caspian's father smiles and then looks to his son. "So, tell me about this blonde beauty." My cheeks burn red under the compliment.

Caspian clears his throat. "She's just a friend."

"Is he lying?" Dune asks me directly.

"I'm being serious. She's in love with—" Caspian stops himself short. I know he meant to say Beck's name. "Prince Aquarius," he finishes with a relieved breath.

"Really?" Dune's dubious. Maybe he knows the truth. "I'm sorry. I thought maybe your marriage with the prince was arranged."

"Well, we're trying to keep our love a secret," I lie with an unconvincing laugh.

"And you're not the slightest bit jealous?" Dune asks his son in a joking manner.

"Marina's like my sister," Caspian tells him with a straight face. Caspian looks me in the eyes with his glimmering silver gaze. "I love her."

I'm relieved to hear Caspian admit he still loves me. I truly love him. He's always been my best friend.

The admiration in his gaze reveals his love may run deeper than friendship.

"No worries when it comes to Aquarius. He's a good guy," Dune assures him.

There's the problem. From everything anyone has told me, Aquarius is a good guy and he'd make a wonderful husband.

Dune rises and swims toward the door. "I'll leave you two to speak. Caspian, I'll be in the guest's caverns if you'd like to find me."

Caspian nods.

When Dune leaves us to ourselves, I don't waste any time. "What happened?" I ask Caspian.

"He told me about the day he saved me. He explained everything."

Caspian breaks into the story of the day he was saved only to lose his father.

"Once my dad was able to release me from the net, his tail caught and he was forced above the Surface. The fishermen were out of their minds. Dad pleaded with them. Despite his despair, the air-breathers kept him restrained. They kept talking about how rich they would become after the government got their hands on him. When my dad tried to escape, one of the fishermen threatened to kill him. Another man knocked him unconscious, saying 'the merman would be worth more alive.'

"The humans kept my dad bound and tangled in the net. He was in a great deal of pain due to the fact he was breathing human air. Night approached and the fisherman on watch was released from his duty by another man named Henry. Henry was an older gentlemen with a soft spoken voice. He told Dune he meant him no harm when he pulled a knife from his pocket.

"'It's unfair what my people will do to you,' Henry had said to my father.

"Henry cut my father's hands free and was working on the net that had his tail when the captain made an appearance. He saw Henry trying to release my dad, so the captain cut Henry's throat. According to Dad, Henry looked to him as he died. Dad took his hand in Henry's final moments and felt his soul leave his body. Henry was a good human with a kind heart. He was the only one who showed compassion for my father. To Henry, he wasn't a creature to be experimented on and left for dead.

"The next thing my dad knew, the sky was growing dark and the waves thrashed. The fishermen's freight was sailing into a storm. The men couldn't control their vessel. It ended up taking on water. The ship sunk and my dad was able to release himself from the net, thanks to Henry. Father said he looked for Henry's body but it was lost to the ocean.

"He said he came to look for me and my mother, but we were gone. Dad didn't know I witnessed my mother die," says Caspian. "He didn't know if we were alive."

I hug Caspian. "He's here now. He knows you're alive and he's not going anywhere." He wraps his arms tightly around me, and once again, I feel at home.

"Princess." Both Caspian and I startle at the guard looming in the entryway of Caspian's room. "I've been informed the Australian Queen would like to speak with you privately in her guest cavern."

My heart drops to my stomach. No. No. Why? I'm one of the most powerful beings in the oceans, so why does my fiancé's mother intimidate me? Maybe because I don't love her son. Maybe she knows our marriage is a fraud and she knows her baby deserves better.

"Do you want to escort me to my destination?" I playfully shove Cas.

His demeanor becomes angry. "No, I have a patrol to organize. I leave in the morning."

"What? For how long?"

"Probably a few days...maybe more."

I struggle with my words. I want to beg him to stay. I want to tell him I need a friend right now more than ever. Being a guard is Caspian's job. He plays an important role in our community. I couldn't ask him to stay. "Cas, I get married soon. I've realized now this wedding is happening whether I want it or not... I need you there."

Caspian sighs. He runs a hand through his short, inky-black hair. "I can't make any promises, Mar."

I nod. I'm saddened by his answer, although I know his job is his obligation. "I know."

"You better go. You don't want to keep your future mother-in-law waiting."

When I exit Caspian's cavern, I'm feeling hollow. We seem to be on better terms, but our friendship isn't the same. Maybe the problem is that neither one of us is the same. I'm a princess, set to marry an Australian prince and rule a kingdom. Caspian serves on the Royal Council and is one of the head guards on the emperor's team. We're leading different lives.

I've reached the guest caverns, but I don't have enough motivation to force myself to swim any further until the queen herself beckons me.

"Princess Marina Kenryk, do come in!" she sings with her thick Australian accent.

I swim a bit further into her cavern. She rests upon her sponge bed with her tail outstretched. Her cavern is lit up brightly with golden lightning orbs. The cavern is bare beside a large sponge bed. We merfolk don't travel with many necessities, so all of our guest caverns are basically bare.

I notice a young mermaid sitting on the other side of her sponge bed. Her hands are folded over her lap and she wears a stern expression. This girl is most likely the queen's traveling story teller.

Unlike humans, we don't have books. Paper wouldn't last

long below the Surface. Instead, we have very well educated merfolk who work as storytellers. They create their own stories and are hired to tell them to anyone who can afford their services.

The storyteller passes by me with her head bowed to the cavern floor.

I paste a smile on my face and tell Laguna, "It's so nice to see you again. I'm sorry I've interrupted your story."

She dismisses my comment with a wave of her hand. "Don't be silly. You've interrupted nothing. If we're being honest," Laguna cups her mouth with her hand, almost to hide her words. "It was boring me."

She laughs, so I follow her lead and giggle.

"You know, it's funny… Cordelia had always said she had a daughter, but I had no idea it was a Kenryk," says Laguna.

She referred to me as her daughter? When I was little, she always ensured I knew I wasn't her child and I was not to call her anything endearing. Nothing was ever good enough for her.

Cordelia allowed me into her mind when I came for Beck. She admitted at times she had felt twinges of affection for me, but soon came to her senses and realized it wasn't love she felt for me but jealousy. Was that another lie? Did Cordelia *actually* think of me as her daughter?

"Cordelia never really treated me like her child until it came to punishing me." I clear my throat. "Is that what you wanted to talk about? Cordelia?"

"No, good riddance. I was ecstatic to hear the news of a Kenryk taking the throne once again. Emperor Zale and Empress

Lynn were our best friends. Wade had known Zale since childhood. They were more like brothers. Zale was first born and only had sisters. Wade was good for him."

A memory of Zale's throat being slit flashes in my mind. I watched Zale die. This is heart-wrenching to hear about his life before slavery.

"Before Zale met Cordelia, I was set to marry the future emperor of City of Zale."

"You were engaged to my grandfather?"

"Technically, yes. Although, I never agreed to the marriage. When I met Wade, I knew I didn't want to marry Zale."

"You could have been the empress… you could have had the crown. Why didn't you just marry Zale anyway?"

"The feeling was mutual. Zale didn't see a future with me. He wanted real love, as did I. Zale gave both myself and Wade his blessing. We were married a month later."

"And then he met Cordelia?" I ask.

"Lynn had been the wife selected for him once I declined, but Zale refused. After the failed engagement with me, Zale chose to find his own love. Cordelia had worked as a servant for the royal family since she was a young girl. Zale knew his father and the Council wouldn't approve of his love for a servant, but nothing stopped Zale when he wanted something. I had the pleasure of knowing Cordelia when she was delightful, young, and kind. We were never close, but I genuinely liked her. Her love for Zale was deep. You could see the passion in her eyes when she looked at him."

"But he fell in love with Lynn." I'm attempting to keep up with this new information.

"The arrangement with Lynn always remained, although Zale's father had made a deal with him. As long as Zale visited Lynn once a month, he could continue to date Cordelia. Ultimately, it would be Zale's choice as to who he'd marry. I think Zale's father knew he wouldn't be able to resist Lynn's charm and beauty. Slowly, Zale fell in love with Lynn. He was torn. His heart was in love with two women at once. Zale chose the woman who made him a better man. He chose the woman who was going to make him a better leader. He chose the woman he couldn't live without. To ease the blow, Zale told Cordelia it was his father forcing him to marry Lynn."

I remember this conversation between Zale and Cordelia. She had shown me this memory while I was in her head. Zale had told her he would lose the throne if he didn't marry Lynn.

"I know the story," I say, surprising Laguna. She looks to me quizzically. I continue, "Cordelia allowed me into her memories once. She showed me her heartbreak... and her revenge. She attempted to kill Lynn at the wedding."

"It was horrific. I saw it directly. It was the first time we all saw the danger Cordelia could conjure from within herself."

The memories flood my mind. Cordelia is gone. I don't want to talk about her any longer.

Laguna changes the subject to her son, obviously weary of discussing Cordelia as well. "Aquarius will make an excellent husband. He's always been a loyal man. I raised him well."

"Maybe you'll understand how I'm feeling since you refused Zale's hand in marriage. I can't marry your son," I admit as I twist my fingers in a nervous knot. "I'm sure he is an honest and kind man—"

"Let me stop you, sweetheart." Laguna waves her hand, dismissing my confession. "Had Zale wanted to marry me, I would have followed through and done my part as a loyal princess. Aquarius is set on marrying you, so you will marry him." She pauses for a moment. "Wade and I have a deal with Emperor Flotsam," she admits.

"I don't understand. What deal?"

"My husband deserves his throne. Both my sons should have claim to a throne," she explains. "Bay will rule the Australian Border one day when my husband passes away. Aquarius will rule City of Zale and all the oceans side by side with you once Flotsam perishes.

"Is that why he truly didn't want to marry Cascade? Because she's only the Grand Duchess and can't claim the throne?"

She waves her hand to dismiss my thought. "It wouldn't matter even if she were the princess. Cascade doesn't possess royal powers, therefore she could never hold claim over you. The crown will be yours. Aquarius will rule as Emperor one day."

The water surrounding me should be boiling. I'm beyond hot with rage. "Does Aquarius know this? Does he know you and Wade have a deal with my uncle?"

"Of course! Once I proposed this idea to him, he couldn't wait to ask for your hand."

Now I have the proof. Laguna admitted Aquarius is only after the throne. He doesn't love me. I have no idea why he would lie and tell me he loves me. It means nothing.

"You proposed the idea?" I question.

"It was either Aquarius or Bay. Aquarius volunteered quickly."

Even though I'm boiling inside, I keep my cool with Laguna. "I'm so sorry, but I'm extremely tired. I think I'll be turning in for the night."

"Oh, but I thought we could chat for a little longer—"

"Maybe tomorrow," I say, fighting the desire to flee. I smile sweetly before turning to leave.

I need to find Aquarius. He'll be staying in the neighboring cavern in the guests' corridor.

Guards are stationed at his cavern entrance.

"Let me through," I demand.

"The prince requested no visitors," one guard says.

I'm raging at this point and nobody is going to tell me no. "I am the damn princess and I demand you let me speak with my fiancé! You might be the Australian king's guards, but my guards could whoop your—"

"Marina!" Aquarius sounds pleasantly surprised.

I push through the guards and brush against Aquarius as I make my way into his cavern. I hear him tell his guards to give us privacy.

"I'm not some prize you can claim!" I poke him hard in the chest.

"What?" He catches my hand before I can poke him again. I swim away to attempt to tame my temper.

"Your mother and I had a little conversation. She informed me you volunteered to marry me after your parents demanded either you or Bay marry into the royal family. You don't love me, so don't claim you do." I cross my arms over my breasts.

"Yes, I volunteered," he admits. "I wasn't about to let Bay put claim on you."

"No one can claim me," I argue.

"That's not what I meant, love."

"I'm so sick of you calling me that! You just want the crown. Well, guess what? Stay in your little kingdom and you'll have one soon enough." I'm beyond bitter.

"Settle down. There's no need for your sass. I'm not after your crown," Aquarius explains. "Yes, that's my parents dream for me. I've never cared much about being a leader... I just happen to be good at it. Bay only wanted to marry you for the title. I basically had to fight him for your hand in marriage." He sighs. "That's why he's acting like a wanker. He's only jealous because I got what I wanted. You."

A smile lingers on his lips. "Honestly, once I met you, I knew I needed you in my life. I've wanted to marry you for the past year. When my parents informed Bay and I they wanted one of us to marry you, I took my opportunity."

"Why should I trust anything you say? I don't know you!"

"Get to know me, Marina. We're getting married. It's happening, so take the time to get to know your fiancé." He runs a hand through his hair in frustration. "You're so damn stubborn. How do you know you won't end up actually liking me?"

"Who do you think you are speaking to me in that manner?" I throw my hands up in annoyance. "I am *not* stubborn!"

"Oh, you're not?" He gestures a surrender with his hands. "My apologies, Princess."

"Don't patronize me," I warn.

"My apologies again." He smirks.

"Stop doing that." I shake my head. I search my brain for the words, but I'm beyond frustrated with this man. "Stop being so… charming. It's annoying."

Aquarius laughs. "I think you're already starting to like me."

I chuckle too loudly. "No! I don't like you."

He's arrogant.

He's too handsome for his own good.

He assumes he knows what I'm thinking.

He doesn't know best.

He handles my stubbornness with grace.

He smiles and my stomach flutters.

He says too many sappy things.

He makes me so angry…

I think I'm starting to like him.

Chapter Eight

[BECK]

"PROJECTS ARE DUE AT THE end of class," declares Mr. Reese. "You have the remainder of the hour to finish, so please use your time wisely."

I finished my assignment late last night, ending up with one-hundred-and-twenty-nine words. Boom. Making word counts.

I'm resting my head on my arms when I hear my name whispered from the front of the class. Slowly, I raise my head, scanning the room for anyone to be looking my way. Everyone is working on their projects. A few are talking to each other. Mr. Reese writes notes on the white board.

"Beck," the voice whispers. Cautiously, I look behind me, but there's nothing but a wall.

"Are you okay?" asks Ella, watching me with a worrisome gaze. Her dark chocolate eyes seem bright in the florescent light. I press my lips together and give her a nod.

Hands slam down on my table top, nearly causing me to fall from my chair. "You didn't think you could get rid of us that easily, did you?" It's Brian. Tyler grimaces from the front of the classroom. He sits on Mr. Reese's desk while Brian leaps onto my table.

No one seems to notice…except Ella. She's still staring at me, watching me closely. I try to ignore her curious gaze, focusing my attention back on Brian and Tyler. Brian hops from one table to another, kicking people's assignments to the floor as he laughs. Once he reaches the front table, he leaps and lands flat on his feet.

The room becomes eerily quiet. I can no longer hear the squeak of Mr. Reese's whiteboard marker. There's no sound from the rustling of paper. I can no longer hear the distant sound of voices. In an effort to test if I've become deaf, I snap my fingers next to my ears. The snap from my fingers is as loud as a loaded gun being fired next to my head. I recoil from the sound, holding my ringing ears.

One by one, each student disappears until there is no one left in the room besides me, Brian, and Tyler. They stare at me from the front of the classroom, both grimacing as water pours from their mouths.

"What do you want?" I ask, my voice quavering.

Brian and Tyler stride toward me, thrusting each chair against the wall, crashing into windows and stone, as the two make their way to the back of the room.

"What do you want?" I scream as they close in on me. I retreat until my back is pressed against the wall. There's nowhere for me to go. My fingers clutch at the smooth wall, my short nails attempting to claw my way out.

"You left us," declares Brian.

"No, no, no," I plead. "You were already gone when—" My words come to an immediate halt when Brian and Tyler's faces begin to morph into a disgusting scene. Their young skin suddenly disintegrates, chunks of their flesh have completely disappeared. Their eyes have been eaten out of their sockets along with many other parts of their body. They've been used as snacks for ocean life.

"This is what happens when you're left to rot in the ocean," says the corpse who was once Tyler.

"I didn't leave you," I claim, attempting to grasp onto any courage I have left.

Tyler leans close; his rotting face only an inch from mine. His putrid smell causes me to gag. Cowering away from him, I bow my head to look to the floor. "You survived," Tyler says.

"Look at us!" Brian demands.

I shake my head. I'm a coward. I can't brave to look at them.

"You're so weak," hisses Tyler. "You should've died."

My knees give out and I collapse to the floor in a heap of trembling limbs. "I'm sorry." The words are gruff, barely a whisper. "I'm so sorry."

Hands lock onto my shoulders and I stiffen. What're they going to do to me? Brian and Tyler are dead, so how can they do anything?

"Open your eyes," a voice demands. But I won't do it. I won't allow them to humiliate me anymore. I squeeze my eyes tighter, trying to will Brian and Tyler away. They have to be in my head. They can't be real. I'm only imagining them.

"Beck, you need to get up!"

Quiet laughter and voices fill the space. Cracking my lids

open, I see Ella and Mr. Reese trying to pull me to my feet, while the class has gathered around my fallen body as they chuckle and gossip about my psychotic demeanor.

Mr. Reese pulls me to my feet and holds me in place to help me keep my balance. "Beck, talk to me. What's happening?"

I rip my arms from his grip. I know he's only trying to help, but I can get up on my own. There's no need for me to look more helpless than I already am.

Storming out of the classroom, I leave my books behind and make my way to the restroom. After checking to make sure no one else is in the space with me, I lock the door behind me. My skin is warm under the embarrassment. I can't believe I just had a psychotic episode during class.

At the sink, I splash cold water on my face and cup a few handfuls into my mouth. Looking at myself in the mirror, I'm shocked to see how unrecognizable I am. My forest-green eyes are bloodshot with dark bags beneath them. The lack of sleep hasn't been kind on my appearance. My mouth is set in a permanent frown while my creased forehead causes me to look as though I'm in a constant state of despair. I haven't shaved in at least a week. With the start of a beard I look as if I'm twenty-something, rather than on the verge of eighteen.

"What the hell is wrong with me?" I ask my reflection. For a split second, I wonder if my reflection will answer. Of course, it doesn't. But with how I've been lately, I wouldn't have been surprised.

Behind me stands Brian—rotted and decaying. In an effort to

make him disappear, I punch the mirror. The glass breaks in the spot of the initial impact, a piece falling into the sink and clinking against the porcelain. I squeeze my eyes shut, attempting to force the bad thoughts and pain away. I collapse to the ground and begin to tear up. My right hand stings, while everything else feels hollow.

I can't do this anymore. I can't live with being haunted by my dead friends. I'm losing my mind.

"Then end it," demands Brian. I crack open my eyes—allowing the tears to flow—and find Brian's rotting corpse squatting in front of me with a shard of the mirror in his mangled hand. "End it," he urges.

I take the piece of broken mirror in my hand. Brian's right. With a few quick swipes to my wrist, I could bleed out in minutes. I could end all of my suffering. But what would that fix? Brian, Tyler, and Nate would still be dead. I'd be dead. My family would be devastated. And Marina…it would break her heart to know I committed suicide.

Marina didn't sacrifice her life so I could kill myself. I'm not a quitter. My mom died when I was seven, but that didn't stop me from growing up and living my life. When Ethan died, I kept on trudging through life—it may have been a sluggish trudge, but I didn't give up. Marina was dead in my arms and I brought her back. All I had was my hands, yet I was able to bring her back when no one else could.

I'm a fighter.

With the mirror's shard cutting into my palm, I grasp it harder while I swing my arm outward toward the figment of Brian's decaying body. The sharp edge slices deep into Brian's decayed throat. Brian lifts his head to stare at me with his eyeless gaze. I don't give into my fear.

Slowly, Brian's decaying form begins to morph back into his thriving lively appearance. The color seeps back into his skin while the eaten pieces of his flesh return to their original presence. As eyeballs form in the empty sockets, blue irises burn into my stare.

"You're not real," I hiss at him.

The gash I caused on his neck opens and begins to stream with blood. The hot sticky mess gushes down Brian's body and pools on the floor. He collapses, with betrayal etched in his cobalt gaze. I can't bear to look at a friend who I left to suffer in the past. I close my eyes, take a deep breath, and open them once again.

Brian has vanished; never really there, but in the back of my mind. I'm alone in the bathroom, holding a fragment of mirror that has slashed open my hand. I toss it to the floor before grabbing my phone from my pocket. Using my uninjured hand, I attempt to make a call to Annie. I'm shaking so badly it's difficult for me to find her name in my phone until I remember she's in my list of favorites.

"Why do I have a bad feeling about this call?" she asks when she picks up.

"Can you come get me?" I cry.

"Why, what happened?" She sounds nervous.

"I think I need stitches."

The dismissal bell rings.

"I'm on my way. I'll call and get you a release note…just be waiting at the doors."

My hand is gushing blood. With quick thinking, I wrap my wounded hand with layer upon layer of paper towels, then shove my hand in my hoodie pocket.

Despite the pounding knocks on the bathroom door I wait a minute before returning to Mr. Reese's class. A few students have arrived in the classroom, but they're not from my hour, so unless they've heard about the incident, they don't know how crazy I am.

Mr. Reese sits at his desk, correcting papers. If there was any way to sneak around him, I would, but I'd have to army crawl on the floor and make my way under four tables until I reached mine in the back. I blow out a breath of nerves, and stride past Mr. Reese's desk, making my way back to my table to pick up my things. I feel Mr. Reese's gaze set on my movements. I flicker my gaze at him before heading towards the door. I'm almost out when Mr. Reese clears his throat.

I slowly spin to face my teacher.

Before he can say anything to me, I take the lead. "I'm going home. Sorry I can't T.A. today."

Mr. Reese opens his mouth to speak, but stops and shuts it before smiling. "I'll see you tomorrow," he says. "Feel better."

That's not what I was expecting, but I force a smirk anyway, and will myself to not faint from the throbbing pain in my hand.

· · ·

AFTER THREE HOURS IN THE emergency room and eight stitches later, Annie and I are back in the car—finally on the way home.

"You need to talk to me," Annie huffs. She's clearly frustrated. "How did you really cut yourself?" she demands to know.

"I told you…" I sigh. Annie knows my story is bullshit. "There were broken shards of mirror in the bathroom and I accidently cut myself. It's really not a big deal," I snap.

"That doesn't explain your bloody knuckles," she debates.

"I punched the mirror, okay?"

Annie slams on the brakes and pulls over to the side of the road.

"What the hell?" My seatbelt has locked me in tightly due to the sudden stop.

"Why?" she asks.

"What?" I'm frustrated. I don't want to talk.

"Why would you punch the mirror?"

"I'm not talking about this! Just drive me home."

"No." She shuts off the car. "We're not going anywhere until you talk to me."

"I'll just walk home." I release my seatbelt and reach for the door when she locks it.

I turn back to her, smirking. "You know I can just unlock my door, right?"

She slams her fists against the steering wheel. "Enough! Beck Alexander, tell me what the hell is going on in your head!"

I'm silent for a moment. Annie has never raised her voice to me. There's not an easy answer.

"I don't know. Okay?"

My step-mom takes a deep breath. "Then explain it to me." Annie is calm now. She tries to comfort me by running her hands gently through my hair.

"I've been seeing things," I finally admit.

"What sort of things?"

"Things isn't the right word...people." I swallow hard. "Cordelia. Ethan. Brian. Tyler. Nate."

Annie's face falls pale. "Cordelia?" her voice cracks.

Without another word, Annie starts the car, throws it in drive, and continues to drive home. I sit back in my seat in silence.

Cordelia is dead, yet she still brings panic upon the living.

Chapter Nine

[BECK]

AT LUNCH I'M NOT FEELING hungry, so I open Mr. Reese's latest assignment and immerse myself in the world of hobbits, wizards, and elves.

The past week has gone back to normal. No hallucinations or dreams. I've kept to myself at home and Annie has stopped prying. For now, I'm just attempting to focus on school.

"Beck," Lily groans, plopping down in the seat across from mine, "I'm not feeling good. Can you take me home?"

"Just take my keys and go. I have a test next hour."

"Do you really have anything better to do? You're sitting here alone reading a book."

"I'm reading it because it's our assignment. Remember the class you're supposed to be participating in?"

"Yeah, I'll watch the movie. Come on, Beck. You can make your test up tomorrow."

I roll my eyes. I'll never win this argument. Sometimes with Lily it's easier to give her what she wants than fight with her. But Dad has been paying extra attention to me lately and if I miss another day, he'll be furious. He'd be more understanding if I'd open up to him, but he wouldn't understand. Annie knows enough.

"Babe, will you please talk to me?" Zach, Lily's ex-boyfriend says, approaching us.

Lily looks to me, pleading with me. Now I get it. She wants to leave school because of Zach.

"Lil, you can't ignore me forever," he pleads.

"I don't want to talk to you."

"Lily," Zach begs as he grabs her arm.

Tossing the book aside, I rise from the table. "Don't touch her," I warn. My voice is gruff, which I hope makes me appear to be more menacing.

Zach ignores me, instead focusing back on Lily, who wants nothing to do with him. "Lil, I swear nothing happened."

"Are you kidding me?" Tears form in her eyes. "There are pictures. There's even a video of you shoving your tongue down Kimberly Jackson's throat."

"Lil—" Zach starts, but I cut him off by saying, "She doesn't want to talk to you. Why don't you take a hint? Or can your small mind not comprehend the word no?"

"Shut up, Hudson."

"Don't talk to my brother like that," snaps Lily. She pulls herself free of his grip.

"Seriously, Lil, how can you be related to him? Do you even know what happened last week with this mental case?"

Lily looks at me with curious emerald eyes. I know she heard rumors. I didn't tell her what happened to me in Mr. Reese's class. How I saw two of my dead friends and ran to the bathroom where I nearly committed suicide with a shard of mirror.

I step toward Zach. "It's not important."

"Oh, it isn't? You collapsed in class, screaming nonsense. And then you ran out. Locked yourself in the bathroom. You broke a mirror! You're a psycho." Zach shoves me hard in the chest, provoking me.

"Is that all you got? You're going to try and hurt me with words?" I taunt him. I want him to hit me. I want him to make the first move so I'll have a reason to punch him back. "I hate to break it to you, Zach, but you've never been very good with words." I smirk. "Because forming a sentence involves the use of your brain—something you don't use very often."

"I'm warning you, Hudson. Get out of my face. This isn't about you." We're face to face. I'm not backing down.

"You're not going to touch Lily again," I warn, my voice gruff. "Do you hear me?"

"Yeah, I hear you...loud and clear." With one quick swing, Zach nails me in the jaw with his fist. I feel as if I've been punched with a brick. Soreness erupts through my face, but I swallow the pain and compose myself. I can't appear weak.

I head butt Zach in the nose with my forehead. He staggers back, momentarily stunned. I can't say that didn't hurt.

"Come on, Zach. Are you going to let me win a fight?" I whisper, so only Zach and Lily can hear me. He clenches his fists at his sides. I smile. "Don't be a little bitch."

Zach charges for me. A crowd has formed around the two of us. They keep their distance but observe with eagerness. It's not every day a fight breaks out at Monti High.

"I've tried to deal with you," says Zach as he punches me hard in the temple. My vision blurs. He grips my head in his hands and slams my head into the table. "You're a loner. You're a loser, Hudson. You killed Ethan."

I fall to the floor. I clench my head as it spins.

Lily slaps Zach. Although I can't see it, I can hear the impact against his cheek followed by his grunt.

My sister kneels down next to me. "Stop this. We're going home." Lily pulls at me.

Groaning, I get to my feet with her help. My sight returns. Zach wipes away the blood from his nose.

This isn't over. I'm not letting him win. I run for him and drop as I close in on him. Swinging my legs to kick his out from under him, he lands on his back. I kneel over him and punch him in the jaw with my left hand—I'm really regretting injuring my right hand last week. Pain shoots through my clenched fist, but I fight through the anguish. And then I'm being pulled off of him and thrown to the side.

Mr. Reese grabs ahold of my shoulders while Mr. Lundberg pulls Zach from the floor.

"Beck, what were you thinking?" Mr. Reese asks as he escorts me to Mr. Lundberg's office.

"Apparently, I wasn't thinking at all," I answer. I did it for Lily…and yes, a little for me, but mostly for Lily.

"Beck, this behavior is unacceptable. You're slacking in class, you're running out unexcused, you're missing several days a week, you're not assisting me during my prep, you quit basketball, and now you're fighting?" Mr. Reese sighs. "I want to help you. You just need to talk to me."

"All people ever want to do is talk," I scoff as Mr. Reese pulls me into Mr. Lundberg's office. He shakes his head with disappointment before shutting the door behind him, leaving me with the principal.

Mr. Lundberg is a tall, stocky man with a handlebar mustache and an intimidating presence, although the smiley face buttons pinned to his lanyard soften up his tough guy look.

"Sit down…" He struggles for my name.

"Beck Hudson," I inform him with an edge to my tone.

He types my name into his computer before raising his gaze to meet mine. He's clearly annoyed with me. "This isn't the time to talk back to your higher authority."

I sit down and say, "I wasn't trying to be smart. I was just informing you of my name."

"Just so you know, I know who you are. It takes me a minute to remember names. But how could I forget you? Former Monticello Basketball star." Mr. Lundberg shakes his head with displeasure and continues. "We're only at the beginning of October, and you have ten absences under your belt along with about a couple dozen tardies."

I nod.

"Why is that?"

I shrug. "I get sick a lot and am a slow walker."

He pinches his mouth into a frown. "You're not heading

down the right track. You'll graduate in less than nine months—that is if you can make up your absences and tardies. Are you ready for the responsibility of adult life?"

I cross my arms and lean back in the chair. "I'm sure I'll figure it out."

Mr. Lundberg folds his hands against his desk. "In the real world, Mr. Hudson, we don't find answers by punching people."

"Look, Zach was upsetting my sister," I explain. "Zach threw the first punch. I was only defending myself. You can check the cameras…you'll see I'm telling the truth."

"I'll be sure to verify your story, but until then, you'll be suspended the rest of this week and next."

"But the fight wasn't my fault!" I argue.

"Do not raise your voice to me," he warns. "You participated in the violence, so you'll participate in the punishment."

I can't say I regret it.

Chapter Ten

[MARINA]

THE PAST WEEK HAS BEEN aggravating.

Wedding preparations have been arranged to City of Zale. High ranking leaders and citizens have been showing up dozens at a time, along with hundreds of people who want to witness the marriage of the royal princess and Australian prince. Really, I think people want to see the girl who was brave enough to kill the empress. It wasn't bravery. It was fear. A fear of losing the man I loved.

For a majority of the days I've been hiding away in my cavern, shying away from the people Sam has sent my way for wedding attire, crown fittings, and coaches who advise me what to say when I marry Aquarius. The advice goes in one ear and out the other.

For the last week I've been trying to justify my plan—to reassure myself it will work. I'll marry Aquarius—who I believe is truly in love with me—and play along with the charade of a happy couple. Then when summer arrives Beck and his family will have returned. I'll leave. No one will have to know. I'll just vanish.

Tomorrow morning I'm getting married. I'll hover before my

city and promise Aquarius words I don't mean. I'll lie to my society. I'll lie for my emperor…for my family. Tomorrow I'll no longer be Marina Kenryk. I'll be Princess Marina Emerson, wife of the handsome Prince Aquarius Emerson of the Australian Border.

Cozying up in the darkest corner of an empty cavern, I coil my tail beneath me and rest my head against the rough wall. It's not the most comfortable position, but I'm not going to complain. This is better than being bothered. No one will find me here outside of the royal caverns.

I feel as if a wall of energy is pressing down on me. The pressure is weighing me down and drowning me in a world I was meant to thrive in. My life is so twisted and I can't seem to untangle it.

Tonight, I don't sleep, despite how tired I am.

. . .

TODAY SHOULD BE THE best day of my life.

Today I get married.

In the early afternoon, Caspian visits me for the first time since he got back from his patrol. We've both been so consumed with our lives that we haven't been able to speak to one another. It's an understatement to say it's wonderful to see him.

A smile spreads across my face when I see him. His face remains in a somber expression, his eyebrows pinched together. My smile fades.

"What's wrong?"

Caspian lingers in the entryway to my cavern. "This is all too real for me," he confesses.

"What do you mean?"

Hesitantly he swims closer to me. "I thought I would have time... but you're getting married today."

"Have time for what?"

Caspian rolls his eyes, frustrated. "I'm losing you. How do you not understand?"

"What?" This truly outrages me. I've always cared about Caspian. I would never let him go. "You're not going anywhere. You're the only one who makes sense. You're the only person I've ever been able to count on."

"There it is." He's smug.

"What are you talking about?"

"To you, I'm just your sidekick. I'm the person you come to when you have a problem, but you don't think twice about me."

I choke on a laugh. This is a joke, right? I've always worried about Cas. "Are you kidding me?"

"Marina," he sighs, "all you ever think about is yourself."

"That's not true," I argue. "I care about you. You're my best friend."

"And you're mine."

"We've both been under stress. You've been working so hard serving as a guard...and now you've discovered your father is alive. It's a lot to take in such a short amount of time. I want to be your friend right now more than ever."

He hesitates for a second and narrows his silver gaze in on me. "I don't want to be your friend, Mar. I need more."

I'm genuinely confused. I feel extremely uneasiness and shocked by his words. "I thought we got over this after we saved Beck together."

"Maybe you got over it. I didn't. I just distracted myself. You never took notice. You were too blind to see who was right in front of you."

"Oh." I'm at a loss for words.

"Do you remember the first time we nearly kissed?"

Of course, I remember.

I remain silent and somber. I don't want him to know I remember.

"It was after the first time you healed yourself with me. You had just been attacked by that tiger shark. I was so scared. And then you healed yourself." He smirks from the memory. "It was the most amazing thing I'd ever seen. I knew I loved you then."

"You didn't love me," I dispute. "You were only amazed by my gift."

"I had been fighting the urge to tell you how I felt for years. And then I feared I would lose you from the shark bite. You survived and I wanted to kiss you. But you pulled away and I knew—I knew you didn't feel that way for me."

I swallow the lump forming in my throat. "Do you still feel that way?"

"No—I mean, at times…It gets confusing. I kissed you before we saved Beck. I felt my love for you, stronger than ever. I do love you, but I see how you look at the human, and it kills me. Now you're marrying a prince. Why do you think I've been avoiding you for so long? The more I stay away, the more my love for you dies."

He laughs to himself to hide the awkwardness, I assume. "You know what? For a while I wished I had left when I had the chance. Maybe that way I could've found my dad and avoided the embarrassment with you—"

A puzzled frown forms on my lips. "What're you talking about?" Caspian had a chance to leave and didn't take it? Why hadn't he mentioned it before now? Would he have left without me?

Caspian's eyes widen as if he's realized he's done something wrong.

"Caspian, when did you ever have the opportunity to leave?" I don't kindly ask. I demand answers.

He shrugs, trying to brush it off has nothing. "About a year after I was taken in by Cordelia, I was given the opportunity to go off on my own. I was young and the death of my parents was still fresh in my mind." He crosses his arms.

"In return for something…" Cordelia wouldn't have given him a chance to leave unless she got something out of it. I know she offered him a deal. Cordelia never did things out of the kindness of her heart.

"She had a request for me." He pauses momentarily. "It was nothing, really."

"It wasn't nothing, Caspian," I spit. "Tell me what she made you do." My stomach takes a leap. Cordelia made people do awful things for her. What did she do to my Caspian?

"She didn't do anything to me," he assures, running his hands through his jet-black hair. "It's what she made me do to you." His gaze meets mine with sorrow.

I gasp. "What're you talking about? You didn't do anything…"

"Cordelia was always worried about you. She needed someone to watch over you. In order for me to escape, I was ordered to follow you."

"That's what Sam and Jackson were for—" And then I'm hit with the realization. Cordelia didn't just let Caspian and I reconnect as collectors; she purposely paired us together so Caspian could spy on me.

I collapse to the cavern floor. Every muscle in my body has given out.

"You used me," I accuse. My friendship with Caspian is a fake. "How could you do that?" I'm beyond raged. My body shakes as I can do little to hide my anger.

"No. I—" He hesitates on what to say. "It wasn't like that at all. I chose to stay."

"Not before exposing my secrets. I trusted you!" I shake my head, not wanting to believe any of it. "You betrayed me," I whisper.

"Marina, let me explain." Caspian swims to my side, but I slither away from him.

"Don't touch me," I warn. He retracts his hand.

I sit with my tail coiled beneath me. My arms crossed, I hug myself, attempting to control my trembling body.

With my back to him, he continues, "She wanted information on you. She only wanted to know what you did during the day."

"So, you pretended to be my friend?" I ask as I choke on the words. My only friend I've ever had and it was never real.

"No," he argues. "I met you after my parents died and you helped me through a hard time. I truly liked you. Cordelia split us up, afraid I was a bad influence on you. I was ordered to follow you when we became collectors together. She knew you'd trust me."

That explains why the slaves were called off of me. Cordelia had Caspian to do her dirty work. I feel sick. "I trusted you." I shake my head at myself for being so stupid. I was idiotic to think Cordelia would allow me to have a real friend.

"Mar." Caspian slithers toward me, but I hold up a hand to halt him.

"Don't call me that," I murmur with my voice no longer projecting sound.

Only Caspian calls me that. It's my special nickname from him but now it only leaves me feeling hollow. "Don't be like that," he insists. "I love you. You know that."

"No, Caspian, our entire relationship is built on a lie." I cry, hanging my head in my palms. "What did you tell her about me?"

"Nothing important. I didn't like snitching on you. I told her you would visit the Surface. I told her about Tad."

"Tad?" Caspian is the reason why Cordelia knew about Tad

being my trader. She was able to manipulate Tad with this information. Caspian is the reason why Cordelia later killed Tad for betraying her.

"I had no choice, Marina!" Caspian argues.

"You didn't have to tell her anything. I mean, what could she have possibly threatened you with? Why would you ever leave Cordelia?" A laugh catches in my throat. "You had no family."

When I see the sadness in Caspian's eyes, I feel an instant regret.

"She was my only family," he declares. "I later decided I didn't want to be out there on my own—to fend for myself."

"Finn," I mutter breathless. "Did you tell her about Finn?" My heart races, waiting for an answer—afraid of the truth.

Caspian was the only one who knew of Finn's existence. If he betrayed me by telling Cordelia about my dolphin, I'll kill him myself.

"No!" he exclaims. Shaking his head, he begins to sob. "That wasn't me. I swear on my life. I loved Finn, too."

"How can I trust anything you say?" I tightly pinch my lips together, afraid I'll vomit. This news is overwhelming.

"It was all over by then." Caspian closes his eyes for a moment. He's trying to compose himself. When he meets my gaze once again, he says, "When we grew closer, I stopped feeding her information."

I'm beyond words. I'm clenching my fists, containing my rage.

"I told her you had gotten better. I was making a positive

impact on you. I knew she knew I was lying, but I didn't want to pretend anymore. Being your friend meant more to me."

"What did she do to you?"

"She didn't do anything. That's what shocked me. She let us remain partners."

Caspian has always been nervous when we would visit the Surface. Every time we visited Tad, Caspian would act as lookout. It's not because he disliked Tad, but because he was afraid of getting caught by Cordelia.

"It doesn't make sense," I say. "Why would she let you off free? You disobeyed an order."

He shrugs his broad shoulders. "I don't know, Mar. I didn't ask questions."

I press my lips in a hard line. How could this be happening right now? I thought Caspian and I were the best of friends. And now I find out it started out as a fake friendship and that he later fell in love with me? "I need to go," I tell him as I push myself from the cavern floor and thrust my tail away from him.

"What? Where are you going?"

"I just need some time. If you forgot, I'm supposed to be getting married in a few hours." I exhale with frustration. "And quite frankly, I don't want to talk to you right now."

"Don't act like that. Why does it matter what I did in the past?"

"Because, Cas... You were my only friend! Do you not get that? I cared about you. I trusted you. And the whole time you used me."

"At first, yes." He's mad. His cheeks have turned a harsh red and he's clenching his fists tightly. "But everything— everything—that's happened with us has been real. You're my best friend."

"I really thought so," I say before swimming away from Caspian, leaving him to his own thoughts.

Chapter Eleven

[MARINA]

I'M GETTING MARRIED TO Aquarius in less than an hour and all I can think of is Caspian.

Beck.

Caspian.

Aquarius.

Everything said about boys is true. They'll ruin a girl's life.

Cascade enters the bridal cavern. I can see her reflection in the mirror as I fix my crooked crown. She looks worried.

I greet her as I continue to struggle with my crown.

"I just wanted to check in with you. How're you feeling?" she asks with a huge smile.

"I feel like a mess." I laugh.

A crown embedded with hundreds of jewels shines brightly as it rests upon the top of my head. The gold chains wrapped around my right biceps sway. A glittery golden paste has been applied to my skin to give me an extra glow.

Her smile quickly fades. She lingers for a moment. "I'd be wary of your fiancé," Cascade warns.

"And what do you mean by that?" I ask, looking back at her in the mirror as I fight to keep the crown evenly upon my head.

Cascade swims forward and takes my hair into her hands. She begins to intricately braid my hair around my crown to give it support. "I shouldn't be spreading rumors, but I've heard from many of our guests that Aquarius was one of Cordelia's many lovers."

My heart sinks. Aquarius wouldn't have been intimate with Cordelia.

Cascade continues to work on my hair. "It's only hearsay. You're my only niece. I only want to look out for you. I know you're not choosing to marry him, but you can choose to be smart."

This makes me wonder about the truth of my soon-to-be husband. No. I refuse to accept this so-called rumor.

Once she has finished my braids, she presses her lips to my cheek and softly kisses me. "You look beautiful, dear." She smiles kindly. "I'll be eagerly awaiting your arrival in the bridal hall."

Cascade swiftly makes her exit, leaving me alone in my cavern to either hurl or faint from nerves.

I'm about to get married.

Waiting at the entrance of the bridal hall are several guards along with my father, Caspian, Dune, and Sam. Dune and Caspian seem to be chummy with one another as they're in the midst of deep conversation. They have over a decade of catching up to do. I swim to my father who is prepared to swim with me down the corridor of hundreds upon hundreds of royal leaders and their families and high-ranking citizens. I can feel my face warming under the pressure.

Jackson embraces me in a tight hug. "I think I'm going to be sick," I admit.

"I'm going to be with you the whole way." His smile is encouraging and reassures me I won't be alone.

"May I have a word with the princess?" asks Sam.

"I'll be back in a minute." Jackson kisses me on the forehead before swimming over to join Dune and Caspian.

"I'm proud of you," declares the emperor with a grin.

"Why? Because I'm following your order?"

"No." His grin slightly fades. "I'm proud because you're going to make one remarkable princess."

I'm shocked. Sam has done nothing but nag me since I started training with him.

"Really?" I ask with bewilderment.

"Yes. Your powers are growing stronger. You have the respect of our people. You're a true leader. I'm grateful to share the royal blood with such an honorable young woman."

"Thank you, Sam." My smile is genuine.

"I know you despise me for arranging your marriage, but I wouldn't have done it if Aquarius didn't have true feelings for you. I heavily debated the idea for weeks. He loves you, Marina."

I look to my intertwined hands. "So I've heard," I mumble.

"He was very persistent." He pauses. "Look at me." Sam gently lifts my chin to look me in the eyes. "I love you very much. I always have. I made the right decision for you. You may not see it now, but you will one day. I promise."

Sam places a kiss on my forehead before he waves Jackson to join me. The emperor swims off to take his place in the wedding hall. As he enters the corridor, the crowd roars to life with cheers and affection for their leader.

I make brief eye contact with Caspian as he passes me to make his entrance with his father. I want to reach out for him, almost to beg him to stop. I could cry. My best friend is a fraud and I'm marrying a man I don't love. I want to hide in my cavern until this is all over.

"Are you ready?" Jackson asks warily.

"I suppose I have to be," I sniffle.

Jackson intertwines his arm with mine and is about to pull me with him when I stop him.

"Wait," I plead. I need to get myself together.

"Speak the truth," Jackson advises.

"What?"

"Forget everything the speech coaches have taught you. Just speak the truth."

I hug my father tightly.

Closing my eyes, I attempt to clear my mind of all the doubts racing through my head. I take a deep breath, and cleanse the negative thoughts. When I open my eyes, I plant a smile on my face, and begin to swim with my father at my side. As we enter the bridal hall and make our way down the corridor, the guests shout my name and cheer joyfully as I pass each row of merfolk. Children wave to me, and it warms my heart. I blow them kisses in which they pretend to catch. To them, I am a role model. I am someone to admire.

At the end of the corridor, I see Aquarius patiently waiting for me to reach him. His jaw is slightly open, as if he's in awe of me. I'm decked out in my royal attire. I look down to the golden waved sapphire ring Aquarius gifted me last week. It's still as beautiful as ever.

Aquarius presses his lips together, flashes me a smile, and follows with a wink.

Bay watches from beside his brother. The presence of Bay makes me feel uncomfortable, especially now that I know Bay wanted my hand in marriage so he could rule beside me as emperor one day.

Sam and Cascade drift out from the front of the crowd and join Aquarius.

Sam will officiate the wedding ceremony. I've been told the ceremonies are fast and simple. Here's for hoping.

The crowd stills and becomes silent when I reach the front of the bridal hall.

"I, Jackson Lee James, consent to the marriage of the princess and prince."

Jackson gives me a kiss on the cheek before allowing Aquarius to gently take me by the hand and lead me next to him.

Aquarius and I turn to face each other with our hands intertwined with one another. When his dark gaze meets mine, I gulp. His eyes are such a deep brown, they're almost black. I find myself getting lost in them. I look down to our hands instead.

"Prince Aquarius Wade Emerson and Princess Marina James

Kenryk are joining together in matrimony today. With the everlasting support of our people, their love will prevail over any evil that may attempt to break their sacred bond."

What is this? Our sacred bond? I squeeze my eyes shut to keep from rolling them.

"Aquarius and Marina have prepared their vows."

Oh no. I didn't prepare a word. I was advised to prepare vows, and with me protesting this marriage, it slipped my mind completely. Now I'll look like a fool in front of my kingdom. How will people follow a leader who can't keep her life together?

It'll be okay. I'll listen to Aquarius and take mental notes.

"Marina, let me start by saying you're the most stunning woman I've ever known. You're brave, and sophisticated, and you challenge me every day. You are everything I've ever looked for in a woman." Aquarius pauses to caress the back of my hands with his thumbs. My first instinct is to pull away from him out of protest, but I'm being watched. And, honestly, it feels soothing. "I've never met anyone quite like you and this is why I will fight for you always. I will never stop loving you. We may not have the titles yet, but you will always be my queen."

Yeah, I can't really follow that…

Speak the truth, my father had said.

I bite my tongue for a moment. I can't be careless about these vows. I must make the people believe it. The problem is I need to make myself believe it first.

"Marina," Aquarius whispers for only me to hear. "You can do this."

I swallow down the lump in my throat.

"Aquarius, my love." Okay, that's a good start. Show affection. "From the day I met you, I knew you were always going to be there for me." He never leaves me alone. "I can count on you to be honest and real with me. I vow to always show you my truth. I'll always confide in you and I promise to never lie. From this moment forward, you are my king." Say something else to really sell it. "From this day forward, I promise to love you more and more each and every day."

Sam's hands illuminate with power. He places his palms over mine and Aquarius' wrists, and with his mind he forms a glowing golden ribbon around our hands. Our marriage will be sealed with Kenryk power.

"Aquarius Wade Emerson, do you take Marina James Kenryk to be your wife?"

"I do," he answers effortlessly.

"Will you sacrifice your life for hers?"

"I will," he says without hesitation.

"Will you devote your endless love to her always and forever until death do you part?"

"I do."

"Please place the chain around her left forearm."

Bay passes his brother the golden chain that will bind us together. I hesitate to raise my arm, but obey. Gently, Aquarius slips the chain up my arm where it rests against my flesh.

"Marina James Kenryk, do you take Aquarius Wade Emerson to be your husband?"

"I do."

"Will you sacrifice your life for his?"

"Yes."

"Will you devote your endless love to him always and forever until death do you part?"

"I do." I guess.

"Please place the gold cuff around his left wrist," Sam directs me.

Cascade passes me the golden cuff. And just as smoothly as Aquarius, I slip the cuff onto his wrist where it fits perfectly. Only the royal Kenryk family wears the golden attire, and now Aquarius will be bound to my family.

"With the force vested in me, I bind you both together with the strength of royal power." And I feel it, too. The force that binds us is strong. When I release Aquarius' hand, I feel the resilient sensation to pull him back to me. "I now declare you husband and wife." He looks to Aquarius. "You may kiss your bride."

This is the moment. This is our first kiss. The crowd remains silent, eagerly awaiting our first act of love.

Aquarius places his hands on both sides of my face, gently cups my chin, and draws me in closer to him. His lips look so soft. I close my eyes and allow my lips to find his. Aquarius' mouth moves gently and slowly against mine. When we pull away, I open my eyes.

I've just married Aquarius.

My name is Marina James Emerson.

Chapter Twelve

[MARINA]

THERE'S A BANQUET OF FOOD served to all guests after the ceremony. It's a delightful selection of shrimp, seaweed, assorted options of fish and octopus tentacles, along with many other menu selections.

The hours after the wedding seem more like a dream. Reality is a blur and I'm drifting through the night.

Aquarius pulls me close to him as hundreds of citizens get their moment to wish us well. Most of the women ogle my new husband when they approach us. Children share their stories of how I've inspired them to be brave. The children make me smile. They're the ones I feel as though I've done my job as a princess.

Cascade approaches us, her arm intertwined with her future husband. King Lincoln Oceanus, the leader of the Northern High Seas wishes us well. When he speaks, I'm surprised by his gruff voice. The Northern King looks angelic, but shows his authority through his tone. Lincoln is a handsome merman with silvery irises and a sparkling tail to match. His tail compliments him well against his dark brown skin. He presents himself with his head held high. Cascade seems content with her engagement.

Queen Nile hails from a small community residing in the

Mediterranean Sea. She attended the wedding with a few personal guards, but no family. Her king died decades ago and she refused to marry again. Her people respected her wishes. At nearly two-hundred years old, Queen Nile is one of the oldest living merfolk. Her pale ivory skin is wrinkled and translucent and her once black hair is a dark gray. While her emerald eyes are bright with life, her tail has lost some of its vibrancy.

The queen extends her frail hand to me and I take it into my grasp. She doesn't speak, but brings my hand to her frail lips and presses a soft kiss to my skin. Aquarius bows his head as she passes us and swims off to join her guards.

When King Galit and Queen Isla Atwater from the Antarctic Waters approach us, I'm thoroughly interested to meet them. King Galit was the man my birth mother, Annie, was promised to when she was a mermaid. This man was the entire reason Annie fled from this world.

It's evident why she refused to marry him the moment he opens his mouth.

"Your mother was a real tease," he says to me. I may not know Annie all too well, but I know for a fact she was no tease. "Maybe you'll be able to seal the deal with this one." King Galit winks at Aquarius who appears appalled by his distasteful comment.

"I won't allow you to speak to us in such a disgusting manner. You will show us the respect we deserve or we will have you escorted out of the kingdom."

I've never heard Aquarius speak with such power. It sends a

chill through my spine. My husband knows how to use his authority.

Queen Isla seems annoyed by her husband, but says nothing.

King Galit holds his big belly and laughs. "The only reason I attended this joke of a ceremony was to see if Oceane's daughter was just as voluptuous as her mother." He examines me further. I can feel Aquarius growing irate. "Not quite," the king comments.

Aquarius summons the royal guards, but King Galit surrenders himself. "No need. Isla and I planned on leaving anyway."

Once the king and queen are out of our sights I comment on how I'd never picture my mother with such an awful man.

"His personality has always lacked intelligence, but he was once one of the strongest leaders in the ocean." Aquarius explains to me. "Mermaids from all over the seas lusted after him. Now, he's a sorry sight. King Galit is a miserable man who sits upon his throne and does nothing for his people while his beautiful wife travels from city to city on his behalf. It's rumored she's been having an affair with a man residing in the Caribbean Sea for a decade."

I'm relieved when I see our last guest approach us.

"Shelly, it's so nice of you to have made it." Aquarius plants an almost hysterically fake grin on his face. "Why exactly are you here?"

I'm surprised at Aquarius' rude demeanor. He's always so professional. "There's no need to be impolite," I advise.

"That's awfully cute coming from you," she disputes with a

snarl.

I've already forgotten this woman's name, but with a permanent scowl embedded on her thin lips, I decide to nickname her Scowler.

"Excuse me? I am a princess and you will not disrespect me with that tone of voice," I declare with an edge of animosity. It's not often I use my title of authority, but something about her rubs my scales the wrong way.

"I would've been a princess by now if it weren't for you."

Wait. What?

"Shelly, enough!" Aquarius demands with a growl.

"I'd slap you if you weren't a prince," Scowler hisses.

"I don't understand, Aquarius. How does she know you?" I ask my husband.

"She's my ex-fiancé," he reluctantly informs me. The regret is written on his face.

He was in love with Scowler? It obviously wasn't for her winning smile. Maybe it was for her blue eyes or her shimmering cobalt tail. Or maybe it was her long brown hair that drifts in waves around her thin face. Maybe, just maybe it was her monstrous exposed breasts with large, pierced nipples.

Nudity is common in my society. Most of us don't feel the need to cover our breasts. It's never been an issue for me, but for some odd reason I'm feeling inadequate next to Aquarius' ex-lover.

I've been silent for too long. Say something!

"I'm sorry I took that title away from you." I attempt to sound sincere, but my words come off as petty.

Scowler breaks her displeased expression momentarily to crack a laugh. "Oh, no. I'll be a princess. I'll just have a different prince."

"You're very determined," I scoff.

This mermaid makes me very uncomfortable. This is my wedding, yet she thinks she can engage with me about how she once slept with my husband.

Aquarius seems to read my displeasure and pulls me in for a side hug. "Good luck with your endeavors," he says almost absentmindedly. He really seems to not give a shrimp's tail about this woman.

Before we can officially bid a goodbye to Scowler, Bay, my new brother-in-law, joins our group. The Australian prince wraps his arms around Scowler, pulls her against him, and kisses her neck.

"Brother, you already know my fiancé," Bay informs with a smirk as he holds Scowler close to him.

Aquarius is silent for a moment before he clears his throat. "I do. Very well, actually."

Bay smirks. "Jealous?"

Aquarius chuckles. "Not in the least. Do have fun with my sloppy seconds."

Scowler glares at my husband as she sucks her teeth, surely displeased with Aquarius' comment.

I roll my eyes, because…gross. I don't want to think about Scowler's hands all over Aquarius. And to top it off, Aquarius was allegedly one of Cordelia's lovers. It's an image I push from my mind.

"If you two don't mind, I would like to be alone with my wife."

No, no. We don't need to be alone. There will be no aloneness tonight.

I follow Aquarius' lead anyway since I'd like to escape Scowler's dirty looks. I can only imagine she's murdered me fifty times in her head.

As Aquarius and I escape Bay and Scowler's presence, my husband apologizes for the unfortunate encounter. "I'm sorry. I don't know what I ever saw in her."

Choking on a laugh, I say, "I have a good idea."

His eyebrows rise in confusion.

I place my hands over my breasts and mimic the enormous boobs of his ex.

"Do you honestly think I'm that superficial?"

I drop my arms to my sides and shrug.

"Shelly—"

"Scowler," I correct, cutting him off.

Aquarius laughs. "Scowler? Huh. I suppose that is quite an accurate description. Anyway, Scowler is from a high-ranking family. My father always liked her, and believe it or not, she has a stunning smile."

Why do I feel a twinge of jealousy when he compliments her? Is he allowed to do that now that he's married to me? I could slap him.

"Oh, she's stunning now, huh?"

"Are you even listening to me? I didn't say she was stunning. Forget it, the point is I ended our relationship after I met you. I had dated Scowler for two years and I was growing bored. She was only with me so she could have the title of princess, and I wasn't happy in the relationship."

"Can I have a word with the bride?" asks Caspian as he taps on Aquarius' shoulder.

"Of course, mate." Aquarius pats Caspian on the back.

I'm beyond done talking with people for today. Especially Caspian.

"No," I say. "I'm feeling quite tired and would like to go to bed."

Without another word, I swim off to my cavern where Aquarius follows, leaving Caspian alone once again.

Once in my cavern, I finally feel free to breathe. The wedding is over. The guests can go home now. I'm done.

Aquarius lies on my sponge bed.

"What do you think you're doing?" I ask.

"We're married now. We sleep together."

"I'm not engaging in sexual activity with you," I argue.

"'Engaging in sexual activity.' Way to kill the mood anyway."

I fold my arms over my chest. "I'm serious."

"Marina, it has never been my intention to force you to do anything. Our honeymoon is about taking a week away from the royal responsibilities and relaxing. Getting to know each other."

"Our honeymoon doesn't start until tomorrow," I remind him, "meaning you can easily find somewhere else to sleep tonight."

"And how would that look? The prince spending the night alone on his wedding night? Would your uncle approve?"

"I don't care whether my uncle approves or not. I married you. I kept up my end of the deal.

"Fine. I'll sleep on the floor, but I'm not leaving this cavern."

"Fine."

Aquarius rolls off the bed and floats to the cavern floor. With a quick thrust of my tail, I shoot myself over Aquarius and sink down onto my spongy mattress. As comfortable as I always thought our beds were, human beds are what I'd imagine sleeping on a cloud would feel like. I miss the human mattress.

"Goodnight, love."

"Night," I mumble.

As I try to fall asleep, I can't help but think about what Cascade had told me. For some reason, what my aunt said is still messing with my head. Was Aquarius really one of Cordelia's lovers? Did she have him fooled? What's he doing with me? Am I his target? If he was Cordelia's lover, is he bitter about her death and now seeking revenge?

And how many lovers has Aquarius had? Meeting one was enough for me.

Scowler. What was her real name? Shelly. She was clearly upset with me for having stolen her love. She can have him. I didn't steal him. He was merely forced upon me.

I sigh. I can't believe I'm about to ask this. "On what level did you know Cordelia?"

There's a definite silence before Aquarius clears his throat. Is he stumped by my question?

"What, love?" he asks.

"Don't 'what, love' me. How well did you know the empress?"

"I met her a few times when I was summoned from home to travel here for meetings. My father had met with her a couple times a year."

"Would you meet privately with her?" I don't do a great job of hiding the bitterness in my voice.

"Sometimes. Only when I was personally summoned."

My heart seems to be pounding against my chest. Why do I care if Cordelia fooled him into thinking she loved him? Maybe because he's my husband and it would disgust me to find out he slept with my awful adoptive mother.

"Most often times than not, my father would travel to the kingdom to represent the Australian Border," Aquarius continues.

I continue to pry. "How long would you stay?"

Aquarius chuckles a bit. "Where are you going with this?"

"Answer the question," I demand.

"A day. Two at the most."

"I never saw you. I would've remembered your face."

I'm met with silence once again.

"You would?" he asks.

"I would what?"

"Remember my face." I can only imagine a smirk is planted

on his lips.

Damn it. "No one can look at your face and not remember it," I say with honesty.

Aquarius laughs. "You like my face," he teases.

I can feel my cheeks turning red. "No," I argue. "I never said that."

"It's okay, Marina. I like your face, too."

"Go to sleep," I roll my eyes, despite Aquarius not being able to see.

"I'm already asleep. This cold, hard cavern floor is so extremely comfortable." There's sarcasm in his tone.

I sigh. "You can sleep in the bed if you stay on your side."

"No, I wouldn't want to accidently touch my wife."

I slide to one side of the bed leaving plenty of space for Aquarius. "Just get on the bed and stop complaining."

I didn't get the exact answer I was looking for. Maybe I don't want to know the truth.

For now, Aquarius floats to the bed and turns away from me. Maybe he's ensuring he won't touch me while we sleep.

Maybe I wouldn't mind a small embrace.

Small.

I said small.

Chapter Thirteen

[MARINA]

DARKNESS. ALTHOUGH IT'S TOO dark for me to see my own body, I can feel my legs, feet, and toes. I'm breathing crisp air. I'm in my human form as I stand in the pitch black.

The blackness has swallowed me whole.

Shivers run through me as it feels as though it's freezing.

Not only is it dark and cold, it's eerily silent.

My heart begins to race. Where am I?

"Hello?" I ask the blackness. My voice is quiet, as if I can't force the words out.

"Help me!" someone screams.

I'd know that disembodied voice anywhere. "Beck!" I yell. "Beck?"

"Help!" he cries.

I'm running for him. I'm stumbling through the black, but I'm desperate to find Beck. "Where are you?"

"Marina!" Beck screams. There's a gurgle to his tone. Is he choking?

"Beck, I can't find you!" I trip over my feet and land hard on my side. I roll over to my back. It feels as if I've hit concrete. Where are we? Where's Beck?

"Marina!" Beck is frantic. I can't tell what direction his voice is projecting from.

With a pain filled moan, I rise from the floor. I force myself to keep searching.

"Beck, where are you?"

There's no response.

"Beck!" I stop to listen for any inkling of which direction I should go.

My only answer is eerie silence.

"BECK!" My scream is bloodcurdling. My throat aches from yelling so hard. I drop to my knees as tears flow down my face. The tears fill my mouth and I taste the salt.

"Beck!" I sob. My voice breaks now, but I don't give up. I force my voice to work. "BECK!"

This time, I scream his name so loudly, I break the dark. The blackness dissipates as I'm yelling for Beck and I'm left standing on the Surface of the ocean. The sun blinds me as the wind hits my waves of blonde hair. It's a serene moment, and then I'm sinking down to the ocean bottom. The ocean swallows me, and I'm drowning. I'm frantically swimming toward the surface, but my human legs don't work. I'm an anchor, plummeting through the water. I can't breathe. I close my eyes to await the inevitable.

When I inhale a breath, of what I believe will be salty ocean water, I wake to find myself in my cavern with Aquarius soundly sleeping next to me.

Beck needs me. I feel it. I have to find him.

. . .

I SNEAK OUT OF MY CAVERN before Aquarius wakes. Lately, I feel as though I have zero time to myself. If it's not a Council meeting, I'm being summoned by the emperor to train, or I'm getting married... I look down to my ring as a reminder of my husband's promise to me. A promise I'll need to break in order to find Beck. I can't escape the kingdom on my own though. I'll need help.

My father comes to mind. Jackson has always been on my side when it comes to my happiness. I'll have his support.

"Princess," a voice calls from behind me.

I roll my eyes, because I'm once against interrupted in my thoughts.

I spin around to face the guard calling for me. I forget her name. It's hard to keep track of the hundreds upon hundreds of guards who serve us.

"Princess, you weren't in your cavern."

"Really?" I ask with a tone of sassiness. I playfully bring my index finger to my chin in an act of thinking. "Maybe it's because I'm right here."

The guard looks confused, but then she laughs. "You're very humorous, princess."

I force a smile. "What can I do for you?"

"You've been summoned to the prison caverns," she informs me with a sense of importance.

I raise an eyebrow out of my own curiosity.

"There is a woman claiming to be Cora Anahi," the guard

says.

My jaw drops. "Anahi? As in Cordelia Anahi?"

She nods. "Yes. She claims she's Cordelia's sister."

"How long has she been here?" I demand.

She shrugs. "I was told a couple of days."

This makes me furious. "Why wasn't I told sooner?"

"Emperor Flotsam doesn't want word getting out about us holding an Anahi prisoner."

"Has she done something to deserve her imprisonment?"

"I don't believe so. Honestly, Princess Marina, I only found out a few minutes ago when I was summoned to find you."

"I want her released at this very moment. She is to not be treated like a criminal."

"Why? She might be a danger to us—"

"No. She's my aunt."

Aunt Cora's visit is one of the only bearable memories from my childhood. She didn't stay long, but for a week, I felt I was loved.

Wasting not another minute, I race to the prison caverns. I search every cell until I see her sitting in the corner of a back cell.

"Marina!" Cora shouts with joy when she sees me swimming to her cell.

I command a guard to open Cora's prison cell.

"You haven't aged a day," I say once I've reached her.

Cora laughs as she swims to me. "I'm not nearly as young as my sister claimed to be, but I do age gracefully, don't I?" Cora grazes my chin with her thumb.

I don't wait another second. I wrap my arms tightly around Aunt Cora.

Like Cordelia, Cora is a homicnidarian. Although Cora's coloring is more of a soft violet, compared to Cordelia's fuchsia colors. She is a Latina beauty much like her older sister. Cora's bell drapes lower in an almost gown-like form. The only tentacles she has are attached to her head replacing hair.

I only spent a short amount of time with Aunt Cora when I was about five years old, but I remember her violet gaze as if it were yesterday. She would look at me with her bright eyes and say "You'll grow to be mighty and beautiful, my princess." I have fond memories of her holding me close at night until I fell asleep. Cora was the one who taught me how to ride dolphins. I've missed her deeply, but was told by Cordelia she chose to leave the kingdom and never return.

"Cordelia's gone. Why would you feel a need to return to the kingdom?" I ask.

"For you, my princess." She caresses my cheek. "I need to speak with your Council immediately. I've been awaiting your arrival. Emperor Flotsam felt it best I be locked away since I have a dangerous reputation being connected with my sister."

"How long have you been locked up here?"

"Two days. I arrived a day before your wedding and Emperor Flotsam didn't want you to be distracted. My little Marina is married!" she gushes with a grin.

"Yeah!" I attempt to match her enthusiasm, but I fail.

"This isn't happy news?" she asks with her smile fading.

I sigh. "We have other things to discuss at the moment."

In less than ten minutes, I've summoned the Council and gathered all of its members with the exception of Caspian. Last night he left to lead another patrol. Maybe that's why he wanted to talk to me after the wedding.

My husband now is allowed to attend a Council meeting because we're officially married.

"I've beckoned all of you to warn you of an imminent danger." Cora looks to Wade and Aquarius. "You two know me. You know my intentions have always been peaceful. I do not mean to bring harm to the royal family."

"Both Aquarius and I can vouch for Cora," Wade says. "We've known her for many years. She lived with us for a few years, even. She means us no harm."

"What is it you've come to warn us about?" asks Sam.

"I can feel a presence within me. I know that sounds odd, but it comes naturally to me. I can feel the life of my sister thriving."

The council gasps in unison.

Next to me, Jackson stiffens. I know he's worried about me. I grab his hand in an effort to comfort my father.

"That's impossible with her corpse being contained here under thorough watch," debates Cascade.

Cora raises her brow. I can tell she's questioning Cascade's claim.

"It's true," I say, despite feeling an uneasiness in my stomach. "Her body is guarded at all times. She's dead."

Cora shakes her head and bites her lip before speaking. "We

homicnidarians, are fascinating beings. Our cells are capable of cloning themselves. For example," Cora pauses to sweep her eyes across the table. She seems to be ensuring everyone is listening. "If I were to cut off my hand, there would be a very high possibility the cells in my hand would begin to regenerate missing portions of my body. I then would have a clone. A new me."

"But Cordelia couldn't have cloned herself. I didn't dismember her at all."

"That was only one example, my princess. If we're injured—which was Cordelia's case—we can release our own cells causing them to grow into a new being."

"So, somewhere, Cordelia's clone is swimming around?" I ask struggling to keep up.

Cora solemnly nods. "Yes. I'm afraid so."

"Can you pinpoint an exact location?" Cascade questions.

"I've been trying, but she must have up a shield. I can sense she's alive and that's about it, right now."

"Cora, you'll be staying in the kingdom until we can locate Cordelia," informs Sam.

"Am I your prisoner?"

He shakes his head. "No. I am truly sorry for locking you away. I was only being cautious." Sam pauses to smile and folds his hands together. "If you would be so kind to meet in my caverns, I'd like to discuss the situation further with you."

"Of course," Cora agrees.

"Cascade, Jackson, and Wade, I need to meet with you as well. Marina, Aquarius will be taking you on your honeymoon today."

"No," I argue. "With Cordelia alive, I'm not going anywhere."

"No, she's not going on vacation," says Jackson. "I'm not comfortable with Marina leaving the kingdom if Cordelia is alive."

"Sitting here won't help any of us," argues Sam.

"I can help," I insist.

Before leaving the cavern with Wade, Cora, and an uncompliant Jackson, Sam demands I leave the kingdom and take a break.

Cascade stays for a moment to speak with me. "If you don't mind, I'd like to have a word with your wife," my aunt says to Aquarius.

Aquarius seems wary, but he kisses me on the head and assures me he'll be waiting for me in *our* cavern.

"How're you feeling about this new information?" she asks once my husband has left the cavern.

"I had a suspicion Cordelia might be alive," I admit.

Cascade gives me a questioning look. "Why would you think so?"

"I've been dreaming of Beck lately. I sense he's in danger."

"But you haven't spoken with him. How would you know?"

"It's just a feeling." I shrug. "I always feel so torn between living below the Surface or above. My life is here, but the boy I love is half way across the world. The ocean no longer feels like home."

"Go to him," suggest Cascade.

"What?" I'm taken by surprise.

"Find Beck," she urges. "If he's what feels like home, go to him. You have the ability, so use it."

"Sam would never allow me to leave, especially to visit the Surface."

"Sam has a meeting in the Pacific the day after tomorrow, so he's taking a small group with him and leaving tonight."

"And he's left you in command while he's away?"

"Yes. I don't see an issue with you taking a small vacation. Get away from the stress here. Go check up on your boyfriend."

I smile, hardly able to contain the excitement. "I promise I won't be gone too long. I just need to find him and ensure his safety."

"Take your time, sweetheart."

After Cascade swims off to her meeting, I make my way to Jackson's cavern and wait for him to return.

In all honesty, I can't face my husband. I'm sure he's wondering why I haven't joined him yet, but I remain in the shadows, hiding from my reality. I can't tell him I'm leaving.

Jackson will have advice for me. Although I have a feeling he won't want me to leave when he knows Cordelia is alive.

Is Cordelia really alive? I have no reason to be skeptical of Aunt Cora.

I'm about to drift off to sleep for a nap, when hours later, Jackson enters his cavern. He's startled by me. "Marina," he laughs, "I thought you would have left for your honeymoon by now."

"No," I sigh, "and I wouldn't have left without saying goodbye."

My dad smiles and swims over to the bed where he coils his tail beneath him and sits with me.

"I'm not going on my honeymoon."

"Maybe I overreacted," he admits. "Maybe it would be best for you to leave. If Cordelia is alive, she knows exactly where to find all of us."

"What do you think about Cordelia possibly being alive?" I question Jackson for his opinion.

"I think you're in danger."

"Every time I turn around I'm in danger. I'm not really fazed by it anymore," I attempt to joke.

"It's not funny. I want guards on you at all times."

This makes me laugh. "What will guards do? If Cordelia really is alive and wants me dead, I'll be dead."

"It's just an extra precaution," he says.

"Dad, I'm leaving. I need to find Beck. If Cordelia wants to hurt me, she'll target him."

Jackson ponders this for a moment. "I don't want you to be so far away from me, but I do want you to stay hidden."

"I'm planning on leaving tonight," I say.

"Where are you going?" Aquarius asks, taking me by surprise. He has appeared in the cavern entrance.

"You don't need to know," I respond with a bit of harshness. Aquarius will only try to stop me.

"I'm your husband. That means something to me." He runs a hand through his wavy hair. "I've been searching for you for hours, Marina. Now I find you trying to leave without telling me?"

"I'll be back as soon as I can," I assure him.

"Be honest with me. Are you going to see him? Beck."

I'm struck speechless. How would he know about Beck? Who told him? "How do you know that?" I ask when I can once again find my words.

Jackson pushes me behind him. I'm not afraid of Aquarius, but it's Jackson's instinct to protect me.

"I'm her husband," Aquarius argues. "You don't need to shield her from me."

"She's my daughter. I'll do what is best for her, and right now, she needs to hide."

"Marina, I know how to protect you," Aquarius pleads. "I can keep you hidden away from the kingdom until we have more solid evidence of Cordelia's presence."

"You didn't answer my question. How do you know about Beck?"

"It doesn't matter how I know. I know, okay. You'll be safer with me. I have a place for us to hide," he tries to convince me.

I shake my head. "I don't have time to wait around for things to be safe again."

Aquarius appears to grow impatient. "You'll be her first victim."

"No, I won't be the first," I debate, only annoying my

husband. "I need to ensure Beck's safety before my own."

"What about your family?"

"Sam is emperor. He holds all the power."

"Does he hold enough power to defeat Cordelia on his own? We don't know how strong she has become."

"Maybe you do," I insinuate. Cascade could be right about my husband. Aquarius could be one of Cordelia's allies.

My suggestion is met with confusion. Aquarius furrows his brows. His lips are set in a hard frown.

I sigh. "Just let me go, Aquarius. I'll be home once I've dealt with my own issues."

"What if I ask you to stay? Do my feelings matter at all to you?"

His pain pierces through me.

Honestly, I don't know what to say. Of course, his feelings matter, but they're not my obligation. "Do you want my honest answer?" I ask.

Aquarius shakes his head. "Do what you must, Marina," he says with defeat.

If Aquarius' feelings aren't my obligation, why do I feel guilty when he leaves the cavern looking as though I just stabbed him in the heart?

Chapter Fourteen

[MARINA]

I'M TORN BETWEEN STAYING here with my husband in order to make him happy or traveling to protect the man I love.

Jackson pats me on the back. "Aquarius will forgive you," he assures me.

"His forgiveness isn't my concern at the moment." I attempt to sound as though I don't care, but I believe Jackson knows the truth. Of course, I care about my husband.

"Sam is traveling to the Antarctic Waters tonight for a meeting," I continue. "If I can escape while he's gone, I'll be in the clear."

"Cascade is in charge during the time Sam is away, how will you get out of her sights?"

"Cascade is the one who urged me to go. She has given me her full support."

"Really?" questions Jackson. "In our meeting, Cascade seemed adamant about you staying in the kingdom."

Why would she tell me the opposite? "Maybe she was only trying to protect herself. If I get caught, I don't want to take Cascade down with me. I wouldn't betray her by telling Sam she told me to leave."

"Sam will be gone for a few days," informs Jackson. "It'll give you enough time for a head start. Once Sam returns, he'll know you left the kingdom without Aquarius. He'll be outraged."

"I can handle Sam."

What I'm worried about is leaving Aquarius. I'm sure he'll be capable of handling himself, but I know it won't look good when word gets out I abandoned him the day we planned on honeymooning.

"How will you find Beck?" Jackson asks.

I haven't thought much about how to get to Beck. "I could swim up the Mississippi river into Minnesota." But once I'm there, how would I ever find him? "Or I could swim to the east coast and then find someone to help me." But again, how would I be able to find where Beck lives?

"Marina, you can't leave until you have a plan. You can't just survive in the human world. You need help, honey."

Then I get an idea. I know exactly who will help me.

"I have a plan, Dad!" I smile brightly. "Don't worry about me."

I give my father a tight hug and kiss on the cheek before I bid him a goodbye. I tell him I'll be back as soon as I know Beck is safe.

Once Sam and his guards have left the kingdom, I sneak out of the castle. A few guards stop to ask where I'm headed since I was supposed to leave hours ago for my honeymoon. I tell them Aquarius and I have changed our minds, instead waiting another day. They don't question me further.

As I leave the perimeter of Mysteria, I finally relax a bit. I'm far enough away from City of Zale that I'm no longer being watched by guards. My father and Cascade know where I've gone. I'm free of Aquarius.

Daylight is fading fast, so I force myself to swim faster.

It's just me and the open water. As I make my way toward the east coast of South Carolina, I have no idea how I will plead for help. I don't know what I'll say, but I know exactly who I will ask for help.

There is only one person who can assist me in finding Beck.

I need to find Dylan Rathbone.

. . .

I SWIM ALONGSIDE THE coast of South Carolina for three hours before I recognize Dylan Rathbone's house. I knew it resided alongside the beach. Luckily, it's a unique looking mansion with most of the walls being windows, a deck wraps around the entirety of the house, and a tunnel beneath the house leads out to the driveway. It's a magnificent house and it's hard to miss despite the darkness. Once I find it, I'm ecstatic.

Only once I've shifted and am walking up to the house do I realize I still don't have a plan. Also, I'm naked... so there's that.

I can't go to the front door. What if one of Dylan's parents answers? They won't let me in. Not after my boyfriend got in a fight with their precious baby.

I'm not entirely sure Dylan will help me.

I stop in the chilly night air to think for a moment. I examine the giant house. There's a staircase leading to the back deck. As I climb the stairs, I spot an open window.

Once I reach the window, I notice there is some sort of barrier between me and the house. I place my hands against the strange tough material. Is it some sort of net?

Shoving my palms against the material with a force, I feel it shifting. I break the netting and there's a cracking pop as the whole barrier falls inward. I'm free to now climb through the window.

I'm in the enormous kitchen. My bare feet clap against the wood floor. I remember being in the dining room not too long ago eating shrimp and steak with Beck's family. I remember smiling and laughing as Lily took a picture of me and Beck. I grin now at the memory.

Soon.

Soon I'll be with Beck once again.

As I make my way down the hallway, I pop my head in every room. There is no sign of Dylan's parents.

At the end of the hallway a light emanates from an open door.

"No! Idiot!" someone screams.

I tiptoe my way closer.

"What the hell was that? Pick up the damn ball!"

I stand in front of the doorway. There's a big TV on the wall. On the screen is a sports game. Sitting on a couch at the end of his bed is Dylan. He holds some sort of controller in his hand. Is he controlling the sports game?

I start to laugh.

"Woah," Dylan screams as he jumps to his feet. "What the fu— Marina? I can see your boobs," Dylan says. "You're naked... and in my room."

I cross my arms over my breasts. "Yeah, don't get any ideas."

Dylan stands in a black t-shirt sporting a yellow logo resembling a bat, while also wearing boxers. Boxers that seem to be growing.

Dylan quickly grabs a pillow from the couch and covers his lower half. "What the hell are you doing here?"

I step forward, but Dylan holds up his hand indicating I should halt.

"I need your help," I plead.

"Well, I need you to put on some clothes."

"Nakedness doesn't faze my people." I stride across his room, closer to Dylan.

"Well, it fazes me." He backs up.

Walking to his closet, I laugh. "You act as though you've never had a naked girl in your bedroom before." I rummage through his closet and pull a shirt from a hanger.

"Of course, I have—" he chokes on his words.

Slipping the shirt over my head, I let it fall to my hips. "Do you feel more comfortable?"

"I will in a minute." He squirms. "Wait. What do you mean by 'my people'?"

"Um—"I stumble on my words. "I just meant... my family."

He seems to come to a sudden realization. "Oh, you're

nudists?"

I shrug. "Sure."

"How did you get in here?"

"The kitchen window."

He hangs his head. "Damn it, I forgot to lock up. My parents would kill me if they knew."

"They're not here?" I question with a bit of enthusiasm.

He shakes his head. "No, they'll be home on Monday. They went out on the yacht for the weekend. I had better things to do than sit on a boat with them."

I flick my gaze toward the TV and the paused virtual game. "Clearly."

Dylan rolls his eyes and huffs a deep breath. "You said you need my help? What makes you think I would help you? You've never done anything but get me punched."

"Your shrimpy mouth kissed me, so you deserved it."

Dylan shrugs. "I guess." He plops back on the couch and resumes his game. "It doesn't mean I owe you shit."

"That's true. You don't owe me anything, but I'm asking you to help me," I plead, batting my eyelashes.

Dylan smirks. "And I'm kindly going to decline."

"But you don't even know what I was going to ask."

"It doesn't matter. I don't want to do it."

There's a distant clatter. "You said you're the only one home?"

"Yeah." He pauses the game. Dylan heard the noise too.

"Stay here," I demand.

I head down the hallway, my feet quietly pattering against the wood floor. Once in the kitchen, I illuminate my hands. I notice a few pots and pans have fallen to the floor. That was most likely the noise I heard.

There's a creak of a floorboard behind me, but before I can turn toward the noise, a hand is placed over my mouth. My breath catches in my throat while my heart pounds fast. I squirm against the attacker's body.

"Marina, calm down," a taut voice orders.

I clamp my teeth down on his hand, tasting blood in my mouth. I bite the attacker, not because I'm scared—okay, maybe a little—but because I'd know that Australian accent anywhere.

Aquarius.

"Damn it," Aquarius mutters as he rips his hand away with an outraged gasp.

Whipping around, I try to run, but he catches me and pins me to the fridge. "You're human!" I sputter.

After shaking away the pain in his hand, he slowly raises his gaze to meet mine as he bites his lip and smugly smiles. "So are you."

I'm wide-eyed and surprised. "You're a hybrid?"

"So it appears."

"But you're…" What am I trying to say? I've lost my thought at the shock of Aquarius in human form.

"Insanely attractive?" He grins.

I glower. "Not exactly the words I was going to use. I can't believe you followed me!" I snap.

Then Cascade's words replay in my head. *"I'd be wary of your fiancé."*

Aquarius sets his jaw with tautness.

I throw my fists down, fully illuminated with an amber glow. Aquarius attempts to block every punch I throw at him, but I'm quick, and make contact with his jaw. "She sent you here, didn't she? You've been playing me this whole time!"

I'm about to throw another punch when I'm crushed against the fridge with a bloody hand pressed to my mouth. Aquarius adjusts himself over me in a manner that forbids me to move. He's crushing my chest, preventing me to scream.

I squirm beneath his strength with no luck of escaping. I'm gasping and moaning for air. "Can't...breathe—" I croak. In return, Aquarius lifts the pressure of his weight slightly, allowing me to gasp fresh air.

"You need to calm down," he demands with a gentleness to his velvety voice. When I raise my knee to kick him, Aquarius catches my leg with his free hand. "Calm down!" he whispers, this time, with a hiss.

If it weren't for the pressure of Aquarius' body still pressing against my own, I could laugh. He wants me to calm down when I can't move?

"Are you going to behave?" Aquarius has a natural way of demanding respect in his tone. His voice forces me to want to obey his authority.

If looks could kill, I'd murder him with my vindictive gaze. I comply with his demand and I nod my head. When he uncovers my mouth, Aquarius wraps his hands around both my wrists, restraining me further.

"I knew I couldn't trust you." I scowl. "I was warned about you."

"What're you talking about? Who told you I couldn't be trusted?"

"It doesn't matter. I know about your sick relationship with Cordelia. What did she do? Send you on a mission to bring me to her? It all makes sense now. You married me, so you could control me. You could be closer to your lover's enemy." I'm rambling, but I don't plan on stopping. "I knew you were full of shit."

Aquarius lets go of me and bursts out laughing. "Are you mad? You think I'm Cordelia's lover?" He laughs so hard, he's gasping for air.

"Well, that's why you're here, aren't you? That's how you're human? She turned you so you could come after me?"

"No, love. I came here to help you. And as far as being a human, I was born a hybrid."

"So, you're following me now?" I huff a breath of annoyance.

"I had no other choice. You wouldn't respect my wishes to stay."

"You're not bringing me back to the kingdom."

Aquarius grabs me around the waist in a gentle, loving manner. "I had time to think and I decided I'll help you find Beck. As your husband, I will always respect your wishes."

"Really?" Honestly, I'm surprised.

"I love you, Marina."

"Stop saying that," I warn, pushing him off of me. I turn away from him, instead looking out to the ocean through the kitchen window. It's easier to hide my feelings when he's not staring at me with his mesmerizingly dark eyes. "Stop claiming you love me."

"I do." I can hear him step closer to me.

"You *don't* love me," I repeat.

I grip the granite counter until my knuckles whiten. Aquarius comes up behind me and wraps his arms around my body, gripping me by the wrists while pressing himself against my lower back.

I'm focused on finding Beck. I don't want to talk about my feelings for Aquarius. No— there's nothing to discuss. I *don't* have feelings for Aquarius.

Aquarius leans forward, brushing his lips against my neck. "Don't tell me how I feel." His hand brushes against my inner thigh, stopping short of the hem of my shirt. Aquarius' closeness makes me uncomfortable and nervous, yet I don't push him away.

Spinning me around, Aquarius holds me hard-pressed against him. I watch him with curiosity. He clearly doesn't want to hurt me. He would've done it already. I watch with nervousness as he brings his face closer to mine with a mere inch separating our lips. "I'll show you how I feel right now."

His arrogance is getting the best of him. "If you'd like your face to remain pretty, I suggest you back off. Now."

"You know I can't do that." He gently presses his lips to

mine, urging me to kiss him back. His lips are soft and smooth as they pry my mouth open, tempting me. My cheeks warm with every second Aquarius' lips are on mine.

What's odd is I don't particularly want to make him stop. Although Aquarius is rude, he's gentle. Touching on different sensations that arise within me. Panicking from the confusion of my feelings, I bite his lower lip. Hard. Aquarius yelps and I can taste his blood once again. I pull his bleeding lip with my teeth before releasing it. Aquarius covers his mouth with his hand.

I push against his chest, urging him away. "Did you think I was bluffing?" I wipe his blood from my mouth.

He doesn't answer. I may have bit him too hard. There's a bruise starting to form on his jaw from where I punched him. It's a nice change to see Aquarius dirtied up a bit.

A small gratifying tremor moves through my body knowing I caused him to be in this disheveled state, although I'm remorseful for hurting him.

"You never cease to surprise me, love." He spits a wad of blood in the kitchen sink. The globule slides down the drain, leaving behind a maroon trail in the silver basin.

I shake my head, attempting to clear my thoughts about the kiss and getting my mind back on my mission.

Beck.

"You said you're here to help me?" I attempt to redirect his focus.

"Yes." He wipes at his lips with the bottom of his shirt. What an animal.

With a sigh, I dampen a paper towel and gently dab the bite on his plump lip. "How will you do that?"

He swallows before responding. "I know how to maneuver around this world. You have nothing. No license, no money, nothing connecting you to a real person."

"Again, how're you going to help me?"

"Before we got married, I had an ID card made for you along with a passport, and I registered you under my bank account."

"You did all this without talking to me first?"

"It was necessary." Ripping the towel from my hand, he begins to clean his own wound.

Placing my hand gently over his injured face, I will my healing power to spread over his injuries. Aquarius is healed instantaneously.

"I would thank you for the kindness, but you were the one who wounded me."

"Don't mess with me." I smirk and poke him hard against his chest.

"Oh, I'll mess with you." Aquarius embraces me and leaves a soft kiss on the top of my head. For a second, I think about hugging him tighter, when suddenly, he falls to the ground unconscious. Standing over him is Dylan holding a baseball bat.

Dylan drops the bat. "I saved you. You're welcome."

My jaw drops along with my husband. I don't have time to say a word. Collapsing to the ground, I'm in a panic. If Dylan hit him hard enough, Aquarius could be dead. "Why would you do that?" I yell as I'm examining my husband for a pulse. I feel one beneath my fingers when I press them to his jugular and sigh a breath of relief.

"He broke into my house!" Dylan screams out of defense. "It's my American right!"

"You could've killed him!" I argue.

"Why do you care? Who is he?"

"He's my husband."

"Your husband?" Dylan seems to be stunned. That's understandable.

Once again, I light up my healing power and mend the dent on Aquarius' head. Slowly, Aquarius stirs. First, his eyes crack open, and I'm met with confusion. He raises his head as I cradle him in my lap.

"What was that? How did you do that? Who are you?" Dylan is freaking out. He's fallen to his knees with his hands grasping his head. "What is happening?"

"Are you okay?" I ask Aquarius.

He nods. Looking to Dylan, Aquarius glowers. "If you ever cross me again, I will bring you to the deepest depth of the ocean and allow a siren to eat your flesh."

Dylan is speechless for a moment, staring at Aquarius in complete wonder. "What... who are you, dude? Who says shit like that?"

"This isn't Beck, is it?" Aquarius asks.

I laugh. "Hardly."

"Someone tell me what the hell is going on!" Dylan screams.

"Humans," Aquarius scoffs while rolling his eyes.

Chapter Fifteen

[MARINA]

AQUARIUS BOOKED US TWO tickets to Minneapolis for tomorrow. He's willing to help, and despite being skeptical, I need his assistance. I think of Dylan as Aquarius drives me to our hotel for the night.

There wasn't much to say to Dylan after Aquarius woke up. Dylan was questioning everything, but I couldn't tell him the truth. My plan for using him for help had failed. I no longer needed him, so I left him wondering.

Dylan doesn't know what he saw. He doesn't understand what happened, so I'm not too worried about him opening his mouth. No one would believe him anyway.

"Why are you really helping me?" I ask Aquarius as he pulls into the parking lot of the grand hotel.

"Stop asking me why I want to help you, and just accept it." He cuts the engine and sighs. "You need to put on pants."

"Why?"

"Because, Marina, in this world, clothes are required."

"I don't have pants."

"Lucky for you," Aquarius says as he reaches into the backseat and retrieves a bag, "I'm always prepared." He hands me the bag. "Here is your new wardrobe. Find a pair of pants and wear them, please."

Inside the bag there are several sets of clothes, but when I discover a pair of sweatpants, I choose to wear them.

"You bought all of this for me?" I ask, slipping the cozy sweatpants over my bare legs.

"My money is your money, so you shall have whatever you desire."

"What if money can't buy what I desire?"

Aquarius looks saddened by my comment. He must know what I desire most is love from another man. My husband hangs his head as he crawls out of the car and walks toward the hotel. I remain silent as I follow him into the lobby. I'm astounded at how perfectly Aquarius maneuvers this world. I watch him in amazement as he checks in, pays with cash, and leads me to our room. He takes action and I admire him for it. I know it seems crazy to be stunned by simple human tasks, but I still have no idea how to be an air-breather.

By the time we settle into our room, and I shower, I'm exhausted. Between the swim from Mysteria, the search for Dylan, and the entanglement with Aquarius, I'm drained. Aquarius seems tired as well. He doesn't protest when I crawl into bed and shut off the lamp. At this point, I'm too tired to care there's only one bed in the room. He rustles our sheets before crawling beneath them and yawning, causing me to yawn in return.

My eyelids are heavy and I feel sleep quickly approaching when I hear Aquarius whisper. "Marina, are you awake?"

I stir with a groan. "Yes."

"I'm sorry," he admits.

"For what?" I roll toward Aquarius.

"Barging into your life," he says quietly. I can only imagine a sad frown plastered on his face.

"You said yourself, you're only trying to protect me."

"I'll defend you until my last breath." Aquarius reaches out and caresses my cheek.

I don't answer his promise of allegiance, but instead push his hand away and change the subject. "When did you find out you were a hybrid?"

Aquarius rolls to his back. "When I was a little fin-biter. I was only six. I had no idea what was happening to my body. It almost killed me."

"How?"

"When the shift occurred, I was in the caverns with my parents. My entire body had gone numb. I couldn't move until the pain arose in my tail. Suddenly, my bones felt as if they were breaking apart. My parents were panicked as I cried for mercy. My tail ripped apart, and a cloud of blood surrounded me. I was in the most..." he struggles for the correct word to describe the shift for the first time, "horrendous pain."

I shudder for a brief moment at the memory of the agony.

"My parents were frightened," continues Aquarius, "although my mother was the one who took initiative and got me out of the caverns. I couldn't breathe. I couldn't hear my mother's voice. I didn't know what was happening to me."

"There was no way you could have." Fortunately, my first shift didn't take me by surprise since Cordelia had warned me of my fate.

Aquarius pulls the covers closer to him. "That was the day I found out I had the ability to shift between worlds. At first, my father accused my mother of having an affair. My father always knew I didn't look much like him. My mother swore her loyalty to my father, but was forced to confess her secret. It turns out my mother was born to a mermaid, but her father was a human. My mother is a hybrid who chooses to live below the Surface."

Queen Laguna is a hybrid? How many of us are there, I wonder? "How did your father react?"

"He was mortified at first to discover his sons weren't of true merfolk blood," Aquarius confesses sounding hurt.

I ask the obvious question. "Does Bay share the same ability?"

Although I can't see him perfectly in the dark, I feel Aquarius shake his head against the pillow next to me. "No, the gene was passed only to me."

"Does Wade still feel the same way about your ability?"

"No, he learned to quickly accept the truth. Obviously, we don't share that family secret with anyone."

"Except for me," I playfully add.

Aquarius reaches through the dark for my hand and intertwines our fingers. The marriage bond is strong between us. I can feel the draw when we're close. This time, I don't let go.

"Well, you're family now," he says. I can almost hear the

smile behind his accent.

"How did you know I was a hybrid?"

"Emperor Flotsam had shared this secret with Wade knowing he could trust my father. The only reason my father told me was because you and I share the same gift. This was only one of the many reasons I knew I needed to marry you. Most of our society despises the human race and would exile the hybrids. We need to stick together. The citizens would never accept a hybrid as their leader."

"Do you want to be the leader?" I question, moving my hand to find his.

He pauses at my touch. "No one has ever asked me that. I think people just assume it's what I want."

I graze my thumb over the back of his hand. "And what do you want?"

"Honestly, I want a normal life."

I softly giggle, causing Aquarius to laugh.

"You're amused by my confession?" he asks.

"With the lives we lead, I'm not sure we could ever live a normal life. We're hybrids. We have two identities."

"We have a choice," Aquarius declares. "My parents always gave me a choice."

I sigh with a heaviness in my chest. "If only we could be both."

"It's difficult, but manageable. When I was younger I only lived as a human in order to visit my grandfather. Now that he's gone, I only escape our world for a little while. I can't be gone for too long or the citizens would suspect a problem."

His grandfather died, too? "What was your grandfather like?"

"Grandpa Sylvan was a very successful man above the Surface. He created an empire for himself along with millions of dollars, which is the only reason I've been able to live so comfortably in this world. My grandfather always helped me transition into the human world. He even bought me a private island off of the coast of Australia when I turned eighteen. I named the island after him."

"What about your mother? Has she transitioned well?"

"Above the Surface is still very much a foreign place to my mother. She only visited her father once a year, twice if he was lucky. She much prefers living below the Surface with my father."

"If you had to choose, would you permanently live as an air-breather or a water-breather?" I spare him the fact that if I had a choice, I'd live as a human with Beck.

"In all honesty, I would give up my throne, and live on my island."

I suddenly realize where Aquarius was planning to take me for our honeymoon. "You were going to bring me to the island for our honeymoon?"

"Yes," he admits. "I was planning on showing you the truth about myself. I didn't want to reveal myself the way I did, but I didn't have much of a choice."

"Well, I admit I shouldn't have reacted so violently," I confess. Thinking about my actions now, I probably shouldn't have punched Aquarius... or bit his lip.

Aquarius yawns before laughing. "I forgive you."

"I didn't apologize. You still deserve it for following me," I tease.

"Go to sleep, my love." Aquarius turns so his back is to me.

"Don't tell me what to do," I joke with a yawn.

Despite wanting to defy Aquarius, I fall asleep as soon as I shut my eyes.

. . .

I'M IN BECK'S ROOM back in the Edisto rental. I rest my head upon his chest, listening to his thumping heart.

"I feel so alone." I tell Beck.

"I'm right here." He holds me close. I feel his warm breath against my skin causing me to tingle.

"I miss you." I push myself up enough to look him in his bright emerald eyes.

"Come here," he says as he pulls me closer to him. He presses his lips to mine and I melt against him. I feel for the hem of his shirt and trail my hands beneath it, wanting my skin on his skin. He tears his shirt off and then peels mine over my head. Beck rolls over me, crushing me beneath him, but I invite the weight.

"Are you sure you want to do this, love?" he asks.

"Yes," I moan.

Beck kisses me again, slowly and softly.

"I told you I'm not going to pressure you into anything."

I open my eyes to be enveloped in the dark. I'm nowhere near Beck. I'm tangled up with Aquarius as my hands are gripped in his luscious hair and he's got me hard by the hips pressing himself against me in the most tempting way.

"Stop, stop, stop." I forcefully shove him away from me. When I roll over to escape him, I fall off the edge of the bed, hitting myself hard against the floor.

Aquarius flicks on the lights in a panic, blinding me for a moment. "Are you all right, love?"

"*Stop* calling me that!" I grunt.

"I'm sorry."

I pull myself to my feet and make my way to the balcony door.

"Where are you going?"

I ignore my husband and step out onto the deck. I need space. Space to think. Space to breathe. Space to scream.

"Marina—" I slam the sliding door.

I made the mistake of not bringing a blanket with me, but I don't care. I sit on the deck and look up to the night sky, full of stars. Finally, I can breathe. Finally, I can think.

I feel guilty for kissing Aquarius while dreaming of Beck.

I mostly feel guilty for liking it.

Chapter Sixteen

[MARINA]

THE FLIGHT ATTENDANT GOES through the emergency procedures, which only results in my growing fear of traveling through the air. My feet—or fins—have never left land or water.

"Nervous?" Aquarius asks, leaning over.

I nod as I exhale and slowly inhale.

What if the plane goes down? What if the plane suddenly explodes? What if—Oh my god. I have to stop...

When the plane starts to move, I instinctively grab hold of the armrests, my fingernails digging into the leather as we begin to ascend into the air. I squint my eyes shut so tightly, droplets of tears form in the corners of my eyes.

A hand is placed over mine to comfort me. Aquarius.

Bravely, I crack my eyelids open to find my husband looking at me with nothing but admiration. I focus in on his dark gaze, and oddly enough, it soothes me.

"I'm right here," he says, comforting me. "You're safe with me."

The plane levels and I feel a calming sensation within me. I take a deep breath. This is most definitely more nerve-racking than the car.

Close to an hour passes before I realize I'm still holding Aquarius' hand.

"Are you still nervous, love?" Aquarius gives my hand a slight squeeze.

"Just a little," I admit. I should pull my hand back, but knowing Aquarius is holding onto me is reassuring.

"Hey, lady!" a boy yells to one of the flight attendants. "Excuse me!"

I take notice of the boy who seems to be causing a scene. I'd say I'm surprised, but when I see Dylan is seated a few rows up from us, I only roll my eyes.

Why is he here? How did he find us?

Next to Dylan is a very large, hairy man who is asleep on his shoulder. Dylan doesn't seem pleased in the slightest and shoves the man's head to the window. But every time, the man shifts his body back to rest on Dylan.

I hear the flight attendant groan before engaging Dylan directly. "How can I help you, sir?"

"My friends are seated back there." He points to me and Aquarius, but we divert our gaze elsewhere as to not associate with him. "I notice there is an empty seat across the aisle from them. I'd like to take it."

"And I'd like my boyfriend of six years to propose to me, but we don't always get what we want," she responds with subtle sassiness.

"Yeah, I don't think I asked about your relationship status," he scoffs. "This man is drooling on my shoulder, and as a paying customer, I demand a new seat."

"That particular seat was purchased, sir."

"No one is sitting in it, so purchased or not, it's empty," Dylan argues, shoving the man off his shoulder once again.

The flight attendant smirks. "I can't allow you to sit there."

"Fine." Dylan crosses his arms over his chest. "I'd like a bag of peanuts."

"We're all out of peanuts," the woman says with a smile and walks away toward the front of the plane.

"How did your friend find us?" questions Aquarius.

"I wouldn't call him my friend. He's more of an acquaintance. And I have no idea."

"He must be pretty good friends with Beck if he tracked us down just so he could tag along."

I frown. "He hates Beck. I really have no idea why he insisted on following us."

Unbuckling my seat belt, I take a deep breath. I'm nervous about getting up and walking while we're in the air.

"What're you doing?" Aquarius inquires.

Slowly, I stand and find my balance before crawling over Aquarius. "I'm going to talk to him."

I wobble down the aisle, but once I make it to Dylan, I kneel down so I'm eye level with him.

"Why're you following us?"

"I'm not exactly following you. I figured when you showed up you were headed to find Beck. I booked a last minute flight. I didn't know you'd be on this one."

"You don't even like Beck. Why would you want to come?"

Dylan sneers as he pushes the man's head from his shoulder. "I have my reasons."

"You're not coming with us," I argue.

"You can't stop me." Dylan smirks.

"You have no idea what I can do," I snap causing Dylan to fall silent, only for a moment.

"Why're you bringing your husband to meet Beck anyway? You really think Beck is going to welcome you with open arms when you show up with...that." Dylan directs his gaze toward Aquarius, who is watching us intently. "He's an upgrade, I'll give you that."

"You're not coming with us."

"I have a picture that would say otherwise," Dylan comments as he pulls his phone from his pocket. He shows me an image of myself reaching in his closet. I'm clearly naked and my bottom is on display. "I go with you or I tell Beck you showed up for a middle-of-the-night booty call—" Wrapping my hands around his neck, Dylan chokes.

"You took a picture of me, you creep?" I squeeze harder. As my rage builds, I feel my power growing within my veins.

Strong hands pull me up to my feet forcing me to release Dylan before I can do any real damage. Dylan coughs, playing the victim.

"Marina, you're causing a scene," Aquarius tells me, holding me against him.

I look around to see several horrified passengers, although the flight attendant wears a proud smile.

"You're nothing more than sea scum."

"So we have a deal?" Dylan asks, rubbing his throat.

As much as I hate the idea of Dylan travelling with us, I don't want to risk Beck seeing a naked picture of me in Dylan's room before I can explain my side of the story. I'll let Beck deal with him once I've said my piece.

"Fine, but only because I want to see your ass kicked once again."

When Aquarius and I return to our seats, I'm shaking. How could I have thought Dylan would be someone who could have helped me? He's slimy.

"What was that about?" Aquarius asks, holding my hand to steady my shakiness.

"Nothing that concerns you," I say a little harsher than I mean it to be. "It was about Beck."

Aquarius falls silent, almost as if he's thinking. He hesitates for a moment to speak, but then sighs. "When we get to Minnesota, what will you do about Beck?"

I bite my lip, not wanting to say the answer. "I'll make him forget," I admit for the first time aloud. "I'll heal him."

Aquarius seems wary. Maybe he doesn't trust me. "I know you still have feelings for him."

"I don't know if my love for Beck will ever disappear," I confess, "but I have to attempt to let him live his own life. Cordelia can't hurt him again. I won't allow her."

"We need to look at this visit as a mission. We're not there to vacation, Marina. We need to get to the island for safety."

I grit my teeth, fighting the anger within me. I want to yell. It kills me to know I must let him go. "I know," I finally whisper.

"I don't want you to be mad. I just need you to understand the situation. Cordelia will only assume you're going to see Beck. She knows exactly where to find you."

"We don't even know what she wants," I argue.

"She's back for vengeance."

Vengeance on me and my family. I turn away from Aquarius and face the window. The clouds are thick today, and the sun has already set. It's hard to see much of anything except for the glimpse of city lights below. For the first time in my life, I experience what it feels like to be a bird flying high above the world.

When we land two hours later, I feel a weight lifted from my chest. We've made it to Minnesota. My breathing slows as my feet touch the ground once again. And of course, Aquarius thought to bring a coat for me. I tug it on against the chilly October night.

Aquarius has already arranged a car for us. He never ceases to amaze me in this world. As Aquarius drives, I stare out the window as other cars pass by and the street lights illuminate the night. The car no longer gives me anxiety, which is a plus.

The car speaks to Aquarius as he drives, another new experience that Aquarius seems perfectly comfortable with. Dylan read off Beck's address from his phone when the voice asked our destination.

"Why're you sad?" Dylan asks from the backseat. To my surprise, his concern seems genuine. "You get to see Beck."

Tears brim from my eyes. I shake my head, trying to clear the thought. "I get to say goodbye to Beck," I mumble as a tear rolls down my cheek.

Chapter Seventeen

[MARINA]

When we arrive at the Hudson's house, my stomach drops. There's a strange fluttering in my gut. This has become a reality. I'm here. I've found Beck.

"I think Dylan and I should stay in the car while you go in first. Break the ice," advises Aquarius.

"Break the ice?" I'm confounded by his metaphor.

Aquarius shakes his head and laughs. He finds my naivety amusing.

"It's only an expression, love."

"Oh." I smile. I take a deep breath and hug my jacket a bit tighter before exiting the car.

The Hudson's outside lights are bright, illuminating their front yard. Their house is beautiful with dark brick, big windows, and a large attached garage. There is a garden on each side of the walkway leading up to the front door.

When the door cracks open, I come to a halt. Is it Beck?

Lily appears at the door and I break out in a large grin. I've missed my friend.

She squeals and begins to run outside. I open my arms to catch her embrace, but she runs passed me. I turn to see where she is running. Dylan is standing outside the car. Lily leaps into his arms as he catches her and holds her close. She grabs hold of his face and plants a kiss on his lips.

My jaw nearly drops to the ground. Lily and Dylan? How though?

Then it all makes sense. Dylan threatened me because he wanted to meet up with Lily. That's why Dylan had the address in his phone. Lily knew we were coming all along.

Lily gives him a few more kisses before finally letting him go and running to me. This time she embraces me with welcoming arms. I hug her tightly.

"I've missed you, girl!" She pulls away to examine me. "You're still gorgeous as ever." Lily smiles and then pulls me back in for another hug.

"You and Dylan?" Honestly, I'm disgusted.

A grin spreads across her face. "Yeah! I contacted him after we got home. I was trying to get in touch with you and thought maybe he'd know where I could find you. Feelings just started to develop. He's a really sweet guy. I think he's just misunderstood." She giggles and covers her mouth.

"I don't think he's misunderstood, Lily. I think he's just a jerk."

Her smile fades, replaced by a grimace. "You don't know him like I do! I thought the same thing for years until I really gave him a chance."

"You should ask him how he got here and then make up your mind as to whether he's only misunderstood."

"What?" Lily frowns.

"Just ask him." I sigh and shake off the horrifying news of Dylan and Lily. "Obviously, you knew we were coming. Does Beck know?"

"No. I wanted it to be a surprise!"

As anxious as I've been to see Beck, there's one person I've been more nervous to see. "Does Annie know we're here?"

"Yeah! She's waiting in the kitchen."

"I'd like to say hello to her first." I swallow the uneasy lump forming in my throat.

"She'll be happy to know that. She's been waiting up for you. Come in! Dylan, come on!"

Dylan walks up to us and grabs Lily's hand. Lily kisses him once more. Although it's dark out, I notice how red Dylan's cheeks have become.

"You know, you could've just told me you wanted to come for Lily," I tell Dylan.

"You would've never let me join."

"That's true." I don't think I can support their relationship when Lily deserves so much better.

Lily hugs Dylan again. "There's something in my room I need you to see."

"Yes, I need to see it," he agrees with a wink. "Right now."

Ew. I don't need to know.

Lily leads us into her family home. I'm glad to get out of the chilly night and into the warm house. I shiver before the warmth invades me.

The entrance of the house is grand. Connected to the entry is a large kitchen with a counter island separating the kitchen and dining room. There's a staircase leading up from the dining area. Behind the staircase, I catch a glimpse of a living room.

Annie sits at the dining table, clearly waiting for me with hands folded against the table top. I suddenly feel a knot twisting in my stomach.

Lily and Dylan pass her to climb the stairs. "Lily, he's not staying in your room," Annie warns.

"I know! Just give us a minute."

My mother looks uneasy. "The door remains open," she demands.

"I know the rules!"

Annie directs her attention back to me. "Marina, I've been looking forward to your arrival all day."

"You have?" I warily step closer to her.

"Yes." Her bright smile is genuine. "I feel terrible about how we ended things."

"You were under a lot of stress—"

"No," she interrupts me, "I'm your mother and I was far out of line. I'm sorry, Marina."

I sit down across from her. She reaches her hand toward me, but I don't take it. I want to forgive her, but I can't bring myself to do it just yet. "What's done is done."

"I want you to know I do love you very much."

I scowl. "You don't even know me."

She retracts her hand, her face burning red. "I wasn't a part of your life, I know. I feel so sick about it. My absence has never stopped me from loving you though. There's nothing stronger than a parent's love."

"Jackson has accepted me for exactly who I am. He truly loves me as his child."

At the mention of Jackson, she livens up a bit and straightens her shoulders. "Do you know where Jackson lives now? You saved all the slaves. I assumed he'd return to his family, but his records are still inconclusive. He's a missing person."

"He remained a water-breather."

"Really? He has so many loved ones."

"He wanted to stay with me. He wanted me to have a father." I smile. Jackson has been a fantastic father. He's always supported me and never judged my actions.

"He's a good man." Her eyes light up as we talk about my father. Does she still hold love for him?

"He's doing well," I add. "Sam appointed him a member of the Council."

"Sam," she chokes on a subtle sob. "How are Sam and Cascade?"

"Sam is tough. He's strict, but is attempting to live up to Zale's legacy. Cascade is marrying soon to the king of the Northern High Seas. She's been very kind to me."

A tear escapes and rolls down her cheek. "I'm glad they're safe now."

I can see the pain her mistakes have caused her. "If it makes you feel better, they don't hate you," I say, attempting to ease her mind a bit.

She wipes at her tears. "I caused a lot of pain when I was exiled here. I still love them dearly."

Behind me, I hear the door open. I turn around to see Aquarius striding towards us.

"Princess Annie?" Aquarius gasps. Annie looks pale when she's referred to as her royal title. "I'm sorry. *Oceane*. I always called you Annie as a boy."

"Everyone calls me that now," she informs him as she wipes a stray tear from her face.

"Do you remember me?" Aquarius takes a seat.

It takes Annie only a moment to think about the man standing in front of her. "Prince Aquarius Emerson." She smiles. "You've grown into such a handsome man."

"I was only six when Cordelia took the kingdom," Aquarius tells me.

"Yes," she sighs. "I remember you and your brother would visit with your father. How is Wade?"

"He's very well. He'd be interested to know you're alive. It was rumored you were human, but the story is you died long ago."

"It's almost been eighteen years since I shifted. Here, I have a husband and kids." She almost stutters at the word *kids* knowing the child she abandoned stands before her.

"You were always such a delight. I have many fond memories of visiting you and your family in the kingdom."

"That was a long time ago." Annie attempts to remain distant from her past. "I understand why Marina is here, but why are you here, Prince Aquarius?"

"I'm accompanying my wife on her travels."

Annie's eyes widen. For a minute, I believe she's speechless. She stares at us with bewilderment behind her honey-colored gaze. "Wife?"

"We married a few days ago," I answer with a solemn nod.

"You're married, yet you came all this way to see Beck? You being here won't be good for him."

"I'm not meaning to intrude on his life—"

"He's suffering from what I believe to be PTSD. He's not okay right now. This isn't the right time for a visit."

"What's PSDT?" I have no idea what that could mean.

"P-T-S-D," Annie corrects me. "It's a disorder someone can develop after experiencing something traumatic. First, there was the car accident. Then, he shifted into a water-breather. It's all very overwhelming. He seemed to handle the accident well, beside the fact he became a homebody, but he hasn't been the same since the transformation."

"But I saved him."

"Yes, but the struggle is within himself now. He's been having nightmares almost every night and hallucinates during the day." She taps her knuckles against the tabletop. "I'm worried about him."

Nightmares. Hallucinations. He's not suffering from PTSD. Cordelia is in his head. Why? I'm not sure at the moment, but I do know if I can't break the tie to his and Cordelia's mind, she'll end up hurting him.

Aquarius shifts closer to me and clears his throat. "You need to tell her," he advises with his gentle voice.

Annie looks uncomfortably between myself and my husband. "Tell me what? Why are you really here, Marina?"

I don't know any other way to break the news, so I blurt it out. "Cordelia is alive."

She shakes her head in disbelief. "You killed her."

I blow out a heavy breath of tension. "I did, but we have reason to believe she survived."

"What does Cordelia have to do with Beck?"

"She still has access to his mind," I explain. "He must be allowing her in."

Annie becomes pale.

"Most likely, Beck can't control it," Aquarius says.

"Of course, he can't control it. He'd never willingly let her in," Annie declares.

"Annie, I have to let him go this time." I'm near the brink of crying. I don't want to let Beck go, but this is the only way I can protect him. "I need to heal Beck's memories of me."

She continues to tap her knuckles against the table. "You've tried that in the past."

"I'm stronger now. Sam has been training me." I take Annie's hands in mine. "I can do this. I don't want to be forgotten, but I've always protected him and I'm not going to stop protecting him."

Annie nods as tears form in her eyes.

"Where is he?" I ask.

"He's sleeping," Annie answers.

"Marina, this can wait until morning," Aquarius suggests, placing a reassuring hand on my shoulder.

"You know I need to do this now."

Aquarius nods. "Okay, love."

Annie leads me downstairs, but stops short of the door. "I'm happy you're here. I'm not pleased with the circumstances, but I've missed you."

Annie opens the door and allows me in before closing me off in the darkness. I can't see, so I light up the room with a golden haze by illuminating my hands. Beck sleeps under a thin sheet while Bandit lay awake, staring at me from the end of the bed. As I walk closer, Bandit begins wagging his tail. I diminish the light in one hand as to not blind the dog. I pet his blocky head and he licks at my fingers.

"Hi, buddy," I say as Bandit nuzzles his head against my hand.

Fading the light in my opposite hand, I'm left in the dark at the edge of Beck's bed. This time around, I don't hesitate crawling beneath the covers with him. I slide into his bed gently as to not wake him.

I shouldn't be doing this. I'm supposed to be in and out. Heal his memory and live my life with Aquarius. That's our plan.

As if by instinct, Beck wraps his arm around my waist. I snuggle closer to him, feeling his warmth. I drown in his heavenly scent and melt against him. I want to live in this moment. I want to remember what his warmth feels like. I want to remember the feeling of his body pinned up against mine. I want him, but I must let him go. I have to heal him. It's for his own safety. Beck is my obligation. He always has been.

Gently placing my fingers against Beck's temples. I clear my mind and conjure my power. When I close my eyes, I direct all of my energy on Beck's mind.

"Marina."

My eyes fly open. No. Beck wasn't supposed to wake up.

"Marina, is it really you?"

Before I can answer, Beck's lips are on mine. I smile against his lips as he kisses me.

This isn't going according to plan. Then again, when do my plans ever succeed the first time around?

"What're you doing here?" he asks.

I kiss him again. Softly this time. "It doesn't matter right now. I'm here."

Beck kisses me harder as he presses his body against mine. My hands move to his hair. I want all of Beck. He's all I've wanted for the past several weeks. He's all I wanted since the day I saved him.

I'm enveloped by him. His kisses move from my lips and down my neck. He pulls at my shirt, letting his hands wander beneath the fabric, and cupping my breasts in his hands. I pull at his shirt, desperate to feel his skin against mine.

And then I remember I'm married.

Suddenly, I stop. My hands go limp and my kisses come to a

halt.

"What?" Beck is breathless. "What's wrong?"

I'll heal myself from his memory in the morning. For now, I want to be with him.

"Just hold me," I whisper.

Beck wraps his arms around me. "Always."

"Do you love me, Beck?"

He's silent for a minute. I almost think he's fallen back asleep, but then I hear him sigh. "I don't know."

Now I'm the one to fall silent.

"I don't know how I feel anymore. I know you mean a lot to me and I'd do anything for you. Maybe that is love."

Chapter Eighteen

[BECK]

I WAKE IN THE MORNING with Marina next to me. At first, I believe I'm dreaming, but when I touch her smooth skin and feel her warmth, I know this is real. Her blonde hair is soft between my fingers. When I press a kiss to her forehead, she stirs, but remains asleep. Marina pouts her lip when she's asleep. I'm not sure why I hadn't noticed when we were in Edisto.

As not to wake my sleeping beauty, I carefully maneuver around her and gently lift myself from the bed. Bandit's already at my door waiting to be let outside.

Quietly, I open the door and release my loyal companion. As I climb the stairs, I hear Bandit growling. It's not out of the ordinary for Bandit to growl at a rabbit or squirrel he'll see in the yard, but Bandit is still inside and this is a vicious growl. I find him standing in the kitchen with his back hair raised. He's mad as hell.

"Annie, you didn't tell me you had a dog!" a man's voice yells in a thick Australian accent.

I turn the corner to find a stranger sitting at our dining room table with a cup of coffee.

"It's my dog," I correct the stranger, before grabbing a tight hold of Bandit's collar and pulling him closer to me. "Who are you?"

"Sorry, mate. I'm Aquarius Emerson," he informs me.

I study the young man who looks to be in his twenties. "Is that name supposed to mean something to me? And what kind of name is Aquarius? You're a zodiac sign?" Maybe I'm being rude, but I don't know this guy and he's sitting at my table at eight in the morning.

Aquarius looks confused. He also looks like a model who walked straight out of a magazine...but, like one who isn't trying to look perfect. His blonde hair is messy, and he has a five o'clock shadow. He wears dark jeans and a white shirt as if he's attempting to model what an average everyday guy should look like. Who the hell is this guy?

"My name means 'water-bearer' where I come from."

"Well, here it means you're unpredictable and stubborn." I surprise myself by knowing this information. Lily really needs to stop leaving her magazines around.

The stranger's gaze focuses behind me. "Marina," Aquarius says with a smile. Why is he smiling at her name?

I turn to find Marina looking distressed.

Bandit begins wagging his tail at the sight of Marina, so I let him go. She pats him on the head before pulling out a chair and joining Aquarius at the table.

"I've met your friend Beck," he says with a smirk.

"How does he know my name?" I ask Marina with an aggravated tone.

She tucks her hair behind her ear, before fidgeting with her fingers. Marina remains quiet. Maybe she doesn't want to say, but I don't care.

Her refusal to tell me only angers me. "How does he know me?" I demand.

"Calm down, mate. She's been under a lot of stress lately," chimes in Aquarius.

"I'm not your mate, dude. She can answer for herself."

Marina reaches for my hand, but I refuse her touch at the moment. She slowly retracts her hand back to her lap. "He helped me get here." She's soft-spoken.

"You're making human friends now?"

"Not exactly." Marina pats the seat next to hers, indicating I should sit.

I don't move.

Marina mopes. How can I resist her pouty face? "Beck, please?" she pleads.

Sighing, I take a seat next to her because I can't resist her.

"Aquarius is a hybrid…like me," she explains.

"Like you?" I look to him. He's a merman? "You mean, there are others like yourself?"

Marina nods.

"We're rare," Aquarius clarifies, "but there are a few hundred of us living below and above the Surface."

"Thank you for bringing Marina back to me," I interrupt, not wanting to hear another word from him.

Marina grabs my hand and brushes her thumb against my

skin. "We have more to tell you, Beck." Her lips are set with a frown. Her bright eyes appear dull. Her shoulders sag. Marina looks as though her words are weighing her down. "I wish I could stay, but there is danger back home."

I don't understand. "That's more reason for you to stay."

She shakes her head. Tears brim at her eyes. "You said you've been seeing things...hallucinations, visions, nightmares."

I nod, filled with apprehension. My chest suddenly feels tight.

"You're not crazy, Beck. Cordelia is in your head," Marina explains.

"What? Cordelia can't be in my head. You killed her. You sacrificed yourself for everyone."

Marina grips my hand tighter. "Cordelia has a sister. Cora knows her better than anyone, and she believes Cordelia had just enough time to clone herself before her death."

I don't mean to, but I begin to laugh. Mermaids. Sea Witches. Hybrids. And now clones?

"Come on! Are you serious?" I even look to Aquarius, who is staring at me with bewilderment. He must think I'm a lunatic for finding this funny.

"Cordelia is a very dangerous threat," Aquarius adds. "She still has a connection to you, and she'll use it if she believes it's necessary to hurt Marina."

This information causes my laughs to turn into a slight choke. "What?"

"Has she threatened you?" Marina questions.

I think back to the incident I thought was only a nightmare. I

told myself it wasn't real. Cordelia had flung me across my room.
It was a dream. Or was she in my head? "You can't escape me
that easily," she had said.

"What is it?" Marina grazes her thumb against my cheek.

"She told me I couldn't escape her easily." My voice is
strained. Suddenly I feel as though I can't breathe. The discovery
of Cordelia living strangles me.

Memories flash in my mind. The pain I felt when she turned
me. My bones breaking. My flesh ripping. The blood…

Cordelia can't be alive.

"Beck?" Marina grabs my shoulders, steadying me. I grip the
sides of the chair.

There's an unsettling stirring deep within my stomach. "What
does that mean? Why can't I escape her easily?"

"It means she'll tap into your brain whenever she pleases,"
Aquarius answers with a dead tone. He seems emotionless when
it comes to my well-being. He doesn't know me, so I suppose I
can't blame him for his lack of caring.

"Look. Thanks for the info, but if you'd kindly take a walk,
I'd like to talk privately with my girlfriend."

Aquarius smiles, but his grin is tainted by a looming
arrogance.

"Aquarius, watch yourself," Marina warns with pleading eyes.

"No. He needs to know," Aquarius argues. He rises so he
stands tall over the two of us. Aquarius looks back to me. "I will
gladly give you a minute alone so you can have a word with my
wife." With nothing more, Aquarius strides out the sliding doors

and takes a seat on the back patio.

I rip my hand away from Marina. "You got married? You made a promise we'd meet up in a year, and this is how you keep your word?"

"I didn't want it, Beck! It was an arranged marriage. My uncle is the emperor! This was his plan to create a strong alliance with the Australian Border." Marina wipes away a few tears that have rolled down her cheeks. "The marriage means nothing. Aquarius means nothing."

"Yeah? Tell him that." There's a bitter edge to my voice. "He was quick to inform me of your marriage."

"He's known from the start I don't have feelings for him." Marina looks away from me towards the ceiling as though she's attempting to keep her emotions under control and stop the tears from flowing.

"How long have you been married?"

"A few days," she answers.

"Have you—" Do I even want to know if she's slept with him?

"Have I… what? Consummated my marriage? No."

"Why not?"

"What part of 'I have feelings for you' do you not understand?"

"So your marriage is a sham?"

"The citizens don't know that. It's all for appearance. I'm loved for killing Cordelia and freeing the true leader. That's why the king and queen of the Australian Border wanted me to wed their son. We're bound to each other and the thrones. Sam is trying to build his empire."

"Does Sam know Cordelia is possibly alive?"

"She is alive." She shakes her head at the disappointing news. "But yes, Cora informed the Council at our last meeting. It's difficult to believe because we have Cordelia's body locked up in a cavern protected by royal guards. The body is proof of her death."

"And this Cora is trustworthy? You believe she's telling the truth about Cordelia having cloned herself?"

"Aquarius and his family know Cora well. Cora has never wanted any trouble. She's lived most of her life in hiding from her sister. After I was born and the kingdom had been seized by Cordelia, Cora came to live in Cordelia's Caverns. Cordelia wanted her sister to join her, but Cora believed her lifestyle was wrong. When Cordelia was rejected, she forbid her sister from visiting the kingdom again. Cora knew the evil within her sister and wanted nothing to do with it. She lived in the Australian Border for a while, before Cordelia's slaves began traveling back and forth. Cora worried she'd be exposed, so she moved. She's only surfaced now to warn us about her sister being alive. She can feel Cordelia's life."

Dylan Rathbone saunters out from the living room. I hadn't seen him when I came upstairs. I was too concerned with Bandit's growls. I don't even care enough to ask what he's doing in my house. I only shake my head and rise from sitting at the table.

"Beck, we need to discuss this."

"Do what you have to do, Marina. I'm over it."

I head towards the door to let Bandit out, and slam it behind me.

Chapter Nineteen

[MARINA]

BECK STORMS OUT THE front door with Bandit. Knowing it's best to give him a minute to cool down, I slip on my coat and join Aquarius outside on the patio. He sits on the step as he scrolls through a phone. Where did he get the cell phone? I'm baffled how he knows exactly what to do in this world.

I take a seat next to him. In silence, we stare out at the woodsy backyard. If I were to live here, I'd probably spend most of my time back here with nature.

"I gather he didn't take the news very well," Aquarius says.

I clench my fists at my sides, furious with Aquarius for telling Beck we're married. "I would've told him in my own time, you know."

"We don't have all the time in the world, Marina."

"You don't get to make decisions for me. I wanted to break the news to him gently."

"So, you like to coddle him? You protect him, I get it. He's nearly a man though. He needs to learn how to protect himself." Aquarius rises to his feet, standing tall above me.

"Without him, I'd be dead. He protects me just as much as I do him. If anything you should be thanking him for saving my life."

"Should I also be thanking him for sleeping with my wife? How do you think I felt all night wondering if his hands were on you…what he was doing to you? It took everything in me to not barge in that room. I gave you space, thinking you were healing his mind."

"We were just sleeping," I argue, dismissing the kissing and groping.

"You took a vow. I'm your husband, not Beck, so the only man beside you at night will be me."

I fall silent at his authority.

A gasp from behind us brings my attention to Lily. She stands with her arms dangling at her sides and her lips parting with the intention of forming a sentence. She hesitates, still puzzled. "Can someone please tell me who this delicious, yet strange man is on my back porch?"

Aquarius smirks at the compliment. I roll my eyes. Before I can answer her question, Aquarius speaks up. "I'm Marina's husband."

Her jaw nearly drops to the floor before her face fixes into a menacing glare. "What the hell? Marina!"

I rise to my feet. "Lily, I know that sounds bad," I try to calmly explain, "but it's not real."

"Oh, it's very much real," Aquarius chimes in.

"Shut up!" I demand. "There's more to the story. Look, I can't explain everything to you. I'm here to help Beck."

"How are you going to help him?"

"You just need to trust me," I snap.

"How am I supposed to trust you when you show up for my brother with your husband by your side?" she scowls.

"Beck has been hallucinating, yes? He's been having frequent nightmares, yes?"

She presses her lips in a hard line before nodding.

"I'm the only one who can help him," I inform her.

Lily looks mystified.

"You just have to trust me." I exit the back porch, leaving Aquarius and Lily behind and circle around to the front of the house to find Beck. He stands in the middle of the yard playing fetch with Bandit.

"Beck, we need to talk," I say, once I've reached him. A sickness creeps in my stomach. How do I overcome the way Aquarius revealed our marriage to Beck in such a rude manner? Although hearing it in any manner wouldn't be easy.

"You've said everything you need to say." Bandit drops his ball at Beck's feet. Beck swiftly picks up the ball and whips it to the edge of his yard where Bandit races to catch it. "You came here to heal my memory," he scowls.

I bite my lip. How do I explain to him this is for the best? "I came here to save you from this life. Cordelia is a threat to you and my family. As long as she has the connection to you, she'll use it to hurt me. You don't deserve this."

Bandit returns the ball and anxiously waits for Beck to throw it once again.

"So that's it? There's nothing we can do to save us? We're

just done."

I can tell he's angry by how much force he uses to kick Bandit's ball across the yard. "Don't put it like that," I plead.

"It's the reality. We're both very different people with very different lives. We were stupid to think this would ever work between us," Beck says, breaking my heart.

"I didn't expect to meet you. I especially didn't expect to fall in love with you," I admit. "I would love nothing more than to forget about my life and start over with you, but I have a father now. I have a family."

"You have a husband," Beck grumbles.

"No," I dispute. "I have a responsibility."

"Since when do you follow the rules?"

"Since I became a princess and people look to me for command. I set an example in my community. I'm worshipped."

"Tell me the truth. Are you trying to make me forget my memories with you so you can live happily with your new husband? If that's the case, just leave. I'll forget you on my own."

His words stab me deep in the chest. "How could you think I would do that to you? I sacrificed my life for you. You think I would just forget you and move on so quickly? You and I have a connection like no other. I'm only trying to give you a better life." I turn away from him to hide that I'm nearing tears. Weakness isn't what Beck needs to see from me right now.

Suddenly, I feel Beck's strong arms wrap around me. "I'm sorry. I didn't mean it like that... What am I supposed to expect when you show up with him?"

"I needed his help to find you. That's it." I hug him tightly.

"Why'd you have to bring Dylan, too?"

This one I can explain easily. "Originally, he threatened me in order for me to agree to take him with…only for me to later find out he's dating your sister."

"What?" Beck lets go of me to see if I'm joking. "You're serious?"

I nod.

"He threatened you?"

"It's a long story. Basically, I showed up to his house in an effort to recruit him into helping me find you. Of course, that was a lost cause. He's only out for himself. As you know, when I shift, I'm naked—"

"Dylan has seen you naked?"

"Yes. It's not a big deal!"

"In my world, it's a pretty big deal—" I place my finger over Beck's lips in order to hush him.

"Anyway, Dylan took a picture of me when I wasn't looking and threatened to show you I was there for a booty call if I didn't bring him along."

Beck pulls my hand from his lips. "He blackmailed you? I'm going to kill him." He storms toward the door, but before he can reach it, I compel him to stop with the little force field I can conjure up.

"Marina, let me go! He took naked pictures of you!" Beck's face is a harsh red and his jaw is set tightly.

Continuing to hold Beck back with my powers, I say, "I

wanted you to beat him. That's really the only reason I let him come. Is he nothing more than sea foam? Yes. But for some odd reason, your sister sees the good in him. Don't let him get in between us. We have enough to deal with as it is…we don't need Dylan to upset us, too."

Beck shakes his head. "You can let go of me."

"Are you calm?"

"As calm as I can be at the moment."

Slowly, I lower the field. Once Beck is released he tightly closes his eyes, blows out a deep breath, and then looks to me with his emerald gaze. "We need to get away," he suggests.

"Beck." I moan with sadness and hug him, "Where would we go?"

"My grandparents have a cabin a few hours north." Aquarius fills my mind. We had a deal. I'd heal Beck's memories and then Aquarius and I would head back to live our lives together. Cordelia is still a lurking danger. The emperor can't know I escaped the kingdom to find Beck.

"What's holding you back from saying yes?" asks Beck.

I shake my head. "Nothing. Let's go." I smile. "Right now."

Beck begins to laugh, but it catches in his throat. "You don't need permission from Mr. Stick-Up-His-Ass?"

I smirk. "I make the rules."

Beck presses a kiss to my forehead. "Get your things and wait in the car for me. I'll be out in a minute."

"We can't let Aquarius know we're leaving," I warn.

"I'm sneaky. Don't worry about it."

While Beck sneaks in the house, I search for my bag in the rental car. As I grab the satchel of clothes and head toward Beck's car, I remind myself I wouldn't have these clothes without Aquarius. I wouldn't be here without Aquarius. Is it fair for me to leave him to worry? If I tell him where I'm going, he'll follow. Beck and I need our space.

"I don't answer to Aquarius," I reassure myself as I take a seat in Beck's car.

I grow nervous as the minutes pass. Has Aquarius caught Beck attempting to leave and stopped him? When Bandit rounds the corner of the house and I spot Beck with him, I sigh a breath of relief. He hasn't been caught.

My stomach flutters with excitement when Beck and Bandit join me in the car. Bandit is more than eager to go for a ride. As soon as Beck starts the car, he cracks the window for Bandit. The energetic black lab shoves his head out as far as he can fit and lets his tongue flop against the glass.

Let the drooling begin!

Chapter Twenty

[BECK]

SNEAKING THROUGH THE HOUSE was no picnic in the park. Although Aquarius was still out on the patio, Aubrey was in the kitchen attempting to make herself toast. For one, she can't reach the toaster. And for two, the last time I caught her using the toaster she was balanced on a stool about to dig her bread out with a knife. She's a little dare devil, for sure. After I scolded her and helped her get breakfast, I snuck down to my room to gather a backpack of a couple pairs of clothes and whatnot. My path down the stairs came to an abrupt halt when I discovered Dylan Rathbone was sitting in the living room. Quietly, I snuck back down to my room and climbed out the window.

Now, Marina and I drive through town heading north.

I know she wants to heal my memory, but I have to change her mind. I can prove to her the visions have stopped. I haven't seen Cordelia or my dead friends in over a week. Finally, I feel normal again. I can live a life without forgetting her.

The cabin will give us a chance to be alone. We can be us without any interruptions from my family or Marina's new husband.

Husband.

I can't wrap my head around Marina being married. It still feels like yesterday we were saying goodbye to one another and promising to continue our relationship in a year. And now she's married.

"Do you love him?" I blurt out. My fingers are tightly gripped around the steering wheel. "What?" she asks with surprise.

"Do you love Aquarius?"

She pauses for a moment. "No, for the millionth time," she responds with a calmness.

"How could you marry him?"

"You don't understand the pressure I'm under," she argues.

I roll my eyes. I don't intend to be so rude. "Make me understand! In the time we've been apart, I didn't run off and get married." I can't bear the thought of Aquarius' hands all over Marina.

She turns toward me. I glance her way before directing my gaze back to the road.

"Beck, my uncle is building an empire. He needs alliances. Aquarius is the prince of the Australian Border and his parents ordered him to marry me. I married him as an order," Marina reassures me as she grabs my hand and brings it to her lips. "I'm sorry. I know that's hard to understand."

I can't resist her sad puppy dog eyes that glow a glittery gold. "You're with me now. That's all I've wanted since you left."

"I love you, Beck," she admits, still holding my hand. "You don't need to say it back. I just want you to know."

I smile. "I know, Marina."

She leans over, pulling at her seatbelt, and kisses me on the cheek. I turn and quickly plant a kiss on her lips.

"You shouldn't distract yourself while driving," she says, gently brushing her hands through my hair.

I chuckle. "You're a distraction."

"How so?" I can hear the smile in her voice.

"You're blonde hair." I glance between her and the road. "Your golden gaze. Your bright smile. Your hands on me. Your lips."

She giggles. You mean…" Marina kisses my neck softly, "this is a distraction?"

"Yes," I groan.

Marina kisses my neck again. "I'm sorry," she whispers in my ear.

"You're gonna make me crash this car."

As I'm about to kiss her again, Bandit shoves his head between us and gives us both wet kisses. "Thanks for the cock block, Bandit."

Marina roughly pets his head and ears while Bandit loves every minute of it.

"Where exactly are you taking me?" Marina asks with excitement.

"Can you ever just sit back and relax? It's a surprise."

"Can I at least get a hint?"

"I'm taking you to a lake cabin."

"A lake?" The tone in her voice sounds worrisome.

"Don't judge. You've never been to a lake."

She begins to play with her hair, twirling it around her finger. "I've heard enough stories to know I shouldn't visit one."

"What're you talking about?" I've lived in Minnesota my entire life. I've grown up swimming in lakes. A lake is nothing to fear, unlike the ocean.

"There are creatures who lurk in the depths of lakes far more dangerous than half the creatures residing in the oceans."

"You're from the Bermuda Triangle. How would you even know anything about a lake?"

"Stories travel about the sirens. They once lived as sea nymphs before they were exiled and executed. The sirens who could escape travelled by rivers, escaping into any body of water that lead from the oceans."

"Lucky for you, Deer Lake isn't connected to the ocean," I inform her.

"Oh." She sits in the seat silently as if attempting to understand. She's ridiculously cute when she's learning about my world. "Why is it called Deer Lake? Is there a high deer population?"

This question stumps me. "Honestly, I've never thought about it. I suppose there is."

"I would like to see a deer." She folds her hands in her lap and gazes in awe at the trees. I forget how innocent Marina can appear. She's a deadly woman, yet she's so gentle in this world.

"It's Minnesota. I'm sure you'll see one by the end of the night."

She's truly gorgeous with her blonde hair flowing down in

waves. Marina tucks her hair behind her ear as she takes in the views of nature as we travel down the highway.

Not only do I want some time with Marina, but I want to show her the cabin I spent most of my summers visiting when I was young. My grandparents' lake cabin holds some of my fondest memories. Before my mom died, we visited for a week here and there between May and September. Lily and I would go with Mom, while Dad worked at his growing orthodontic practice. My mom always tried to visit her parents whenever she could. Since my mom's passing, Dad doesn't like to visit the cabin. My grandparents have always extended the invite to him and Annie, but he's always felt uncomfortable with the idea. So Lily and I now visit every few months while Grandma and Grandpa are home.

There's a low rumbling sounding from the seat next to mine. Marina grabs ahold of her stomach and laughs. "Whoa!" she exclaims.

In return, my stomach grumbles. "What kind of road trip would this be without burgers and fries?"

"I don't like burgers. What's fries?"

"The fact that you're even asking me that is just sad. You never even tried your burger last time at the barbeque. That one was a dry mess. I'm telling you this place won't let you down."

Luckily, we're only a few minutes away from one of the tastiest burger places I know. Mom used to stop with me and Lily every time we drove up north.

I drive thru and order us a couple of double cheeseburgers,

fries, and root beer floats. If the pancakes blew Marina's mind, the burgers will send her over the edge of her seat.

Once we have our food, I park the car so we can eat.

"What's this?" Marina asks as she takes a sip of her float. Her eyes light up with joy. "It's amazing."

I scoop up a spoonful of ice cream from my float and take a bite. "It's root beer and ice cream."

She mimics my actions and scoops up ice cream from her cup. When she takes a bite, she's careful not to use her teeth. She obviously learned from her brain freeze snow cone incident to eat slowly. "I didn't think the human world could be any more amazing. Clearly, I was wrong."

"You need me in your life," I add playfully, but Marina freezes. With a frown she sets her root beer float back in the cup holder.

"I do need you in my life," she confesses.

I don't want to spoil the mood. We don't need to talk about healing my memory right now. This trip is for us to reconnect. Which I know is exactly the opposite of Marina's plan. "Without me, you'd never taste a burger." I pull her food from the bag and hand it over. "Dig in."

She seems hesitant as she rips the wrapper from the burger. She looks disgustedly at the meat patties and fillings. "What is it though?"

"Will you trust me?" I take a big bite from my double cheeseburger.

With two hands she cradles the burger. I debate whether or

not to take video of this moment. Marina takes a bite and chews slowly, contemplating the flavors. She nods, takes a bigger bite, and begins to moan as she chews.

"Right?" I take another bite.

"What am I eating?" she moans louder.

I'm laughing so hard my stomach hurts. Bandit is in our faces begging for scraps, but it doesn't faze Marina as she scarfs down her food.

"It's cow meat," I inform her.

"Cow is delicious!" As she finishes off her cheeseburger, she begins shoveling the fries in her mouth.

"Slow down. The food isn't going anywhere. We're in no rush."

"I've been eating seaweed and squid for weeks. Let me have this."

After finishing off her fries, she returns to scooping the ice cream from her float and sipping the remainder of the root beer.

"My girl knows how to eat," I comment with a proud smile. When she smirks I notice a small driblet of ice cream in the corner of her mouth. I reach to wipe it clean, but she's too cute and I end up kissing her instead.

Marina's lips taste sweet from the sugary drink. As I kiss her, she moves her fingers through my hair and cups my face. Before I can pull away, she bites my lip slightly, causing me to go crazy. My heart is pumping and my blood is rushing to places I can't begin to control.

The steamy fun comes to an abrupt stop when a family passes

our car and pauses for a moment to gawk at us. Marina and I laugh as the mom pulls her child along, while the husband only shakes his head.

Marina sits back and replaces her seatbelt. She groans. "I think I'm in a food coma."

I'm forced to turn the AC on full blast in order to cool off and think straight once again.

Marina ends up falling asleep for the remaining hour of the trip, and to my surprise Bandit makes the three-hour trip without needing a potty break. As I pull into the driveway, Bandit becomes rambunctious and wakes Marina from her nap.

The cabin isn't huge by any means, but is rather spacious. The log cabin is two stories high with a deck that wraps all the way around and resides on a hill overlooking the lake.

"Surprise," I tell Marina once she's fully become aware of her senses. She yawns and stretches.

Bandit can hardly contain himself from the excitement. When I let him loose from the car, he runs in circles around trees, barks at his echo, and finally relieves himself on a few select bushes.

The key is hidden in a fake rock that sits in a planter of plastic flowers. They are a bit weathered from the sun, but at seventy, my grandmother doesn't care for a real garden.

Marina's mouth gapes open as I pull the key from the rock. I explain to her that I'm not a wizard of any sort, it's a fake rock with a hidden compartment for the key. She cradles the faux stone, examining it with perplexity. It's interesting to see the things of this world that amuse her.

I push the door open. "So, are we gonna go inside or stare at this rock all day long?"

Marina blushes and places the stone back in the pot before stepping through the doorway. Bandit runs in after us, heading straight upstairs for his favorite bed.

The entry opens into the dining room, kitchen, and family room. In the back hallway, there are two bedrooms and a bathroom. Upstairs is a balcony overlooking the second floor, along with a master bedroom and bath with a deck overseeing the lake.

From the kitchen there is a magnificent view of the lake. My mom always volunteered to wash dishes after dinners just to stare out at the water. My grandma would argue with her insisting she was a guest, but my mother would always pitch in with chores. Lily and I on the other hand would be too occupied playing outside or swimming in the lake.

Marina wanders toward the hallway in the back of the cabin. I give her a minute to explore on her own while I reminisce the memories.

At age six, Lily and I would sleep on air mattresses in the living room and stay up late watching Scooby-Doo. Although my grandparents had two extra bedrooms, Lily and I always chose to "camp" out in front of the couch. A smile spreads across my face at the memory of the relationship I once had with my twin sister.

I find Marina observing the dozen photos of our family on the wall. There's a black and white photo of my grandparents at their wedding, when they were young and vibrant. Of course, there are a couple of the cousins and my uncle's family. One of my favorites though is a family picture of my mom, my dad, Lily, and I gathered together in front of the lake. My mom is holding a four-year-old me while Dad holds Lily. We all have huge grins plastered on our faces as the sun beats down on us in the hot July weather. I love Annie like a mother, but I'd do anything to bring my mom back.

"Your mother was beautiful," comments Marina, her gold eyes lighting up.

I smile because my mom was very pretty with fair ivory skin, bright blue eyes, and brunette hair that fell in waves to the middle of her back. It was hard to see her lose such beautiful hair when she underwent chemotherapy in the months before she passed.

Marina hugs her sweater closer to her and shivers. The cabin has been closed up for a month, so there's been no heat through the house. I grab her a blanket and lead her to the family room where I start up a fire in the wood stove. Grandpa always ensures there is a stockpile of dry wood in the front closet in the case family does visit in the winter months.

"You want to watch a movie?" I ask Marina as I finish up feeding the fire.

"Movie?" she repeats.

I bring my palm to my face and shake my head. "I have so much to teach you."

We both know we need to talk, but more importantly, we just need some time to be together, so I pick a few of my favorites and cuddle up next to Marina with the blanket. As we watch Batman defeat Penguin in one of the greatest Michael Keaton films ever made, Marina is awestruck at the motion picture. She's captivated by the plot and with every shocker, she gasps. She's a hybrid princess, yet she finds Batman to be astounding.

We watch a couple more of my favorite superhero movies before Marina and I begin to grow hungry and our stomachs grumble. One thing I didn't think about for the trip was stopping for groceries. I don't trust most of the boxed and canned foods in my grandparents' pantry since they usually tend to keep things that expired ten years ago. Why do all grandparents think a box of crackers from fifteen years ago doesn't perish?

I remember a local bar and grill not too far from the house. My grandparents used to take my family out to eat there anytime we visited. I could definitely go for one of their steaks with potatoes right now.

Before we leave, I pat Bandit on his big blocky head. He's sad to see us go, but I always come back. He should know that by now.

It takes me a little longer than expected to find the bar and grill. It's been a while since I've been up north, and the GPS is spotty.

Once we're there, we're quickly seated. Marina smiles at the waitress, who informs us her name is Ashley, hands us our menus and asks for our drink orders.

"What do you have?" asks Marina, entranced by the options as they're named off to her. "Umm... this is just so difficult." Ashley laughs as she waits with her pen to paper. "I'll try the raspberry lemonade."

"That's a great choice. It's my favorite," Ashley says with a smile before she goes off to get us our drinks.

"Why're you so happy?" I ask Marina.

She shrugs and gazes around the restaurant. "I'm just happy to be here."

The bar and grill does have a nice up north feel to it. I thought maybe the animal heads hung on the wall would be off-putting to Marina, but she doesn't seem to mind.

"I'm happy to be with you." Marina reaches across the table to hold my hand.

"You know, it could be like this all the time," I say, rubbing her hand with my thumb.

Her gaze becomes sorrowful. "I wish it could always be this way, I do."

"You're the only one stopping us from being together."

She pulls her hand away. "What do you not understand? I'm giving us up in order for you to have a real life."

"The visions have stopped. I'm fine."

"Cordelia is in your head. I know it."

"Then why hasn't she made an appearance lately? Why would she stop invading my mind?" I argue.

"I don't know," she whispers in response.

"She's gone," I assure her.

Marina shakes her head but doesn't continue the conversation. She instead examines the menu. Her face his furrowed in what I think is anger. I've never been great at reading girls. She's huffing her breaths, but I ignore it and look at the menu, too.

Suddenly, she slams the menu down on the table. "Do you really think I want to say goodbye to you? I said goodbye once before, and hoped I'd never have to let you go again. This isn't what I want."

I throw my menu down on the table creating a loud slapping sound. Marina jumps, surprised by my outburst. "Then don't heal me," I whisper with rage. "If you don't want to let me go, hold on. If you don't want to be a princess, don't go home. If you don't want to be married, stay with me. You always have a choice, Marina."

"Cordelia is alive," she whispers back with just as much outrage.

"She's bound to the ocean. Stay here. I'll be safe with you."

She grunts with her teeth gritted together. "You're so stubborn. I can't protect you from what's in your head."

Our server approaches our table with our drinks in hand causing both of us to fall silent. Marina and I smile as the waitress takes our orders as if we weren't talking about brainwashing me only a minute ago.

"What's a mozzarella stick?" Marina asks the waitress, who seems puzzled by her question. "I've just never had one before," Marina explains.

"Oh... well, they're delicious. It's just a deep fried cheese stick served with a marinara sauce."

"I'll take an order of mozzarella sticks... and I'll try the loaded potato skins because those sound interesting... and I want the barbeque ribs."

"You get two sides with the ribs."

"Oh!" Marina further examines the menu. "I'll have the mashed potatoes and gravy… and corn. That's a funny word. Corn. Corn. Corn." Her laugh is so innocent. "If you say it enough, it doesn't even sound like a word."

"Marina," I snap light-heartedly.

"Right." She clears her throat. "That's all."

"And for you?" Ashley turns to me.

"I'll have the steak—medium-rare—with the mashed potatoes and asparagus, please. We're sharing the appetizers."

Ashley smirks and takes our menus.

"I'm sorry," Marina says. "Beck, please, can we just enjoy our dinner without talking about this right now?"

I nod. "We're gonna have to talk about it at some point though."

"Tomorrow. We'll discuss everything in the morning."

My phone buzzes in my pocket, but I ignore it. Lily has been texting all day to ask me where I took Marina. Obviously, Aquarius is furious with me. Well, I'm a little bitter about him marrying my girlfriend, so he can suck it.

"What've you been doing lately?" Marina asks.

"Not much," I say. "I was suspended from school for punching Lily's ex-boyfriend."

"Did he deserve it?"

"More than anyone."

"That's my man!" She grins.

"How's Caspian? Still grumpy?"

Marina purses her lips. "Honestly, Caspian and I have grown apart. I feel like I don't know who he is anymore. He basically confessed his love for me. We also got into a huge fight. I don't trust him. Which really hurts. He's always been the one constant in my life."

"I'm sorry, Marina. I know he isn't very fond of me, but he's a good guy…" I shake my head, "merman, I mean."

"I got you," she assures me. "I guess it's just time we move on from one another."

"But you have your dad now."

Her smile returns. "He could've gone home to his family. He could've returned after so many years, but he chose to stay with me."

"You're his daughter." It's a no-brainer that he chose to stay with his child.

"I know. I just would never expect him to continue his life with me when he had the choice."

"He loves you. You weren't there to see him when he thought he lost you."

"I know I just find it odd.

"You find loving your dad odd?"

"It's hard to explain. Like, I know I love you because I saved you. I feel as though I was meant to be with you. It's a feeling I can't deny. When I'm with you, everything feels right. With Jackson, I never established a relationship with him. He just loves me."

"It's that simple when it's a parent's love."

"I can't fathom it."

"You will one day," As I respond, I realize she very well could have a child with Aquarius. My appetite changes when I think about Aquarius on top of her.

Ashley brings us our food with the help of another staff member. Luckily, I have Dad's credit card for this dinner emergency.

Marina gasps as all the food is set in front of her.

Ashley jokingly asks us if we need any boxes right away, but I tell her we'll be fine.

"I don't like the way she insinuated I wouldn't eat all of this," Marina comments, wrinkling her nose out of annoyance. I take a mental note of how cute she is when she's annoyed. "It's because you don't look like you can eat all of this." I laugh.

"She can watch me if she'd like." Marina shoves a potato skin in her mouth and moans. She says something, but it's inaudible with all the food in her mouth.

"What?" I ask as I cut into my juicy steak.

She swallows and wipes her mouth. "Human food is the most amazing thing I've ever experienced." Marina picks up a mozzarella stick and takes a bite. When she pulls it away, there's a trail of cheese oozing from where she bit. She follows the trail with her mouth before finishing the whole stick. "I lied. This is the most amazing thing I've experienced."

"Are you even tasting anything?" I question as I take a bite of my steak. The flavors melt in my mouth.

Marina has now dug into her ribs. With a mouth full of barbecue, she says "I'm tasting everything!"

I never thought a girl with barbecue all over her face could be so attractive.

Chapter Twenty-One

[MARINA]

MY STOMACH HURTS. IT very well could be the mozzarella sticks, loaded potato skins, rack of ribs, mashed potatoes, and the corn I ate, but I think it's mostly because I don't want this night with Beck to end. I don't want any of my time with Beck to end. Being with him once again only validates how much I need him in my life. He grounds me. He makes me feel human. I know I'm meant to be in this world when I'm with him.

We've just arrived back at the cabin, but I'm too full to move from the car. When Beck kills the engine, I reach for his hand. "Thank you for dinner."

"You can thank my dad," he jokes.

"I ate too much," I admit, holding my bloated stomach.

"You think? I don't know where you put it."

"In my defense, I need to eat the good stuff while I can."

Beck chuckles. "You definitely ate it all. I think the waitress was surprised you finished."

"I know how to eat my food like a real woman."

Beck pulls at me, hinting for me to join him in the driver's seat. Awkwardly, I crawl over into his lap and straddle him. He runs his hands from my hips up into my hair, urging me to kiss him. I don't fight the urge. His lips press hard against mine, but move slowly before trailing down my chin and neck. I grip at the back of his neck as he begins to nibble at my collarbone. I'm about to kiss him again when he abruptly stops.

"What's wrong?"

Beck looks panicked. "Did you leave a light on?"

"No?" I mean, I don't remember leaving any light on.

Beck opens the door and urges me off of him. As I plant my feet in the driveway, I demand for him to tell me what's going on in his head.

"Someone's inside," he responds.

"You think someone broke in?"

"Maybe. I have the key with me." He feels his pocket for the key and retrieves it.

I walk ahead of him and light up my hands, ready for an easy battle against an intruder.

Beck runs in front of me and blocks my way. "What do you think you're doing?"

"Protecting you," I simply answer.

"Stop doing that! I don't need you to protect me. I'm the man. I do the protecting."

The light in my hands fade. "But you don't have powers."

"I don't need powers—" He rolls his eyes. "Just stay behind me."

"Fine," I scoff. I'll stay behind him ready to fight a trespasser.

When Beck and I walk through the door, I'm surprised to find Aquarius sitting at the dining table.

"What're you doing here?" I'm outraged. I can feel my face turn red from the anger. "Stop following me!"

"Marina, calm down," he demands. His jaw is tightly set and he is obviously very displeased with me.

That won't stop me from arguing with him. "No! Every time I turn around, I find you."

"Technically, it was me who found you," informs Lily as she walks out from the back hallway with Dylan. Bandit happily trots behind them.

"Why did you have to come here?" asks Beck. "I ignored your texts for a reason."

"Annie's worried about you," she answers.

"Could everyone please stop worrying about me? I'm okay! How did you even know I was here?"

Lily crosses her arms over her busty chest. "Annie checked to see if you left a trail behind with the credit card... It wasn't hard to figure out where you were going after you stopped for lunch."

"Shit! That was stupid on my part," Beck admits.

"Marina," Aquarius growls. "I need to speak with you, *now*."

Beck steps forward. "Whatever you need to say, you can say in front of me," he snaps. I lay a hand on Beck's chest in an attempt to calm him. His heart is pumping hard. He needs to take a deep breath.

"I'll just be a minute," I assure him.

I head upstairs feeling overwhelmed. I love a man I can't marry, and I'm married to a man I don't love. My husband is upset with me for sneaking off with my boyfriend. Does every woman have this problem? It's exhausting.

Aquarius follows close behind me so we can converse in private.

"What the hell was that?" Aquarius asks with an angry edge in his tone. "That wasn't our deal. If you can't follow your part of the agreement, this isn't going to work."

"Then leave. I can handle myself."

"You really want me to leave?" He studies me, curious to know if I'm bluffing. Well, I'm not. Or at least I don't think I am...

"Would you leave?" I counter, crossing my arms against my chest.

"No," he simply answers.

I huff a deep breath. "Then why are we having this conversation?"

"We need to be able to trust each other. I was worried about you."

"I was with Beck. I was safe."

"How was I supposed to know that? Anything could've happened to you while you ran off with that stubborn bloke."

"You're only jealous," I snap.

"Of the puny human?" He chuckles. "No. I just don't understand your fascination with him. But I am your husband...and he is not."

I wear a permanent scowl. "He's not puny... just because he's shorter than you doesn't mean he's any less of a man. Beck has risked far more for me than you ever have, so back off."

Aquarius' cheeks redden with fury. "You have no idea the risks I've made for you," he growls.

I cock my eyebrows, honestly surprised and curious, but I remain annoyed. "I never asked for you to do any of that."

"But I did." His voice remains soft despite him being angered.

"Look, I'm not going to measure you and Beck up and choose which one I think is better. I love Beck and that's that. You need to deal with it."

My words are callous, but necessary. Although, if they're necessary, why do I feel hollow as I descend the stairs to find Beck, leaving Aquarius alone with the truth to set into his thick skull?

I find Beck downstairs in the living room with Dylan and Lily. "So how did this even happen?" Beck points between Dylan and Lily who are cuddled up next to each other on the couch.

Lily grins at Dylan. "I originally contacted him about helping me get in touch with Marina, but he didn't know much. We just started texting every day. Dylan has helped me work through a lot of my emotions."

"Huh," Beck scoffs at Dylan. "You never seemed to be the sensitive type."

Dylan smirks. "What, because I made fun of you for crying one time? Get over it, bro."

"My mom had just died!"

"I was a kid! I didn't know any better."

"Dylan, what did we talk about?" Lily reminds Dylan as she squeezes his hand.

"Make friends with Beck," he replies with displeasure.

Beck snorts out a laugh. "Make friends with me? Yeah, I think I'm good."

"You've never even given Dylan a chance," argues Lily.

"I've never given cocaine a chance either, but I think I'm good on that also."

Lily rolls her eyes. "You're mad at me for finding someone who truly cares about me, yet you're dating a girl who's married? No offense to you, Marina." Lily seems to honestly be apologetic about her stab at me.

"If I told you the truth about my marriage, you wouldn't believe me."

"Try me," she challenges.

"Okay." I smirk. "I am Princess Marina Kenryk, descendant of Zale Kenryk, emperor of City of Zale. I'm daughter of Princess Oceane Kenryk, aka Annie Hudson. Prince Aquarius Emerson is the son of King Wade Emerson, ruler of the Australian Border. Together we are bound in matrimony to strengthen our family's alliance. We're both hybrids on the run from the sea to save your dear brother from an evil homicnidarian named Cordelia Anahi, aka my former mother, who demanded I kill Beck and collect his soul. I'm now here to heal his memory of myself and his entire ordeal of becoming a water-breather in order to force Cordelia out of his head."

Both Lily and Dylan stare at me for what feels like minutes. "What?" Lily finally asks with an amused smirk planted on her lips.

"Did you need me to repeat that?" I sass.

Her smirk fades as confusion sets in. "No… I got it… but what?"

"I'm a water-breather," I say, but Lily still stares. "Mermaid," I clarify.

"Annie is her birth mother," informs Beck.

"When I met Beck, I was meant to murder him," I say.

"She's here to save me, but by saving me she has to leave me," explains Beck.

Dylan bursts out laughing. "Um, I'd like to know what kind of drugs you two are on…Why have you not been sharing?"

Lily bursts out with laughter. She can't control the giggles as she holds her stomach and tears escape from her eyes. "You guys are definitely high."

"This isn't a joke. I'm telling you because I trust you enough to not tell my secret," I say quietly. I look to Dylan, "Not you, but if you were to say a word, I'll feed you to the sirens myself."

Dylan's amused smile fades. "What's with y'all and sirens?"

"Oh my god. Are you pregnant? That's why you married Aquarius." Lily snaps as though she's figured out my life. "He's the father!"

"What? How would you ever think I'm pregnant from everything I just told you?"

"It makes more sense than you being a princess mermaid from a royal family sent here to originally kill my brother."

"She makes a valid point," Dylan declares.

"Marina," Aquarius snaps, "the less humans who know the

truth the better."

"Hey!" snaps Lily. "Don't you dare refer to me as a human. I have a name!"

"Try to stop me, Aquarius," I challenge as I slip my pants off, take a seat on the floor, and outstretch my legs.

"Why're you taking your clothes off?" asks Lily, her tone matching her confusion.

"Don't do it," warns Aquarius with a glare.

"Do what? What's happening?" Lily's mouth is gaping open, her eyes wide as she awaits what will happen next.

"Wipe that sick smile off your face," Beck warns Dylan.

Dylan throws his hand up in surrender. "Hey, I'm not the one getting naked."

I close my eyes, take a deep breath, and will myself to shift. The transition is no longer painful or gory. The transformation is quick as my feet turn to fins, my legs morph together and form golden glimmering scales, and my gills appear below my ribcage. I give my tail a wave.

Lily's ivory skin becomes a ghostly white.

"Holy shit." Dylan is astounded. His hands are running through his hair, pulling at the roots as if he's testing himself to make sure he isn't dreaming. "HOLY FU—" Dylan's words are cut off by Lily as her eyes roll backward and she falls unconscious into her boyfriend's lap.

"I told you not to do it," sighs Aquarius as he shakes his head.

"Well, I didn't know she'd pass out!" I dispute as I make the shift back to human with little effort. I race to Lily's side. She's breathing. Her heart is pumping. She's only in shock. She'll wake up. "Take her to a bed and let her sleep it off," I order Dylan.

"Wha—What are you? Who are you?" Dylan stumbles from his disbelief. When he stands, his legs buckle, and he, too, faints.

"Humans," grumbles Aquarius before he reaches down and pulls Dylan up and over his shoulder. Dylan is out cold, same as Lily.

While Aquarius hauls Dylan's unconscious body to a guest bedroom in the back, Beck carries his sister and places her beside her boyfriend.

Once we're outside the room and Aquarius has closed the door, he says, "They'll sleep it off. What were you thinking? They didn't need to know."

"Lily is my friend," I dispute. "She deserves the truth."

"You're here to heal Beck's memories, not create new ones with his family and friends."

"You don't need to speak on my behalf," argues Beck.

"I can't do this right now," I burst out with frustration.

Aquarius steps forward closing space between us. Beck steps in front of me, shielding me from my husband. "You need to do this right now. This is why we're here."

"I'll heal him in my own time. I'm too tired tonight."

"Come to bed, Marina," urges Beck as he gently pulls me toward the stairs.

I nod. "You'll be sleeping in the guest room next to Dylan and Lily," I inform Aquarius.

He strides to me, and pulls my arm into his grip. "You are my wife and you will not sleep with another man."

I rip my arm free, infuriated at his domination. "Your wife makes her own decisions and will do as she pleases without permission from a man."

Aquarius tenses, his jaw set tightly. He squeezes his fists at his hips. "Marina," he begs. It hurts me to make him sad, but I never asked to be thrown in between two men's lives.

"You got what you wanted. You married me. I'm your wife!" I explode with rage. "Beck will be healed soon enough and I'll be all yours. In the end, you win. So shut up!"

Beck wraps his arms around me from behind and lays his forehead against the back of my head. "Calm down," he urges with a whisper.

I spin around on my heels and embrace Beck. I need to calm myself. I'm losing my mind between trying to keep my promise to Aquarius and wanting to spend time with Beck before I say goodbye.

"Marina." The gruff tone in my husband's voice indicates he's furious, but I don't turn to face him. Beck continues to hold me tightly. "I think I have been extremely patient and lenient toward you and Beck, but this is crossing a line. I can't spend one more night with my mind reeling with the thought of him defiling my wife."

I rest my head against Beck's chest and sigh deeply, attempting to clear my mind. I understand Aquarius is frustrated, but how does he think I feel? I'm losing the man I love. I need to make every minute count.

Slowly, I turn around to look my husband in his dark eyes. He's near the brink of tears, causing my stomach to drop. Shaking my head, I force my guiltiness away. "What I do with Beck is none of your concern."

"It's all of my concern, Marina!" Aquarius snaps. He runs his hands through his wavy hair. He's irritated with me and hurt by my actions, I know.

"Let's go to bed," Beck whispers from behind me as he holds his hand out for me to take.

"Marina," Aquarius chokes.

I can feel the pull toward him. It's our bond. The urge to embrace him is strong, but I fight against it. I can't make him feel better right now.

"You need to give me time," I tell him before taking Beck's hand in mine.

I climb the stairs with Beck and follow him to bed. Bandit, of course, follows us and doesn't waste time making himself comfortable.

Beck closes the door behind us and immediately wraps me in a comforting embrace. Then I begin to sob. The tears hit me out of nowhere and my stomach clenches in a tight knot. I pull at Beck's shirt, clenching it in my fists.

"Calm down. Shhh," Beck whispers in my ear as he rubs my back.

"I can't," I cry. "I can't stop."

"It's not fair. I didn't ask to be married," I sob. "I didn't ask to have to choose between my husband and my boyfriend." I look to

Beck, my tears blinding me. Beck rubs the wetness away with his thumbs. "I'm going to lose you and I'm hurting him."

"You love him," Beck says with sadness.

"I didn't say that," I sniffle.

"No, you didn't." Beck kisses the top of my head.

I pull away from his embrace and strip off my shirt before crawling beneath the warm blankets.

Beck slides in next to me, still wearing his clothes. I cuddle up next to him and he holds me tightly.

Running my thumb against his lips, I trace the outer line of his mouth.

"I've missed you so much," Beck whispers against my fingertip.

"I've missed you, too." I snuggle closer to him and lay my head on his chest. "I didn't know if I'd come here and find you'd forgotten about me."

His chest rises and falls rapidly. Is he laughing? "Marina, you're not someone I could forget easily."

He pulls my chin up, so he can face me. Beck lowers his mouth to mine and gently caresses my lips. Slowly and gently, I kiss him back. Our bodies meld together and for a moment I forget about the danger that surrounds my life. I let the pressure of Cordelia being alive melt away. I will the anger of Sam away. I will Aquarius' crestfallen look from my mind. In Beck's arms, I'm free and far away from the people who dictate the decisions in my life.

"Will Lily be okay?" I ask, regretting how I shocked her with my transition.

"She'll survive," he answers.

"Can I trust Dylan with my secret?"

"Most definitely not."

A heaviness fills my chest. "I'm going to have a lot of explaining to do in the morning," I say as I begin to nod off.

Chapter Twenty-Two

[BECK]

IT'S THE NIGHT OF ETHAN'S death. I sit in the back seat of Ethan's car. I know I'm inside of a dream, but I can't escape its memory.

"I'm sorry I made you go out. I know you're having a hard time," Ethan tells me as we drive down the highway. We're wearing our Halloween costumes. I smile when I look at Ethan as a *cereal* killer with his bloody cereal boxes and plastic knives.

"Nah, the truth is I wanted to break up with her for a while," I speak of my ex-girlfriend.

"You never told me that."

"I wanted to make it work, but I'm sixteen. I don't need a serious relationship."

"Yes! That's what I'm saying," Ethan says.

"Watch it, dude. You know Lily's in love with you," I warn.

"She's been in love with me since first grade when I shared my fruit snacks with her." Ethan laughs, but suddenly stops with a sigh. "Lily's my girl. She always has been."

"That's what I thought."

Ethan pulls into the turning lane. In the opposite lane is a truck racing toward us. I see it coming fast and veering into the wrong lane. Ethan doesn't notice the truck right away…even if he did, there's nothing he could do. I scream a gut-wrenching cry as we're blinded by the headlights.

When metal meets metal, Ethan's head is obliterated at impact. Still watching from the backseat in my dream, I watch as the airbag deploys and smashes the memory of me in the face causing blood to flow from my memory's nose.

And then we roll.

The wreck seems to move around me as I remain still in the backseat. I'm dreaming after all. This is only a memory. This *was* me.

The memory of me cries as the window shatters around him and the glass cuts deep within his arm. His head slams against the doorframe abruptly stopping my bloodcurdling screams. The car finally rests again in the deep ditch, wheels on the grass. The memory of me looks to his dead best friend.

Ethan's face is beyond recognition. His neck is ripped open. Shards of glass stick out from his flesh. His blood is spurted all over the windshield and the airbag,

"Ethan!" the memory cries.

Ethan doesn't respond.

The memory of me cries from the loss and the pain.

I remember the pain. It was blinding.

Suddenly, Dead Ethan looks back at me in the backseat. I slide as far away from him as I can.

"Look at what you did to me." Ethan's voice is gruff.

"It wasn't me," I mutter.

"You. You did this."

I shake my head. "I didn't do this," I yell.

"Beck?" Marina's voice fills my head.

"I didn't kill you," I argue. I didn't...

"You'll pay for it," Ethan snarls from his toothless, blood-soaked mouth.

"Beck?" Marina appears next to me in the car. "Beck, look at me." Marina pulls my face to hers, forcing me to look at her and not my dead best friend.

"Marina?"

She presses her lips to mine. "You're okay," she says. As she kisses me, the scene begins to fade into blackness.

I force myself to open my eyes.

I'm back in the bedroom, Marina's hands cup my face as she kisses me.

"Beck, wake up." It's Marina.

"Marina?" I kiss her back with urgency. My hands wrap around her waist and hold her tight to me. "Are you real?"

She kisses my lips softly. "Does it feel real?"

"Extremely... That's what scares me." The visions and dreams always feel real.

"I'm real," she assures me with more kisses, but I don't believe the words. My mind is only playing tricks on me again.

I push the illusion of Marina off of me. There's a yelp when something hits the floor. I flick the lamp on.

"Why would you do that?" she yells from the floor. "Look what you did to my elbow." She rubs at her reddened flesh. She gets back to her feet and moves to sit back on the bed.

"Stop," I warn.

She halts. "Stop what?"

"You're not really here. You're up here—" I tap my temple with my index finger, "—messing with my mind, just like the others."

"Beck?"

"No. No. No," I mutter. "You're not really here."

"Beck." She grabs my face. I avert my eyes to the ceiling to avoid looking at the illusion of the one person who keeps me grounded. "Beck, I'm right here. Look. At. Me."

I shut my eyes, willing the image of Marina to disappear.

"Beck," she whispers, her breath tickling my skin. At the heat of her, the hair on my arms stands on end. Her cheek brushes against my face before her lips are kissing mine. Delicate hands grasp at the back of my neck, pushing into my hair. Despite my best effort to lose the hallucination, I press my hands to Marina's back.

She's so warm. She surges to life beneath my touch, kissing me deeper and grinding harder against me. "Beck," she breaks the kiss. "I'm here."

"It's really you?" I'm hesitant to believe her. Then again, I have to take note that she's not trying to kill me like the other hallucinations.

"Mhmm." She pulls away from me with a furrowed brow.

"You're real."

Marina runs her hands through my hair, comforting me. "Was this like the other dreams and visions?"

"No, this time it was a memory. Except... Ethan talked to me after he was dead. He blamed me for his death."

"It wasn't Ethan. It was Cordelia. She's manipulating your thoughts," Marina explains. "Tell me about the previous visions."

"Brian—" I croak. When I squeeze my eyes shut, I feel tears escape from my lashes and stream down my cheeks. "I was in class when they appeared." My voice is thick.

"Who?"

"Brian and Tyler. They emerged out of thin air. When they stalked closer to me, their flesh began to peel off and disintegrate. Their eyes were eaten out...they told me I didn't deserve to survive."

"Beck—"

"I was screaming. Screaming for them to stop. Screaming for help. Screaming just to scream...I'm not sure." I pinch the bridge of my nose, attempting to hide my weak tears. "The next thing I knew my teacher was hovering above me telling me to snap out of it. I shoved myself up, ran to the bathroom and locked the door behind me. Then Brian appeared in the mirror behind me. I just wanted him to go away, so I punched the mirror and it broke. The shards fell to the floor and I collapsed alongside them."

I swallow hard and continue. "Brian kneeled down next to me and picked up a shard. 'End it,' he said, handing it to me. I almost did."

All the color has drained from Marina's face. She clutches her mouth, looking as though she'll be sick. "Beck," she whispers as she hugs me tighter to her.

I don't want her to pity me. I don't want her to think of me as pathetic.

"I was so close. I fought it…I slashed Brian's throat instead. And then the bell rang."

"I'm so sorry."

I sit up and look to her, confused. "You have nothing to be sorry for."

"I wasn't here," she clarifies. "I chose to leave you and I wasn't here when you needed me."

"You're here now."

"I am."

I pull her into my lap and hold her close, never wanting to let her go.

Chapter Twenty-Three

[MARINA]

WHEN I WAKE TO FIND an empty spot next to me in bed, I panic. Where's Beck? I race downstairs only to find Beck sitting with Lily and Dylan at the dining table eating pancakes and bacon. Bandit lies on the floor waiting for scraps. Aquarius works in the kitchen, not acknowledging me as I enter the room.

Lily kisses on Dylan, but when she sees me, her emerald gaze grows dark with uneasiness.

"Good morning," I cautiously say. The last thing I want is Lily to be afraid of me.

"Aquarius went out this morning and bought a couple of groceries," Dylan says taking a bite of pancake, but avoiding my gaze.

"I couldn't sleep…you know, worrying about how my wife was in bed with another man." There is an angry edge in Aquarius' voice, and to be honest, I don't blame him. I've been an awful wife. "I also was hungry," Aquarius adds, flipping a pancake.

I'm surprised to see Beck eating food made by Aquarius. "I can't resist bacon," Beck admits as he crunches into a strip.

Aquarius approaches me with a plate stacked with fresh

pancakes and crispy bacon. "For my queen."

I sigh when he refers to me as his queen, although he vowed to me I'd always be his queen. I bid him a thank you and take the plate from him. I can't deny I'm starving.

I take a seat with the group and don't hesitate to dig in. Aquarius' pancakes are sweet and fluffy. The bacon is crunchy and salty. My stomach has been happy this weekend.

For the most part, Aquarius seems calm. I know he couldn't have forgiven me so soon. Maybe he is finally understanding I only need time.

Lily clears her throat. "So you're really a mermaid?"

I nod. Lily looks to Beck for reassurance. His strong jaw twitches as he swallows and simply nods. Lily's gaze flickers back to me and then to Aquarius.

"I touched it," confesses Lily with a red face.

Pausing on the pancakes, I stare at Lily with confusion. "You touched what?"

"I touched your husband's—"

"You touched HIS WHAT?" interrupts Dylan, slamming his fork down on the table with a loud *clink*.

"Babe, let me finish," pleads Lily.

"I allowed her to touch my tail," Aquarius finishes the conversation. "She was asking me a million questions this morning and I shifted for her. She wanted to touch it."

"When you're in a relationship, you are forbidden to touch any part of any man…including mermen!" Dylan argues.

"But it's so big!" Lily exclaims.

Dylan's jaw drops. "I can't believe you just said that to me." He's obviously appalled.

"The tail! His tail is so big!" Lily attempts to kiss Dylan again, but he pulls away.

Beck sits at the table looking extremely uncomfortable.

Aquarius looks entertained as he watches Lily and Dylan bicker. A smug smile is planted on his lips as he chews his bacon.

Lily continues to beg Dylan for his forgiveness. Ultimately he accepts her apology as long as she doesn't touch anymore mermen tails. She hugs him with agreement.

"I'm still struggling with how this can be real. You're not supposed to exist." Dylan informs me.

"Says who?" I ask.

"Logic. Mermaids are only a fairytale."

"Clearly, we're more than a children's tale," says Aquarius.

"How. How is it possible?" questions Dylan. "There's people who search the oceans! Scientists...no one has ever found any evidence of mermaids."

"You would know that how?" I dispute. "You're just a teenager. Even if these so called scientists found anything they wouldn't be running to tell you."

"We remain hidden because we don't want to be found," comments Aquarius. "It's not hard to remain hidden when seventy percent of Earth is water."

"You're really married to him though?" Lily asks me, not seeming to care how we exist, but only wanting to know the juicy details.

This time, Aquarius remains silent, waiting for me to validate our relationship status. I frown. Beck, noticing my apprehension, grabs my hand, squeezing it tight, and traces his thumb in small circles over the back of my hand. He's reassuring me that whatever is going on between Aquarius and I—which is nothing—has zero to do with how we feel about one another.

I exhale, blowing my bangs away from my face. "Yes, we're technically married." Emphasis on the technically part.

Lily winces. "But he's, like, thirty…"

Aquarius sucks his teeth, clearly annoyed by her comment. "I'm twenty-four," he snaps. "I turned twenty-four back in August, okay? Marina turns eighteen on the twelfth of November, so there's only a six year difference."

"Six years and three months," scoffs Beck.

"Isn't your birthday in December?" asks Dylan. He's amused. "You're dating an older woman."

"It doesn't matter," snaps Aquarius. "Marina's my wife."

"She's my girlfriend," disputes Beck.

I hang my head back, annoyed by how they argue over me as if I'm property. "Pretty soon, you're both gonna be single."

"Marina," says Lily. "Who are you, really?"

And with her question, I know I'll have to tell her everything.

. . .

IT TAKES MORE THAN two hours to run through everything with both Lily and Dylan. They have many questions and I answer every one with patience.

I started by telling them how I grew up with Cordelia and how I didn't know who my parents were. I then went into detail about Harbor and Caspian and explained how Harbor was the one who killed Brian, Tyler, and Nate. When I told Lily I was ordered to kill her brother she began to cry. To know what my true intentions were frightened her—as it should. I was set on killing Beck...but I didn't. There's a silver lining.

And then I told her about Annie. She laughed at first, but stopped when she realized it wasn't a joke. She couldn't comprehend how the woman who was her step-mother could be my mother—a former water-breather. I explain to both of them how and why Annie was exiled to the human world. Lily then asked about her half-sister Aubrey, who to the best of my knowledge, doesn't have the ability to shift. Annie was human for many years before the birth of Aubrey and Malcolm is just Malcom. A human.

To finish off her questions, Lily asked if vampires exist. I, of course, answered with "no" because the idea of a night creature thriving off human blood is preposterous.

Aquarius and Beck join us in the family room. Aquarius takes a seat at the opposite end of the couch while Beck cuddles up next to me. Lily smirks and bites her lip as she looks at Aquarius. "You're like sex on legs," Lily whispers in a hoarse tone. I can only imagine what Lily is fantasizing about in her head.

"I'm right here," argues Dylan.

"I'm sorry, baby. You can't take it personally. Obviously, I'm attracted to you…it's just—" Lily pauses to study my husband once more. "He belongs in a movie or something. Normal people don't look like that."

"Thank you, Lilian." Aquarius smiles. Aquarius directs his attention toward me. "If you're going to tell her the truth, you should probably include the reason you're here."

"You said you can help Beck with his visions," Lily adds with eagerness, snapping out of her Aquarius trance. She wants to help Beck just as much as I do.

"Cordelia—"

"Your dead mother," Lily struggles to keep up.

"Yes… she's not exactly dead. We don't know where she is at the moment, but we have information from her sister that she's very much alive. Cordelia is the one manipulating Beck's mind. The reason he's been having these visions is from when Beck was enslaved. Cordelia still has access into his mind."

"You had said your dad was a slave. How is Cordelia not in his head?"

"Honestly, I think it's because Beck is human. He's vulnerable to the spell," I respond.

"So in order for you to save him you must heal his memory?" Lily is following perfectly.

"Yes. I need to heal any memory of me and my world from his mind. It's like restarting his brain. Cordelia will no longer have access to his mind once it's wiped clean."

"Then what're you waiting for? Help him!"

"It's not that easy, Lily," Beck explains. "I don't want to

forget Marina."

"So you'd rather live your life tortured by the visions and dreams?"

Beck pinches the bridge of his nose, and hesitates to answer. "I can live with it if it means Marina and I can be together."

"Beck, you're living in a reality you've created," intervenes Aquarius. "What happens when Cordelia chooses to kill you?"

"Marina will bring me back." Beck's answer is calm.

"So you'll force her to watch you die over and over? What if there's a time she can't save you?" Aquarius questions. Although I hate to admit it, my husband makes a valid point. To each power there's a limit.

I grab Beck's hand. "It's true, Beck. I'd rather live in a world knowing you don't remember me, but are safe and alive, than live in a world without you."

"How is this choice not up to me?" Beck pulls his hand from mine. "I'm the one with the witch in my head!"

"Ultimately, the choice is yours," I assure him. "I won't heal you if you're not willing."

Aquarius sits at the end of the couch with his arms crossed against his chest. He shakes his head, clearly upset. The silence in the room is deafening. Lily seems shocked by the whole ordeal. Beck is frozen next to me. Dylan holds Lily as they process all the information. When Aquarius storms off into his guest bedroom, I fight the urge to ignore his anger, but I break and follow him.

"What's wrong with you now?" I ask once I've caught up to

him.

"This was supposed to be simple. You were supposed to heal his memory and then we could return home... and now you're giving him an option?"

I shut the door not wanting anyone to overhear our conversation. "If Beck is unwilling, I *can't* heal him. I won't force him to forget. He swears his visions have disappeared. Maybe he can lead a healthy life without being restored."

"So you can live a life with him?" Aquarius counters.

I don't know how to answer, so I remain silent.

Roughly, Aquarius rubs his eyes and face before running his fingers through his hair. "You know Cordelia better than anyone. Once she has no more use of someone, she executes them. She will kill Beck if you don't save him."

"We're not certain of that. She hasn't killed him yet. Clearly, she needs him for something. I just can't figure it out."

"You're running out of time," Aquarius warns.

"I'm so tired of you pressuring me to heal Beck. I know you want me all to yourself, okay?"

"Is that what you think I'm doing?" He sounds offended. "I want you to love me for me, not because you feel forced. I've never wanted to pressure you into anything. If you want to let Cordelia kill Beck, fine. That's what will happen if you keep letting her invade his head. I don't want to see Beck die. Your heart will die with him."

I can feel myself beginning to break down as my chest tightens and my knees start to tremble. "I can't say goodbye," I admit with a choking sob.

Aquarius strides over to me and wraps me in his strong embrace. "I'll be here for you when it's over." Aquarius rests his forehead against mine.

"You're not Beck." I sniffle.

Aquarius pulls away from our embrace. "Why am I not good enough for you?"

"That's the problem, Aquarius…you are good enough."

He cocks his head to the side. "How's that a problem?"

"You shouldn't settle for good enough. Why would you sell yourself short of what you deserve?" He listens but doesn't say a word. Aquarius looks to me with hurt written all over his face. "You deserve to be someone's entire world, not someone's good enough."

"I don't believe you. Deep down, you feel something for me. You try to disguise it, but I see it in your eyes when we're alone. I get it. Beck is your first love, and you're trying to hold on to it…make it last. But admit it, what we have is different. It may not be a love yet, but it could be."

He presses a light kiss on my forehead. "One day, you'll look at me and you'll only see *me*. I'll consume your world. I promise you that, my queen."

. . .

AT DINNER, I SIT IN the middle of Aquarius and Beck while Lily sits with Dylan across from us. I was grateful the two of them made dinner together. I never imagined Dylan being a cook when he was spoiled his entire life. I do have to say he and Lily make a tasty spaghetti and meatballs.

As I sit next to Beck, I feel a gut-wrenching sickness in my stomach. After speaking with Aquarius I knew I couldn't deny my obligation much longer. I plan on having a discussion with Beck after dinner. I would have done it earlier, but everyone agreed on watching a movie, so I wasn't about to spoil the fun, plus, I'd jump at any excuse to postpone the inevitable.

My thoughts are interrupted at the soft touch of someone's hand grazing my right knee. With Beck being on my left, I know it isn't his hand giving me goosebumps.

I glance down to find Aquarius skimming his hand against my knee, trailing his fingers up my inner thigh. Luckily the table hides his hand. I don't need a boyfriend/husband war on my hands. Aquarius has never crossed a line I've drawn and knows if I say "no" I mean it. He's just testing me—trying to see what he can get away with before I snap.

Aquarius wears a smug smile as he chews his food and listens to Lily talk about—well, I don't know what she's talking about. I'm a bit distracted at the moment. Aquarius' touch reaches higher and in an effort to stop him, I clamp my thighs together, although he doesn't remove his hand. So here I am at dinner with my boyfriend next to me and my husband's hand trapped between my thighs.

Grasping a fork in my hand, I lower it beneath the table, and prod at Aquarius' groin. I make little effort to be gentle about it.

Instantaneously, Aquarius removes his hand and clears his throat as he chews. He straightens up, but doesn't move away from me.

Next to me, Beck picks at his noodles with little interest in actually eating. I lean over and ask him if he's okay. He only nods. His forehead is creased in anguish. I massage his back in an attempt to comfort him. He grabs a hold of my knee and applies a little pressure. He smiles. "It's just a headache."

"Do you want me to heal you?"

He rolls his eyes playfully. "It'll pass."

"We need to discuss the elephant in the room," says Dylan.

My face is screwed up in bewilderment. Elephant? First of all, why would there ever be an elephant in a dining room? And second of all…what?

Next to me, Aquarius stifles a laugh into his napkin. I look to him, still puzzled. "Are you laughing at me?" He nods, still chuckling.

"It's an idiom," informs Beck, rubbing at his temples roughly. "He doesn't mean a physical elephant."

"It's kind of like when we say, 'you mess with the bull and you get the horns,'" chimes in Lily.

"In our world," says Aquarius, "the expression is, 'when you play with the shark, you get the teeth.'"

"Oh!" Idiom. Got it. And right now, I kind of feel like an idiot.

"I've always wondered if you were a natural blonde," teases Dylan. "You just verified my curiosity." Lily elbows him in the stomach causing him to cough. "For real. What's the plan?"

Dylan asks.

"I think I'll discuss the plan with Beck in private," I respond as I take another bite of a meatball. Dylan seems to enjoy being a part of a group, but he doesn't need to be involved in every matter.

Dylan shakes his head. "I didn't mean the plan right now. Once you heal Beck, what's your plan?"

For the first time I realize I haven't made a plan for returning home to find Cordelia. I've been so consumed with Beck I haven't thought about how I need to protect my family.

"I assure all of you Marina will be safe under my care," promises Aquarius.

Beck slams his hands down on the table. "You're so full of shit!"

Aquarius remains calm. "Beck, I'd risk my life for her."

Beck's emerald eyes glow with rage. "I've already risked everything for her... and you want to take all of it away from me."

"No," argues Aquarius. "Cordelia is taking it away from you. Cordelia is the enemy, not me."

Beck moans out in pain clutching his hands to his head. His ivory skin flushes a deep shade of maroon. I reach out my hand for him, but he pushes my arm away. "Stop, Marina! It's just a headache. I don't need your help."

His words cut deep, slicing me open. My hand falls limp at my side.

Beck rises from his chair and says nothing more before

heading to the stairs. His footsteps fall hard. Everyone at the table remains quiet for a few minutes. I want to storm upstairs after Beck, but I decide it's best to give him his space.

Chapter Twenty-Four

[BECK]

MARINA COULD'VE EASILY healed away a headache, but it's nothing I can't handle myself. I'm beginning to nod off when I hear a voice say my name. It echoes through my room a few times in a haunting tone.

"Marina?" I ask.

"Shouldn't you recognize my voice by now?"

And what scares me is that I do recognize the voice. I could never forget the voice of the woman who caused me so much agony.

"Cordelia."

"You're a smart human, I'll give you that." She sighs. "I'm still saddened by losing you."

"What do you want?"

She laughs, sending chills though my body. "For right now…just your mind."

My head begins to pound fiercely. I collapse to the floor in a heap of throbbing agony pulsing through my body.

I can hear Cordelia in my head…not just her voice but her thoughts. Our point of views are two different beings until they're not. Until they're morphed into one body. My body. Cordelia and

I are combined into one mind. I'm no longer myself. I have no control over my own actions.

Hello, my name is Beck Hudson...

This is equivalent to the feeling of being enslaved. I'm psychically here. I'm capable of thinking, but I'm unable to say or do anything I want. Cordelia exists in my mind as though my own thoughts are chained up within my own head.

I realize she was the cause of my hallucinations. It must have been her creating the images of Tyler, Brian, Nate, and Ethan in my head. She was the reason for my insanity. I denied it for so long. I didn't want to believe Marina and Aquarius.

"Calm down, my dear," I say aloud by force.

Wait. I didn't say that though. I attempt to speak but am unable to say anything. What's happening to me?

I laugh in response to my thoughts. But it's not me who's laughing, it's Cordelia. "You'll be just fine, honey." Cordelia laughs, using my body as a temple. "I only need to borrow you for a minute."

What do you want?

I slide from the bed and walk to the dresser and look in the mirror. I can clearly see this isn't me. It's my physical body, but my gaze is menacing. Glowering back at me in the mirror is a stranger. "A distraction," I answer—*Cordelia* answers.

There's a quick flash of an image. It looks to be a face. Cordelia's face flashes in my mind and then as fast as she appeared she's gone. It was Cordelia, but she looked twenty years younger. She was smiling and looked innocent. Why would she show me herself?

My fist smashes into the mirror with all of my strength, causing pieces to fly. I've reinjured the same hand that broke the boys' bathroom mirror only a week ago. Cordelia forces me to kneel and pick up a shard from the floor.

What're you doing?

I'm coerced into lifting the shard of mirror so I can see my reflection. My lips curl into a smirk. "You'll find out soon enough."

As I descend the stairs, I find everyone still finishing their dinner. Marina is the first one to notice me. She looks worried. Bandit is at the foot of the steps growling, causing everyone to now stare. Bandit can sense the danger. I beg Cordelia to keep everyone safe. I don't want her to force me into hurting anyone.

Cordelia compels me to stop. I stand in the open space of the dining room and kitchen, my body still, with my hand digging into the shard of glass. There is a sharp pain growing in my palm where the glass is digging into my hand.

Lily gasps when she sees what I'm holding.

"Beck," Marina whispers as she moves to stand, wanting to get to me. Aquarius stops her and pulls her into his arms.

Bandit circles me, growling.

"Beck?" Marina cries, fighting Aquarius' restraint.

"Hello, princess—or can I still call you daughter? It's such a pleasure to see you again," I say with the influence of Cordelia.

"Beck?" Lily asks with tears forming in her eyes. Dylan grabs her hand, fear filling his gaze.

Aquarius and Dylan are the girls' protectors now. Good. I want them to shield Lily and Marina from whatever I may do.

The only person I look to is Marina. She stares wide-eyed at me, still fighting against Aquarius. She can't break his hold despite her screaming at him. "Let me help him!" she screams. She desperately claws at Aquarius' arms, drawing blood, but he holds tight.

Bandit is furious. He's viciously growling and barking at me. He can sense the evil within me. When he lunges, Cordelia forces me to stab him deep in the stomach with the shard of mirror. Bandit lets out a screeching yip and falls to the hardwood floor.

Lily's screams are bloodcurdling as she runs to Bandit's side.

I can't breathe. I'm suffocating beneath Cordelia's grip. My dog is dying on the floor from my hand and I can't save him. I can't move. I can't scream out for him. I can't tell him it wasn't me…it was Cordelia.

"Let me save him," Marina screams as Bandit bleeds out on the floor. His whimpers grow quiet as the pool of blood on the floor grows larger.

I begin to laugh—*Cordelia* begins to laugh.

Marina's rage grows angrily. With one hand, she thrusts me against the wall and pins me there with her powers. With her other hand, she shoves Aquarius away causing him to stumble backwards. Marina races to Bandit's side pulls him in her lap and wraps him in her amber glow to heal his wounds.

I want to cry for my Bandit. I want to tell him I didn't mean to do it. I would never hurt him. I love him more than anything and I could've killed him.

Bandit groans before breathing heavily. He yips a few times before rising to his feet. His yips turn to whimpers as he cowers away from me, frightened. He's thick with blood, but it seems Marina has successfully healed him. Lily continues to sob as she forces Bandit into a hug. Our dog accepts her comforting embrace.

I'm still pinned to the wall, but that won't stop Cordelia.

She forces me to raise the shard to my throat.

"Cordelia," Marina screams, "don't do this to him!" Aquarius pulls Marina into a tight embrace, forcing her away from me for her own safety. When she's pulled away, the force holding me is released. I fall to the floor.

Lily still holds Bandit, who seems dazed, but Dylan has joined them. He huddles with Lily, holding her in his arms.

I press the shard deep into my flesh near my left ear. I want to scream as the razor digs in my skin, but I remain silent.

Marina and Lily are crying as though they're being murdered, both trying to escape Aquarius and Dylan's grips.

Marina's skin glows a bright gold, her arms are restrained by Aquarius, but her fists are clenched in a tight ball. With a quick flick of her wrists, she throws Aquarius off of her and she charges for me.

Everything happens so fast.

Marina runs for me, her hands extended outward, reaching for me. Her blonde hair, swaying behind her. Her golden eyes pleading for me to stop.

The mirror burns as I cut across my throat. The hot blood spills from the wound and spews out, drenching my shirt and pooling on the floor near and around my bare feet.

Time seems to slow as my life drains from my body. I'm falling, but the hardwood floor feels minutes instead of seconds away. I no longer feel the pain. I no longer hear anything. I only witness what's playing out in front of me.

Lily is screaming, tears running down her flushed cheeks. Dylan holds her as she falls limp in a bundle of numb limbs. He screams something, but I can't read his lips. He looks to be in serious distress with his face red and sweaty.

Aquarius runs for me. Marina falls to the floor, frozen with shock. Her gaze meets mine; her golden irises wide and written with terror as I collapse to the floor. I've never seen her so frightened.

Time returns. I'm pummeled with the feeling of being very aware of my situation. I'm dying. Cordelia has killed me. No— Cordelia has forced me to commit suicide.

My body falls hard against the floor, but Aquarius catches my head before it hits. He presses his hands over my wound and applies pressure. Marina crawls to my side, pulling me into her lap. My blood is painted on her ivory flesh. As horrific as it is, I see the beauty of dying in the arms of the woman I love.

As my eyes drift shut, I feel her tears spill down my face.

I'm met with the dark. Total blackness. Where am I? My scream is met by an eerie echo. I move towards the echo, stumbling my way through a corridor of terrifying darkness.

"Beck," a woman says.

I don't need light to know who this voice belongs to. It's my mother.

The blackness around me evaporates while a new scene forms.

The sun is high in the sky with not one cloud to be seen for miles. Waves crash onto the beach then retreat back into the ocean. My six-year-old self sits in the sand with my mom. Her long brunette hair is pulled up into her sun hat. Her blue eyes are bright with life. She smiles, revealing her dimples. Little Beck sits in her lap as she laughs and yells to my father who has Lily on his shoulders as he wades out into the ocean.

"Are you sure you don't want to go play?" she asks the younger me.

Little Beck looks up to her freckled face. "There are monsters in the water," I say in my childish tone.

Mom smiles and kisses a younger me on the head. "Baby, the world is full of horrors, but your dad and I would never let anything happen to you."

I kneel next to the memory of my mother. I forget sometimes how beautiful she was. Tears emerge in my eyes. "You lied," I croak. "You didn't protect me when you died. Ethan died. When I died."

A hand reaches out for me. Mom's hand.

"Mom?" I wrap my hand around hers. She feels as real as I remember. Soft skin with light freckles splattering her flesh. "Please, Mom. I think I'm dead."

"Beck," she says, watching me with admiration, "you have a bigger purpose in life than to die by your own hand. Remember, baby, you're strong."

"Mom, I miss you." I pull her hand to my face.

A golden haze envelopes us as the beach scene begins to vanish.

"I love you," she says.

I sniffle. "I love you, Mom."

I'm thrust back through the dark until I'm brought back into the world. For a brief moment there is a serene fog of amnesia, much like the moment you wake in the morning with a fresh slate. I lay on the hard floor, soaked in a warm substance. Aquarius and Marina look down over me, along with a sobbing Lily. As Lily wipes away her tears, she's left with streaks of blood on her cheeks. Dylan pulls her into his arms and wipes the blood away.

"You saved him," Aquarius says praising Marina.

She healed me.

"Beck, what the hell?" Lily croaks, horror written on her face. Her body is trembling with fear, but Dylan holds her tight, whispering in her ear.

Marina forcefully kisses me as if I'm the air she seeks to breath. As her mouth moves against me, the throbbing in my head returns and quickly intensifies. Against my will, I wrap my hand around her throat and whip her off of me.

"You killed me," I hiss.

With confusion, Lily asks, "What?" She pushes Dylan off of

her so she can get closer to me.

I turn my head in order to narrow my gaze on Marina. My face is warming and I know it's a harsh shade of red. Cordelia forces me to grit my teeth together as if I'm some rabid animal. "Beck?" Marina whispers with question. I push myself up, leaning against the wall.

"Cordelia," Aquarius accuses as he pulls Marina against him to shield her.

"You're more than a pretty face, Prince Aquarius."

Marina shoves Aquarius away from her. He attempts to grab her, but she escapes and scrambles toward me. She grabs my blood-soaked shirt and shoves me to the floor.

"What'd you do with Beck?" she demands, her face inches from mine. I want to tell her to get far away from me, but despite how I feel, my body remains in a calm demeanor.

I begin to laugh a dark, menacing chuckle. "I didn't do anything with him," Cordelia answers. "He's still right up here." She forces me to tap on my temple.

"Get out of his head!" Marina demands, slamming me back, causing me to hit my head hard on the floor.

With both hands, I grip her throat. She chokes out. I roll my body over hers, crushing it as I continue to strangle her. Arms wrap around me and pull me from Marina. I'm thankful in this moment that Aquarius is larger than me. He should be able to keep me from doing any damage.

Marina whips me into the wall with her powers. My back smashes into the plaster, knocking the breath from my lungs. I fall to the floor.

"I killed you," screams Marina, striding closer with rage. Her hands glow brightly.

Despite possibly having a few broken ribs, I sit up and notice a hole in the wall. "You can't kill me, honey."

Marina closes the space between us and grabs me by the throat, slamming me into the wall with the strength of her mind. "Why would you reveal yourself?" Marina questions. "Everyone believed you were dead."

"I've never been one to hide." I smirk.

Lily screams out for Marina to stop hurting her brother.

"It's not Beck," Dylan sounds as though he's questioning himself.

"Why're you doing this?" Marina squeezes my neck harder, cutting off the little air I had left in my lungs. I want to choke out for oxygen, but silently suffocate beneath her grip.

"Marina, you're only hurting Beck. Cordelia isn't here," Aquarius reminds her.

Slowly, Marina's grip on me loosens as she calms her mind. Her arms fall to her sides.

"No, I'm not here. You're right, Aquarius. But maybe you should think about why you're really here," Cordelia says through me.

A fury of pain burns across my skin, suffocating me. The agony sizzles through my veins and eats me from the inside out. This time my screams are audible.

The weight of Cordelia is lifted from my mind and I'm

released from my internal prison. The burning comes to an abrupt halt.   I inhale a deep breath, but am pained by my sore body and broken bones. I cry out in pain and I begin to sob from the memory of stabbing my dog and slicing open my throat.

"Distra—" I begin to say, but can't get the word out.

"Beck? Beck, is that you?" Lily races to my side, tears spilling down her cheeks.

Marina slides next to me and rests her hands on my chest. As she envelopes my body in her healing glow, I feel myself strengthen. I feel my ribs pop back into place and my head stops throbbing.   The entirety of my agony vanishes, but the painful memories remain.

"Beck?" Marina cries with joy. Her lips are on mine, urging me to kiss her back. I shove my arms in her hair and kiss her back, expressing my love for her. I begin to tremble as I come to the realization of what just happened to me. Cordelia was in my mind, controlling my movements. I could've killed Bandit. I could've killed my sister. I could've killed myself.

Marina pulls away, but hugs me closer. "Beck, I'm so sorry."

"Somebody better tell me what the hell just happened!" screams Lily, who is still shaken up. Dylan strokes her hair, but she refuses his affection, only wanting answers.

"I'm the distraction!" I cry out as I regain my thoughts.

"Distraction?" Aquarius repeats.

"Cordelia is using me to distract Marina," I explain, heaving as I attempt to settle myself. I turn to Marina. "Cordelia wanted you to come to Minnesota…"

Aquarius slams his fist against the coffee table. "Why didn't I realize that? Cordelia wanted you far away from the kingdom, Marina. She's planning something."

Marina gasps. "Cordelia knew I'd sense Beck was in danger."

"Get this Cordelia bitch out of my brother's head now!" Lily demands.

I now know that I'll never be able to escape the grip Cordelia holds on me unless Marina heals my mind.

Chapter Twenty-Five

[MARINA]

Beck rests his head in my lap. I run my fingers through his hair, comforting him.

Bandit approaches with caution. He sniffs at Beck's fingertips, but when Beck reaches up to touch his dog, Bandit snarls.

"Bandit," Beck chokes back tears.

Carefully, I raise my hand, inching it closer to Bandit's head. His snarl disappears as he sniffs my hand and gives me a quick kiss. Placing my hand on Bandit's blocky head, I close my eyes and will away the bad memory of Beck slicing him open.

Once Bandit is healed it's as though nothing happened. Bandit shakes his body and plops down on the floor next to Beck.

A grin is planted on Beck's face. "I can't lose him," he says petting his fury companion.

Lily sits with her knees to her chin, rocking back and forth. Dylan kneels behind her, rubbing her back in an effort to console her. Aquarius sits at the dining table, his face written with horror. I've never seen my husband look so worried. It puts a knot in my stomach knowing Cordelia lured me here. And for what reason?

A silence haunts the air. We all sit with one another, but don't dare look each other in the eyes. We don't speak a word of the horror. Maybe we're all ignoring the fact we're all smothered in blood.

After a few minutes, Beck pushes himself to sit up and looks at Aquarius. "Can I talk with you...in private?"

Aquarius nods, rises from the table, and follows Beck out to the deck. They close the door behind them, but I go stand near it.

"What're you doing?" asks Lily. Her voice is hoarse from screaming.

"Listening," I simply answer.

I crack the door open enough to see the backs of Aquarius and Beck. They stand looking at the woods. Aquarius' arms cross his chest while Beck nervously grips onto the deck railing.

"I have to let her go," Beck says.

Aquarius remains silent for a moment before nodding. "I know it won't be easy."

"How do I know the healing will work? I never invited Cordelia in my head. How will I know Marina can keep her out?"

"Think of it like a locked door. If the door is closed and locked, no one gets through. Once the door is unlocked anyone can come in and out as they please. After you shifted into a water-breather, your horizon was widened and that door was unlocked to a new perspective. Cordelia forced herself into your mind when you were enslaved. Now, your brain has an open channel allowing Cordelia into your mind. The door isn't always open. She's only able to enter when you're vulnerable. Hence why you've been having visions and nightmares," explains Aquarius.

"Using your analogy, she broke into my head?" Beck attempts to understand what exactly is happening to him.

"Yes. If Marina can heal that experience from your mind, Cordelia is once again locked out."

"How do you know all of this?"

"Cordelia's sister is a close family friend. She has the same powers as Cordelia. The only difference is Cora uses her gifts for good."

Beck slumps his shoulders and shoves his hands in his pocket. "Cordelia is punishing not only me, but also Marina. She's still bitter about her attempted murder. Healing my memory won't affect me. I won't remember Marina and as much as that saddens me now, I won't know to be sad about it once I'm healed. Marina on the other hand will have to mourn me."

"It'll take time for her to move on from you, yes."

Tears brim from my eyes. The thought of losing Beck is heart-wrenching.

"Where will you go?" Beck asks.

"As much as I want to protect her and keep her away from any possible danger, she'll insist on going home to fight Cordelia—wherever she may be at the moment. I can't be selfish. Marina is the only one who can defeat the evil of Cordelia."

Tears roll down my cheeks as I listen to Beck and Aquarius. I know I must protect Beck by healing him and I must return home to protect my family, my new husband's family, and the citizens of City of Zale. I have an obligation to my people. I'm neglecting my responsibility as princess just by being here with a human.

"I know you love her. I know you will protect her and I honestly do take comfort knowing she'll be safe with you. I can't stand the thought of losing her. I won't remember anything about her. Not her smile when I walk into the room, or how she tucks her hair behind her ear with such precision." Beck pauses to chuckle under his breath. "I won't have any memory of how she can scarf down a cheeseburger." Aquarius, too, laughs. "I won't remember how she bites her lip when she's thinking or how she looks at me with such admiration. I won't remember how she's risked her life for me on so many occasions..." Beck's voice catches and he chokes on his words.

Aquarius clears his throat. "I don't take pleasure in your pain. I know Marina loves you, but I also know she can love me one day. Until then, I will give her time. I only want her to be happy."

"You're making it really hard to hate you," Beck admits.

Aquarius laughs and slaps Beck on the back in a friendly manner. "Trust me, I really wanted to hate you too."

Beck sighs with a sorrowful heaviness. "I want to forget Marina."

I want to forget Marina.

His words settle, much like the venom of a sea urchin—painful and paralyzing.

I've literally had bones break and limbs tear in the process of transformation. Cordelia has electrified my entire body in prickling spasms. My stomach has been sliced open. I've drowned. But nothing has been more painful than hearing Beck say that he *wants* to forget me.

Grasping the wall for support, a choke of agony makes its way out of my mouth. Little specks of black blur my vision, yet I still see Beck turn around and peek through the cracked door. He knows I'm listening.

"Marina, wait," he urges, racing to the door.

A wave of anger washes over me and my vision returns. Slamming the door in his face, I lock it, and slide to the floor. Uncontrollable sobs burst from my chest, threatening to suffocate me from the inside. Beck pounds his fists against the door, begging me to let him in.

Arms wrap around me and hold me close. It's Lily. I cry on her shoulder, soaking her sleeve with my tears.

"Marina, I know you don't want to leave him, but this will be best for him. You haven't had to watch the visions taunt him endlessly, day after day. I just watched my brother slit his own throat. This needs to stop."

"I know," I blubber. I can't be selfish. I can't allow him to die because of me. "It just hurts to know he *wants* to forget me."

"He didn't mean it like that," Lily assures me. "He just knows it's the only way.

At the door, I can hear Beck pounding.

"I'm struggling with whose side I should take on this one," says Dylan. Like, you're crying on the floor, but Beck's beating his hands bloody on the door." Dylan bites his lip. "Yeah, I'm gonna let him in." He strides to the door and unlocks it.

Beck drops to the floor next to me, and scoops me in his arms. I sob against him. He's still blood-soaked, but I don't care about the mess. All I care about is his arms around me, protecting me.

"Marina, you know I didn't mean I want to forget you." Beck is desperate to explain. "I'm just ready to be… normal. I want to wake from a full night of sleep. I want to go to school without being haunted by my dead friends. I want to be able to close my eyes and not see Cordelia lurking. I don't want to remember hurting Bandit," he cries. "I don't want to remember the pain of slicing my throat." Beck wipes the tears from his eyes with his thumbs.

I swallow down the lump in my throat. "I don't want to see you hurt." My eyes still sting from the tears that continue to stream down my face, their saltiness invading my mouth. "I want you to live the happiest of lives. I want you to succeed in everything you do." My breath hitches in my throat. "I want you to have a wife and a family. I want nothing but the best for you, Beck."

Beck cups my face in his hands. "Listen to me, Marina. Don't worry about me once you're back home. You have to forget about me, okay?" I lean into Beck's hand as I weep. He pulls me into a tight embrace. "Aquarius truly loves you, Marina."

I cry harder because I know it's true. Aquarius has stood by my side, even when I completely disregarded his feelings. He's promised to give me time. He's been patient with my stubbornness. He's perfect.

"We were meant to fall in love, but I don't think we were meant to be together," Beck says, pushing me over the edge of heartache. I hug him harder, never wanting to let him go.

I pull my forehead from his chest. "I need to heal you now…before I change my mind."

I feel heavy with grief.

This is it.

This is goodbye.

. . .

[BECK]

MARINA IS WRAPPED IN my arms. Her lips press against mine softly and my hands tangle in her hair. I glance to Aquarius who has turned away. He gives us this last moment together. I close my eyes and kiss Marina with more urgency. She presses into me as if she'll never let me go.

A shot through the head of pulsing agony makes me stagger backward, clutching my head. "She's coming back," I warn, falling to my knees.

Tears flow from my eyes as my entire body is engulfed in flames. The searing pain envelopes me. Blood-curdling screams escape my throat as I burn.

I roll around on the floor in an effort to extinguish the fire burning across my flesh. Cordelia's going to kill me.

"Marina, please!" I scream. In my last moments with her, I'm forced to beg for her mercy. I am weak. "Make me forget!" I scream, as a shrill sound like the wailing shriek of a storm siren overtakes my mind, threatening to burst in my skull.

Lily's screams, Marina's cries, and Bandit's barks disappear as the pain becomes too much to handle. Suddenly, there's no sound. The pain has vanished, replaced by a numbness. I'm cold.

Marina grabs my face and forces me to look in her gold gaze.

"I love you." Her mouth moves, but I hear no words. There's a deafening silence around me. Black spots dance around her pain-stricken face.

"I love you, too," I attempt to say, but am so weak I don't think the words are audible. I'm beginning to black out. I can't keep my eyes open for long.

Marina's body glows with an amber essence, and then she closes her eyes.

Chapter Twenty-Six

[MARINA]

BECK'S MEMORIES FLASH in my head as I heal his mind and I'm overwhelmed by his feelings. Opening his eyes on the beach the night I saved him and seeing me for the first time. Me on the beach naked and needing a savior. Our walk to Botany Bay. Our moment on the beach when we fell into each other's arms and *almost* kissed. The night we first kissed in his bed. The moment I told him the truth and he shifted. Cordelia's caverns and all her slaves. And then I'm reliving the moment Beck tried to crush me under his strong grip. I can see how hard Sam and Caspian fought to keep him alive from the hoard of slaves. He's on the beach and my body is brought to shore. I'm lifeless. Beck won't let me die. He fights for me until I'm breathing.

And then I can't take his memories anymore. I can't handle the loss of the man I love. So I take everything away, leaving gaps that will need to be filled and explained to him. The one thing I don't take away is Dylan. Beck needs a friend and I believe he can find one in Dylan. This experience has changed Lily's boyfriend for the better. Beck won't understand the blooming friendship, but that will have to be something he'll come to recognize in time. Beck will believe he has a slight case of amnesia. Lily can easily explain it as a hit to the head.

Every image of me, everything and anything he's ever thought about me, and every moment we've spent together has been eradicated. Nothing remains in his mind.

Nothing.

"I stripped him of his bloody clothes and did my best to wash off the dried blood," Aquarius informs Lily and Dylan once he's carried Beck to bed. "You'll have to get him into the shower before he wakes."

"How long will he be out?" Lily asks.

"At least a couple of hours. It'll take time for his mind to adjust to the change." I sniffle back tears. "I need a minute," I choke.

I climb the stairs to see Beck. He lies in bed where Aquarius covered him in a blanket. Beck looks so peaceful. Finally, he's free.

I take hold of Beck's hand in both of mine. It's warm and rough and brings me a sense of comfort. Tears well up in my eyes as I think about how he no longer knows me. How he wanted to forget me. With the memory fresh in my mind, his declaration still cuts deep in my heart. I know he only wanted to be free of the pain.

By forgetting, Beck is now safe from Cordelia's manipulation. Beck's free to live. I'll never cross his mind. He won't smile at the sound of my name. He won't remember how extraordinarily special he is. But I'll know.

I'll hold dear the time we spent together. I'll forever

remember the boy who saved my life. The boy who showed me how truly strong I am. The boy who sang to me in the car. The boy who taught me to be human.

"I will always love you, Beck Hudson." I gently kiss him on the forehead.

I stand up straight in an attempt to compose myself and act as though I'm okay as I descend the stairs. I blink away the tears and force a smile with little emotion that relays I'm fine. Aquarius looks to me with a sorrowful gaze. He opens his arms, offering comfort, but I instead, shove him away from me. I fall to the floor in a bundle of limbs and flooding tears.

With his sturdy arms, Aquarius pulls me to him. Rejecting his affection, I punch his chest with my fists. "Don't touch me," I warn, but Aquarius doesn't let go. "I hate you," I hiss.

He presses his chin to the top of my head, attempting to embrace me tighter. "You don't mean that," he mumbles, sounding almost unsure of himself.

No, I don't mean it, but at the moment, I don't care. Aquarius stood in my way of happiness. I'm being unfair, I know. But I can't help but feel hateful for being forced to make Beck forget. Without Aquarius here, I would have ran off with Beck. We would have made a life together work.

Yet in one minute, our time together was wiped away. There's no longer a future for us. There's no longer a past.

"I do. I hate you," I tell Aquarius, meaning to cause him pain. The same pain I'm feeling right now. "Let me go. I have to say my goodbyes."

Reluctantly, he releases his hold on me. In order to get up, I shove my weight against Aquarius, leaving him on the floor while I make my way to the kitchen.

Lily and Dylan sit wrapped in each other's arms at the dining room table, watching me with subdued gazes.

Lily breaks from Dylan's embrace, strides to me, and wraps her arms around me as she cries. I return her tight hug. She's the same height as Beck, but slimmer, and my chin rests against her shoulder as easily as it does on Beck's.

"Don't make me forget," she sobs. "I want to remember." The tears escape now, rushing down my cheeks and escaping onto Lily's back. "You have to do something for me. You have to fill in the gaps for Beck. He'll be confused. Your dad and Aubrey can't say a word about me. You and Annie will need to figure out how to convince them not to mention me."

"We've got this under control. I called Annie to come here and help me get Beck home. Are you sure you can't wait for her?"

I shake my head. "No. I don't want to risk Beck waking while I'm still here. Aquarius and I need to get home anyway. I have a family to protect too."

She nods with understanding. "Marina, you're my best friend," she admits.

I squeeze her tighter because I realize she's mine, too. "This isn't the end for us." I grab her by the shoulders and force her away for a moment so I can look at her. "I swear to you, I'll find a way for us to see each other again."

She throws herself into my arms. "You do what you need to do. Worry about you and Aquarius and your kingdom." Her gaze flickers to my husband, who quietly lingers near the door, waiting for me. "When you're safe," she continues, "then you can worry about me." Her reassuring smile puts me at ease. As I turn to leave, she leans in next to my ear, so only I can hear her. "You know, Beck loves you."

"Not anymore." I swallow back my disappointment and attempt to hide my tears. A defeated sigh breaks through my tightly pressed lips. "It doesn't matter," I admit. "The first time I healed his memory it failed. This time will be different. I've become stronger. I have a better hold on my power. He's not going to remember me."

"What about Cordelia?" Dylan asks.

"We're going to find her," Aquarius answers. He seems confident.

"She can't hurt Beck any longer," I promise as I step toward Dylan. He looks to me with a new perspective. Is it respect?

I place my hands on his face and close my eyes.

"Wait. What're you doing?" Dylan pulls away, but my power forces him to freeze in order for me to concentrate.

"Marina, stop!" Lily demands.

"I don't trust him. He can't know who I am—" I pause to look to my husband, "who we are."

"I promise, Marina. I swear I won't tell a soul," Dylan pleads. "I want to remember. I want to be a part of something bigger than myself."

"Why should I believe you?" I ask, pressing harder against his temples.

"I would never betray Lily. If I were to tell your secret, she would never forgive me, okay?"

In this moment, I don't know what to do. As I've said before, I do believe this experience has changed Dylan for the better. If I heal him, I'm afraid he'll return to his selfish ways. "Beck will need a friend more than ever right now. Be that friend," I tell Dylan releasing him from my hold.

"Beck hated me before..." Dylan begins.

"Prove to him you've changed," I interrupt.

"Are you sure about this decision?" Aquarius asks me.

I smirk. "I think Dylan knows if he were to betray us, he has an awaiting date with a siren."

"Really? The siren threat again?" Dylan crosses his arms.

"It's a promise," Aquarius says.

I focus my attention back to Lily. "You need to help Beck adjust into normalcy once again."

"I will," she promises.

. . .

THERE IS A NEW URGENCY to get back to the kingdom. Danger looms over my family and everyone in City of Zale.

"Cordelia knows I'm in Minnesota. As of right now, she's not expecting me to come home. She knows I would never leave Beck's side," I tell Aquarius as we buckle ourselves in our seats.

"Now that I've healed him, we only have a day, at the most, before she realizes what has happened. I've taken Cordelia by surprise once again and I'm coming for her."

Aquarius starts the engine with a rumble. "Let's go home."

The drive through the night is haunted by a gloomy silence. I have nothing to say. I feel broken. I feel empty.

On the side of the road, a pair of glowing eyes appear in the ditch and Aquarius slows the car as we pass. I get a quick glance of a deer standing with its baby before they retreat in the woods to safety.

My heart warms at the sight of the deer I'd so wanted to see while I was here. My heart sinks again when I realize Beck isn't here for me to share this moment.

Aquarius and I board our plane by midnight. Once we settle in our seats, Aquarius grasps my hand, intertwining his fingers with mine. As the plane fills with more passengers, I grow nervous. I'm thankful for the first-class seats, so there's only Aquarius next to me.

I remain silent. I feel badly for how I treated Aquarius back at the cabin. I was upset and not thinking clearly. My husband has been nothing but good to me. He had even treated Beck with respect. He didn't deserve for me to yell at him.

When the plane begins to move, I grip his hand tighter. As we ascend, I close my eyes and hold my breath. I hate this. I hate this. I hate this!

"Open your eyes," urges Aquarius. His voice is soothing.

We've leveled out. I take a deep breath. "I'm sorry," I

whisper to him after a few minutes of thinking of what to say to him.

"For what? You can close your eyes if you really want." He chuckles under his breath, causing me to smile despite the circumstances.

"I don't hate you. I—I'm sorry I said that...I didn't mean it."

His thumb grazes over my skin. "I know."

He brings my hand to his lips and gently kisses me.

"I just can't believe it's over," I say. I feel void inside. I can't shake the fact Beck will wake and have no recollection of me.

"I think you're looking at the situation in the wrong way, love. It's not over. This is a new beginning. Beck is free from Cordelia's harm and you no longer need to worry about his safety. We'll find Cordelia together and she'll be punished for her actions. I'm going to protect you."

"Protect me from what? If Cordelia wanted me dead, I'd be dead. She's known exactly where I've been this entire time. I'm not what she's after. She sent me after Beck for a reason... we know this. We just don't know for what reason yet."

Aquarius scrunches his face up in thought, causing little wrinkles to appear near his eyes. "I've been wondering something. Cordelia wanted you to find Beck... that's why she invaded his mind. She knew you'd feel something was wrong. But how would she have known you left the kingdom?"

"I don't know. I mean, I haven't seen any Cordelia clones, so unless you have, she wouldn't have known."

"Everyone believes us to be on our honeymoon."

"Not everyone," I admit. There were a couple people who knew I was on a search for Beck.

"You told someone beside your father you were looking for Beck?" His eyes widen as he releases a heavy sigh.

My heart is pounding.

"Who did you tell?" he demands to know.

"Jackson, and—"

Suddenly it hits me. Cordelia isn't a clone. Cordelia stole a body. She's posing as someone in the kingdom.

"Cascade," I gasp, my jaw dropping. "Cascade is Cordelia."

Aquarius is quiet, but his mouth is slightly gaping with shock. "Cascade appointed herself the supervisor over Cordelia's remains."

"Cascade was the one who informed me you were one of Cordelia's lovers," I comment.

Aquarius nearly gags. "I wouldn't touch those tentacles if my life depended upon it. She was only trying to mess with your mind before the wedding."

"Cascade urged me to visit Beck."

My husband looks pensive as he absorbs the revelation. "She had a plan, but needed you out of the way. You were the only one suspicious enough about Cordelia's death to investigate it."

"But why not just kill me then?"

"That would raise too many questions."

"We need to get back. Right now." I move to stand, but Aquarius tightens his grip on my hand, urging me to settle down.

"What do you expect us to do, Marina? Jump from the

plane?"

"I mean..." I bite my lip before finishing my thought, "we could."

"We're not jumping from the plane!" He sighs heavily. "You just need to take a deep breath. We'll be to Florida in a few hours. Mysteria is close enough from the coast... We'll be home by dawn."

I rest my head on his shoulder. "Thank you, Aquarius." My eyes are tired, but I'm too frantic to sleep.

My aunt has been murdered by Cordelia, her body overtaken by evil.

Cordelia has claimed Zale, Lynn, and now Cascade. I need to find my family before she kills more of the ones I care about.

I'm the only one who can stop her.

Chapter Twenty-Seven

[MARINA]

AQUARIUS KEEPS HIS PROMISE and gets us back to Mysteria by the break of dawn. He's flanking me, attempting to keep up.

"What's our plan?" he finally asks once the golden lightning orbs from the kingdom are in our view.

I ignore him as I haven't thought of a plan yet. I've just been so desperate to know if my family is safe.

"Damn it, Marina. Stop." The authority in his voice causes me to come to a sudden halt. I do have to admit Aquarius has what it takes to be a leader with only the use of his voice.

"We can't blindly swim in there planning on killing Cascade—" He shakes his head at his mistake. "I mean Cordelia." What if your aunt is still alive in that body?"

I hadn't thought of that possibility. "What do you mean? Like, Cordelia is only using the body as a capsule?"

"It's possible. We don't know if Cascade is alive or not. You're the princess... how would it look if you executed your family member without hesitation?"

"She's Cordelia!" I argue.

"No one knows that, but us."

"What do you suggest we do?" I inquire.

"We return without causing a scene. We've just returned from our honeymoon and we play it safe until we can have a private conversation with Cora and the emperor."

I close my eyes to block out the world and debate this plan in my head. Aquarius is right. We must carry out the facade that we were on our honeymoon. Although Cascade/Cordelia knows the truth and will ask me if I found Beck. I open my eyes to find my husband patiently awaiting a response. "What if Cordelia suspects something?"

"You won't let her... as far as you know she's Cascade, your loving aunt."

"She's not expecting me back. What if she questions me? She knew I was going to find Beck."

"Then tell her you found him... you healed him. That's it. Keep it simple."

"And when we find my uncle?"

"When we find Emperor Flotsam, we tell him everything we know. Then we form a plan." Aquarius offers me his hand with an endearing smile.

I take his hand. It's a simple gesture, yet I'm comforted by him with just one touch. Aquarius is endlessly devoted to me. I'll never forget Beck, but maybe I can be open to Aquarius in the future. I love Beck, but I can't deny that something inside of me burns bright for Aquarius.

Together, Aquarius and I make our way to the kingdom. The guards greet us upon our return and ask about our honeymoon. I tell them we had a great time. Most importantly, I tell them we're madly and deeply in love with one another.

So far, no problem.

"Prince!" Dune yells from a nearby cavern. "How are you and the wife?"

"The wife is just fine," I snap with annoyance.

"We had a beautiful vacation." Aquarius smiles.

Cascade appears in the cavern entry. She must have been meeting with Dune. Actually, I hadn't realized it, but Dune has been spending a lot of time with Cascade. Does he knows the truth? Does he know Cascade is Cordelia?

"You're back so early!" exclaims Cascade, her golden eyes lighting up brightly. Maybe it's paranoia, but I seem to sense the evil within my aunt.

Not knowing if Dune knows Cascade's secret, I twist the truth. "I got homesick."

"Eager to see your family?" She throws her hands over her heart and smiles. "That's so sweet."

Aquarius places his hand at the small of my back. "We hate to be rude, but we're very eager to settle back into our cavern. We're quite exhausted." I'm thankful my husband is always quick to take control of a situation.

Dune stares at us with his dark silvery gaze. He almost looks menacing with his lips fixed in a frown. I look to the cavern floor just to avoid the eye contact.

"Before you go, doesn't your favorite aunt get a hug?" Cascade twists her mouth into a conniving smirk.

Aquarius wraps his hand around my back to my waist and

pulls me closer to him. He's wary of me getting close to Cordelia's capsule.

Cascade stares me down as she waits for me to embrace her. For the first time in months, I feel a sickening in my stomach. Only an uneasiness I've ever felt from Cordelia.

I pull away from my protective husband. I'm going to continue to play the part of a clueless Marina.

"It's so nice to see you." I force a smile as I embrace Cascade. She wraps her arms so tightly around me, my ribs threaten to crack. In this moment, I know I've made a mistake. I've made myself vulnerable to the monster.

Cascade leans in closely, her lips brushing against my ear. "I've missed you, my darling daughter," she whispers, sending chills through my spine.

"Mother," I whisper. I freeze from the realization of being wrapped in Cordelia's arms. Will she crush me with her power? She can kill me so easily. I'm weak beneath her grip.

To my surprise, she lets go.

My body trembles.

Why'd she let go?

I stare at her in awe, questioning her with my eyes. None of this feels right. Cascade plants a sweet smile on her face, causing me to feel sick.

"Marina," urges Aquarius, "I'm sure Emperor Flotsam would love to see us."

"Yes, my brother has been very worried about you," Cascade says with concern in her voice. "I hear you didn't tell him you were leaving on your honeymoon."

I still can't speak. I can't find the words. I only stare in bewilderment.

"Love?" asks Aquarius, grabbing my hand and intertwining his fingers with mine.

"I— um…" I shake my head, attempting to clear my mind. "I'll make sure to apologize for our sudden departure."

"You be sure to do that," insists Cascade.

Slowly, I swim away from Dune and Cascade with Aquarius by my side. When I'm out of their sight, I thrust my tail so I shoot through the corridors of the castle.

"She knows?" Aquarius questions, but the certainty in his tone tells me he's already well aware.

"Oh, she knows." I swallow the lump forming in my throat. "I don't know what she's planning, but I need to get the kingdom under lockdown."

Aquarius suddenly stops, pulling at my arm, and causing me to shoot backwards. "You're not doing this alone!"

"I have to start the lockdown!" I argue. "Cordelia will get away before I can stop her."

"Are you strong enough to hold City of Zale under lockdown?"

"No," I admit. "I need you to find Sam. He's the only one with enough power to finish what I've started."

He shakes his head. "If you over exert yourself it could kill you."

"I won't push myself to death. I'm not arguing with you about this. I need you to go find him right now!"

Aquarius scoffs, but then quickly kisses me on the lips. "Be careful." He swims off in the direction of Sam's caverns.

I have to admit I have absolutely no idea how to place the kingdom under lockdown. Sam never once trained me to do something so strenuous. Who am I kidding? I can't even create a successful force field. But I know I must try.

When I make it outside the castle, I swim to the top of the lightning orbs. The entire kingdom is lit with a golden haze. The force field needs to reach to each of the lights, forming a dome around City of Zale.

I hover above the lights with my arms extending from my sides. Closing my eyes, I concentrate on the power flowing through my veins. My gifts should be as easy as shifting. They should come naturally. The force leaves my fingertips with a tingle. The barrier grows and moves over the lightning orbs. I feel myself strengthening, but I know I must move faster to ensure Cordelia can't escape. I push myself to extend the power.

Glancing down, I find the force field has moved to cover almost all of the castle and is inching its way over the citizen's caverns.

Yes! Sam was right. The power does come easily the more I conjure it.

But the further the force grows, the harder it is to control. The power surrounds me, and I've pushed myself further than I have ever in the past.

The force field begins to retreat and as much as I push, I can't hold it. I tremble as I attempt to save the power I've created. I feel the pressure weighing down on my body like an anchor. I'll lose what I have of the force field if I don't stop pushing myself.

Instead, I choose to hold what I have of the barrier until Sam can find me.

Minutes, feeling like hours, pass before I catch a glimpse of a gold-scaled tail thrashing through the water. I'm growing weak as I continue to fight the urge to release the wall of energy.

Sam passes through the barricade, while Aquarius is trapped beneath the force.

"Sam," I whisper with a weak smile. "I can't do it." I'm beyond exhausted, but I don't want the power to snap back. I keep holding on.

Sam lights himself up with the amber essence and spreads his power over mine, extending all the way around the castle, the citizens caverns, and the remainder of the kingdom. The lightning orbs' light shines brightly off of the reflection from the wall of energy. He placed City of Zale under lockdown within a minute without seeming to exhaust himself in the least.

I let go, knowing Sam has the lockdown under his control. Sinking through the force field, I drift downward until Aquarius catches me with his strong arms. He hugs me closely to him and kisses me on the forehead. "You did so well, love."

"I couldn't do it," I whisper, feeling sleepy. Regaining my strength will take a minute in order to heal myself enough to fight.

Cordelia must only have access to her mind-manipulating

powers while using Cascade's body as a vessel. Cora explained how Cordelia could have cloned herself... but if she cloned herself, why wouldn't she just transfer her soul to that new body? Unless the clone was reborn. The clone started from an infant, meaning Cordelia would need to borrow a body. The clone is in hiding. We find the clone and we can end Cordelia.

"Sorry it took so long. Emperor Flotsam took some convincing."

"He believed you," I huff, still attempting to regain my energy.

"It wasn't me. Cora had a feeling Cordelia was using Cascade's body. She convinced him to have faith in us. He's desperate to save his sister if she's still in there somewhere."

Pushing my gift, I spread myself in the amber glow, and conjure my healing ability to work over my body. The weakness escapes me, replaced by a newfound strength. Aquarius lets me go when he sees I've been rejuvenated.

Sam sinks below the barrier.

"Marina, I'm exposed. I won't be able to use as much of my power to fight when I'm holding the force field."

"I can't do this by myself!"

"You've defeated Cordelia in the past. That wasn't me. You can do this." Sam is confident.

Out of the corner of my eye, I notice a glowing violet entity floating closer to us. Cora. Sam points to her off in the distance. "You're not alone."

"Cora was gathering our fighters," informs Aquarius.

"You're going to find Cascade and save her," Sam promises.

With Sam holding the force and Aquarius by my side, I swim downward closer to the castle. At this point Cordelia must know we're under lockdown. If she's trapped inside Cascade's body, she won't be able to fight her way out. This is the time to strike.

Unexpectedly, I hear an agonized gasp behind me. When I turn to find my husband pierced through the shoulder with a harpoon. He sinks as a cloud of blood surrounds him.

Before I can scream, Dune swims out from the shadows and catches Aquarius. He wraps his tail around my husband and traps him in his grip. Against Aquarius' throat, Dune holds a spear head.

"No," I cry, desperate for Dune to listen. Zale's death flashes in my mind while the fresh memory of Beck slitting his throat plays in my head. I can't witness Aquarius die in front of me. I've lost almost everything. I can't lose him, too.

When I move closer, Dune presses the head of the spear deeper in Aquarius' skin. Aquarius groans out in pain, although he looks close to fainting from the agony of his shoulder wound.

"Dune, he'll die!"

"I don't want to kill Aquarius," Dune assures me. "I've looked after this boy as if he were my own son, but when the empress calls upon you for help, you obey."

"Cordelia has brainwashed you," I attempt to calmly explain. "Don't let her manipulate you into killing someone you love."

"I've loved her since the day she saved me from the humans."

"It was a storm..." I sound unsure as I'm confused by his

confession. Caspian told me Dune was saved by a random storm.

"Yes, but it wasn't a regular storm. Cordelia created it. She saved me." He speaks about Cordelia with respect and admiration.

Cordelia created a storm… she saved Dune. Cordelia knew Caspian's father was alive. She knew Caspian wasn't an orphan. It's all making sense now.

"What about your wife?" I question, still very aware of the weapon placed against my husband's throat. I need more time to think of a plan, so I distract Dune with questions.

"Nerissa died long ago. She couldn't handle losing me, so she took her own life."

"Why would she do that when she had a young son? Who would've wanted Nerissa out of the way?" I know the answer to my question. Cordelia killed Caspian's mother. It's obvious.

"No," Dune shakes his head violently. "Cordelia wouldn't have killed her."

"Cordelia killed your wife—the mother of your son… and after Nerissa was dead, Cordelia took Caspian. Is that why you obeyed her for so many years? You didn't want her to hurt Caspian?"

The more seconds that pass, the closer to death Aquarius becomes. He's losing a lot of blood and I'm losing my window to save him.

"Mar," a voice urges from behind me, "just let us go."

Caspian. My best friend swims out from behind me, joining his father's side. Aquarius looks tired; he fights to keep his eyes open. My heart drops into my stomach with worry.

"We don't want to hurt you or your family," promises Caspian, breaking my focus from my dying husband.

"Who are you? You've joined the woman you've despised your entire life?"

"My father explained everything. Mar—"

"Don't you dare call me that," I snap.

"Marina," he corrects, "we've been looking at Cordelia all wrong. She's our savior. She saved our society from a corrupt family. She saved you when you were born and raised you. She only wanted to be a mother."

"Cordelia is nothing but evil. She's caused havoc on my entire family and manipulated countless others. She enslaves people and steals the dead's souls. She's no savior."

"She only wanted the best for you. Cordelia feels betrayed by you." Caspian has become submissive to Cordelia. This is unbelievable.

"I'm done with this conversation." I light up my fists, prepared to fight my former best friend.

"No," Dune warns, pressing the spear into my husband's neck, drawing more blood.

The rage within builds as I fight to control my urge to murder Dune where he hovers. I shake from holding the power within me.

"You're going to release the barrier around the kingdom, so Cordelia can leave freely. She promises to never return or contact you."

"Cordelia will never give up," I respond through gritted teeth.

"Cordelia only wants to live, Marina," Caspian explains as if I'm a small child. "She accepts you've disowned her."

Aquarius can no longer keep his eyes open. He's growing weaker from all the blood loss. I'm on the verge of losing my husband and my mind.

I outstretch my hands. "Enough," I growl. "You don't get to negotiate."

"Release the force field," demands Dune.

"Allow me to heal Aquarius first," I counter

Dune slices deeper into Aquarius' neck. My husband's eyes roll backward as his soul begins to leave his body. I can see the slight glimmer around him. I have mere seconds to save his life.

Rage takes over my body. I want Dune dead and I don't care about the consequences. The image of Aquarius dying in front of me is enough to create a hurricane deep in my veins. With my hands outstretched in Dune's direction, I build up a wall of energy. Dune is terrified and trapped. Caspian's screams only inspire me to cause more destruction. I summon the strength through my body and release it through my palms. As the power exits through my fingertips, the tingling returns. I hit Dune in the chest with my force, thrusting him backward causing him to release Aquarius. Confining Dune within a sphere of my strength, I bring my hands together in one quick motion. The force field collapses together, Dune's body crushing beneath my strength. He's instantaneously obliterated in a burst of red.

Aquarius is sinking quickly and I waste no time to swim to

him. As we're sinking, I rip the harpoon from his shoulder and thrust it away. Wrapping Aquarius in my healing power, I conjure all my energy on healing him. Am I too late? Is his soul gone? Did I waste all my strength on killing Dune? I focus on healing the wounds Aquarius has endured.

When we reach the sandy ocean bottom, I feel defeated, but continue to surround my husband in the amber glow. His harpoon injury has closed along with the slit across his throat. Why isn't he waking?

Still enveloping him in the healing gift, I grab hold of his shoulders I shake him violently and slam him against the ocean bottom. "Wake up!" I demand. "Damn it, Aquarius. Wake up!"

I begin to cry, desperate for Aquarius to wake. I'm losing hope as I shake him with no response.

"Aquarius, I love you." I sob. "I do. I love you."

Collapsing in the sand next to him, I consider giving up. What am I fighting for at this point? Cordelia has taken my best friend, indirectly killed my husband, and murdered almost all of my family...

"Had I known it took dying for you to love me, I would've considered it long ago," Aquarius croaks.

"Aquarius?" I shoot myself above him to examine him. His eyes are still closed. I healed him, but couldn't replace all of his energy. It'll return with time.

When Aquarius cracks his eyes open, I'm met with his dark, stunning gaze. He cracks a smile. I don't resist the urge to kiss him. Aquarius kisses me back hard despite still being weak. His arms are wrapped tightly around me as our lips move together soft and slowly now. I begin to cry knowing I had nearly lost him.

"You love me." He grins so wide his eyes wrinkle at the corners.

Pressing my forehead against his, I laugh, and wiggle my nose against his. "I do. I'm sorry it took losing you for me to realize it."

Even in all my training I had never created a force field so powerful to obliterate an object. For Aquarius, I obliterated Dune with ease. Aquarius is my motivation. It's not that I didn't have the power within me. It's because I couldn't find my incentive. I killed for my husband.

A swishing passes by our heads and lands mere inches away in the sand. The same harpoon I had pulled from Aquarius has been thrust in our direction. Caspian rams into me from behind, knocking me off of Aquarius.

"I'll never forgive you for this," Caspian cries as he pulls the harpoon from the sandy bottom and aims it at me. Aquarius doesn't waste time swimming in front of the weapon, shielding me.

"I'm stronger than you, Caspian." Caspian is more than aware of my strength and ability.

"Yes, but is he?" Caspian thrusts the harpoon aiming it at Aquarius' heart this time. As Caspian releases his grip, I envelope the weapon with my mind and crush it into sand.

"You'll regret this," Caspian warns, his face as cold as ice.

"I think you'll regret betraying me."

With one mighty lunge, Caspian shoots himself upward, heading for the top of the castle. I chase him, but when I find Aquarius has followed, I stop.

"Hide," I demand from him.

"You're not going alone," he argues, continuing to swim after Caspian.

"Stop!" I'm surprised when Aquarius halts. "Don't think I'm not appreciative when you protect me because I am, but sometimes I have to do things on my own. Dune used you against me. Cordelia will do the same."

I press a gentle kiss to his lips and shoot away, leaving him behind. If he respects me, he'll do as I've told him.

At the castle entrance, guards float lifeless all around me. They're too far gone for me to save. Tens upon tens more guards rush in as hundreds more surrounds the vicinity of the castle. When I spot Jackson in the crowd of guards, I nearly break down with tears of joy.

"Marina!" he exclaims with pure joy as he swims to me and embraces me. "Why are you back? You need to get out of the kingdom."

"No! I came back for you... for my family. I'm not abandoning you."

"We can detain Cascade without a problem—"

I shake my head. He doesn't understand. "We have to find the clone."

Jackson seems confused. "There's still a clone?"

"There's no time to explain. Cordelia is only borrowing

Cascade's body until she can transfer her soul into the clone. The clone is our answer to ending Cordelia."

"The entire castle is under siege. Sam has the kingdom under lockdown. She's not getting out," Jackson promises.

"Cordelia would be stupid to be hiding out in the castle. She has to be in the citizens caverns."

Jackson contemplates this for a moment. "There's hundreds of families living in that reef. How would we know where to start?"

"I know a compass."

Cora Anahi will help me locate her sister.

Chapter Twenty-Eight

[MARINA]

CORA WEARS A PERPLEXED expression with her lips pinched in concentration. Her hands are extended outward as she feels all the energies within the reef's caverns.

"It's odd. I'm not only feeling my sister's presence, but a new being... the clone." She smirks.

"You found her? Where is she?"

Cora quickly shushes me. "Hello," she says softly into the air. Her eyes are closed as she continues to feel the energy through her fingers. "You don't need to be afraid any longer."

"What're you doing—" With the flick of her hand, Cora quiets my father by clamping his mouth shut.

"Come out. We'd love to meet you," Cora urges with a smile. And then she opens her shimmering violet eyes. "Hello, sister."

When I look above us, there is a girl hovering in the entryway of a cavern. She looks to be about sixteen. I've seen this girl before... Cordelia showed me this girl when I was in her head. This girl is Cordelia. Cordelia's clone.

"How is she a teenager?" asks Jackson, shocked.

"Cordelia must have sped up her aging. This way she'll remain a teenager for a longer period of time. Her mind is young, but she'll be strong. She's at a vulnerable stage," Cora responds.

Cora motions for the young Cordelia to join us. The girl seems wary of us, but swims a bit closer. Her fuchsia tentacles sway below her bell as she hovers, still hesitant to join Cora. Behind her, Caspian appears.

"Praia," he beckons with a coaxing voice.

They named her? This poor girl has no idea what they've planned for her.

"Caspian, who is this woman?" Praia asks, frightened.

"I'm your sister," Cora gently explains. "I'm here to take you home."

"I don't have a sister," Praia says with a soft-spoken voice. "I am home."

"Praia, they're only trying to confuse you," Caspian lies. He holds out a hand, urging her to return to him.

"Mama?" Praia calls. She sounds petrified. "Mama, where are you?"

Cordelia appears behind Caspian, still using Cascade's body as her vessel. She swims out and hugs Praia. "I'm right here, baby," she says to comfort her clone.

"Who are they, Mama?" Praia appears extremely distraught. The worry in her fuchsia eyes is evident as she tightly hugs her "mama."

"They're trying to take you away from me," Cascade says before giving Praia a kiss on the forehead. She pulls Praia's face close to her own. "Don't let them take you from me."

Praia's attitude changes from a helpless, confused girl to a homicnidarian filled with rage. Praia fans out her tentacles and shoots herself upward. Electricity shoots through her body, lighting herself up brightly.

Cora becomes defensive, illuminating her body with her violet energy, but remains calm. "We're not here to hurt you, Praia."

"Praia," I intervene, "this woman isn't your mother. You're nothing but a body to her. Cordelia has been posing as Grand Duchess Cascade Kenryk for the past two months. She's been waiting for you to grow enough to take over your body as her capsule."

Praia doesn't look convinced. Of course, she wouldn't want to believe her mama is only using her. Cordelia has convinced her younger self she is her protector and guardian.

"You tell me lies," hisses Praia as she shoots a wall of energy in my direction. I outstretch my hands and absorb the power she's thrusted at me, pushing it out and away from myself.

Praia shutters at my ability to reflect her power. "Mama?" she questions. Praia has no idea who she's dealing with. She may have powers, but she's young and has no clue of the extent of her magic. If Cordelia takes over Praia's body, she'll be able to hone into the unlimited power.

I look to Caspian, who hovers behind Praia. He catches my gaze and our eyes lock. Caspian's face wears a sorrowful expression while his mouth is fixed with a frown. Deep down, he must know this is wrong. He must feel the knot in his stomach telling him not to follow Cordelia's plan.

I glare at him. "You're going to do nothing while Cordelia kills Praia for her body?"

Caspian remains silent.

Cascade/Cordelia swims forward. "No harm will come to Praia. I would never hurt my child. Just as Cascade is still thriving within me."

"Cascade is alive?" It pains me to know she's been trapped with Cordelia in her own body.

"Not for long." Cascade/Cordelia smirks.

"You've killed enough," says Cora. "When will the bloodshed end?"

"Perfect Cora," scoffs Cascade/Cordelia. "Mommy's favorite. Little miss innocent. Yet, you remain young… someone has been consuming human souls." She laughs.

"I only take from the dead. I never hurt the living." Cora remains patient with her sister.

"You were always such a rule-follower. Boring." Cascade/Cordelia mockingly yawns.

In my peripheral vision, I notice Jackson swimming over the citizen's caverns and coming down fast at Cascade/Cordelia. I never noticed him wander off. He's formed a plan of his own and it's up to me and Cora to help him. Cora seems to take notice as Jackson descends on Cascade/Cordelia and is quick to shoot toward Praia. Caspian doesn't notice until it's too late to stop the collision. Cora pulls Praia into a tight embrace absorbing all the shocks Praia releases.

Caspian thrusts his tail and shoots in Jackson's direction. He's planning on saving Cascade/Cordelia, but I won't let him get too far. I thrust out a wall of energy in front of Caspian. He crashes into the invisible barrier and crumples to the ocean bottom.

"Mama!" screams Praia as she fights against Cora. Her body is illuminated with a fuchsia glow. Praia whips Cora away with the flick of her hand. Although Cora remains young by consuming human souls, she isn't as strong as her sister since she only consumes the minimum. Praia can overthrow Cora, even at the young age of sixteen. I don't want to know how strong Cordelia will become once she overtakes Praia.

Cascade/Cordelia no longer fights against Jackson. "It's time, my child. You've grown strong enough."

She'll transfer her soul and there's nothing we can do.

Jackson pins Cascade/Cordelia down, but it won't matter. We can't restrain Cordelia or Praia's mind.

"Praia, don't allow her in," I desperately warn her. "You're strong enough to fight her power."

"We're trying to help you," Cora gently urges.

"Caspian?" Praia cries.

"You know what to do," Caspian says with little emotion.

How did I allow so much distance between the two of us? How did I not see Caspian develop into an entirely different person? Where is his heart? What happened?

"Praia," I beg. "Think about it. She's kept you hidden away, not allowing you freedom outside the caverns."

"It was for your safety, Praia," promises Cascade/Cordelia.

"Mama?" Praia's voice quavers. She sounds unsure of her

belief in her mama.

My heart races.

Praia closes her eyes and calms herself. Her tentacles rest and her arms sink to her bell. "Et nos unum sumus."

Cascade's body lurches forward as Cordelia's soul exits. Praia opens her glowing fuchsia eyes. The moment Cordelia's soul enters Praia's body, she jolts and her eyes glimmer a bit brighter. Praia's innocence quickly transforms into malice. Her lips are fixed into a smirk. Praia is gone.

"Marina!" Jackson yells. "She's alive! Cascade is alive."

Cascade thrashes against Jackson. She looks to be in tremendous pain as her screams fill the silence and she finds her own voice once again.

"She only has minutes to live. Neither you nor Flotsam will be able to heal her. Only I will release my hold on her once I'm safe outside of the barrier," says Cordelia

"And me," adds Caspian.

With a wave of her hand, she dismisses him. "You're no longer needed."

"My father fought and died for you! You can't abandon me," argues Caspian.

Cordelia scoffs, but momentarily pauses, seeming to think. "I suppose you could be of some use to me." She flashes a grin and places her hands on her bell. Her confidence has returned in her new body. "Fine, once Caspian and I make it far from the kingdom, I will release my hold on Cascade."

Cascade's thrashing halts and she falls silent.

"She fainted," informs Jackson as he holds her close.

"Her body shut down from the intense agony. Will you allow Cascade's blood to be on your hands?" asks Cordelia.

"I will break the barrier for you," I tell Cordelia. "Under one condition."

Her laugh is menacing. "You're not in the position to be striking deals, my dear."

"Maybe not. For Cascade's life, I will release you, but Caspian isn't going with you."

"After he has betrayed you, you'll still forgive him? Pathetic," she sneers.

"I never said I forgave him."

"Marina," begs Caspian as he begins to swim backwards. "Just let me go."

I glance at Cora; she already knows to trap him with her powers. Cora holds him beneath a barrier of her own.

"Maybe there is a little of me in you," Cordelia says to me with a malicious smirk. "You learned a thing or two from mommy after all."

I throw my hands out in front of me with a mad fit of fury, spreading my power across a portion of Sam's barrier. I break a section, weakening the wall of energy. "Get out," I demand with a burning rage beneath my skin.

She outstretches her hand. "You could still come with me."

I killed her! I still want to kill her, yet she wants me to join her? I narrow my eyes at Cordelia. "You better slither to the deepest trench in the ocean, because if I ever see you again, I will end you… and it won't be as painless as last time."

Cordelia presses her lips together and nods. Does she finally understand I will never become the daughter she always desired? "It's such a shame. I could teach you so many things." She swims forward, grips my face in her hands, and presses a gentle kiss to my forehead. "You will join me one day. I promise you I'll find a way."

Although I'm struggling to hold my strength against Sam's barrier, I don't show it. My hands are beginning to tremble, but I remain calm. I don't know how long I will be capable of weakening the wall.

"Get. Out," I demand.

Cordelia turns to Caspian, who is still trapped within Cora's hold, and blows him a kiss along with a little wave. "Do me a favor and kill him quickly. He always was one of my favorites." She quickly escapes through the hole in the force field. I release my hold on the barrier, and sink to the ocean bottom to rest my body for a moment.

I released Cordelia.

I could've ended her. At what cost? Cascade's life. My family shouldn't have to suffer any longer because of my decisions.

Jackson still holds Cascade in his lap, brushing through her hair with his fingers. I join him and eagerly wait for a sign of life.

"She was my friend." Jackson is somber. "It wasn't real."

I rest my head against his shoulder. "Cordelia has a way of convincing us of the illusion she creates."

"We know it better than anyone," he adds.

The worry begins to settle in when Cascade doesn't wake after a couple of minutes. I've given Cordelia a head start. All she needed was a chance to escape. Once Sam discovers Cordelia escaped, he'll send out search teams until she is located.

"She should be far gone by now," Jackson comments, squeezing Cascade's hand.

Another minute passes before my heart drops to my stomach. I've made a mistake. Cordelia lied to me. She broke our deal.

Just as I've given up hope, Cascade cracks her eyes open. She seems groggy, but she's awake.

"Cascade?" Jackson caresses her cheek.

"Jackson," she cracks a smile. He pulls her into an embrace and she begins to cry. Jackson holds her tightly as she sobs.

I'm happy to see her wake, but am saddened by the thought of how she's suffered in her own body for so long.

Praia's suffering.

I whip around to face Caspian, who is still imprisoned in Cora's power. He assisted Cordelia. He knew the former empress was posing as my aunt and did nothing to stop her from hurting others.

The wrath burns deeply beneath my skin, threatening to explode around me. With no mercy, I pull Caspian from Cora's grip, and thrash him against the ocean bottom with my mind. I outstretch my hand which only helps me control the energy. The force from my body has caused him to dig into the sandy bottom leaving behind a cloud of muck.

"You've killed Praia," I hiss.

"Marina, please. She's not dead!"

I whip Caspian against the cavernous reef. He groans as his back collides with the rough wall.

"You nearly got Cascade killed. You knew Cordelia was using her body. You knew she was using Beck to distract me."

"I swear, I didn't know about Cordelia until you had already left. I would've told you—"

I slam him against the reef once more, feeling the anger grow stronger within me. "You would've told me nothing." Beneath my power, I crush Caspian into the ocean bottom. "Who are you? You're not Caspian. That sea wench and your psycho father turned you into a monster."

"You killed my father. Do you think you're any better? You murder in cold blood, yet you act like you sit high upon the throne? You're more monstrous than I'll ever be." Caspian's words are abrasive, but I feel no remorse.

I only see rage. My skin warms beneath the thought of Cordelia forcing Beck to slice his own throat, Dune stabbing and nearly killing my husband, and Cordelia stealing Praia's body. Caspian had a hand in all of it. He's just as evil as Cordelia. If he wants to follow her, he'll be punished for treason. "I killed Dune and I'll just as easily kill you. Caspian, you mean nothing to me."

"Marina—" He chokes as I slowly begin to crush him beneath my energy. I want him to feel every moment of agony. He will suffer as Praia is suffering now. He'll feel the pain both Beck and Aquarius felt. He will die a painful, merciless death for betraying my family.

As Caspian's skin turns a harsh red under my crushing power, I don't think about how he was my only friend, or how I would've trusted him with my life, or how he kissed me because he needed to know what it felt like, or how he confessed his love for me. I don't think of the Caspian I knew; I only think of the traitor he has become. This person I don't know. For this person, I have no empathy. This person I will kill and still sleep soundly tonight.

Arms wrap around my waist and force me away from my ex-best friend, but the anger is blinding. I fight against the embrace with the intent to kill. I'm thirsty for revenge.

"You need to stop this, love. Killing him won't right his wrongs," Aquarius whispers in my ear, his lips brushing against my skin. He hugs me tightly and hums a soft lullaby until I begin to calm. Cora imprisons Caspian once more with her powers. He looks weak and clinging to life.

Sam appears with his army of guards. He orders them to take Caspian to the prison caverns where he'll remain until the Council can decide his fate. The emperor rushes to his sister's side. He wraps Cascade in his arms before he swims off to the castle with her. Sam doesn't acknowledge me as he passes. I can only imagine how furious he is at me for allowing Cordelia to escape.

Aquarius kisses me on the forehead. "Caspian will be tried and sentenced. You're not a killer."

"I killed Dune." My voice is steady and calm, and my heart as cold as ice. I feel no remorse for killing Caspian's father. Should I be worried for not feeling guilty?

Aquarius kisses me again before resting his chin on the top of my head. He's silent for a moment. I can only assume he's reflecting upon his former guard attempting to murder him. "You saved me."

Tracing my fingers up his back to his neck where I intertwine my hands to embrace him, I say, "You're my king."

Chapter Twenty-Nine

[MARINA]

THE COUNCIL FEELS EMPTY without Caspian. I haven't gone to see him in the prison caverns, nor will I visit him. Caspian died when he joined forces with Cordelia. Instead, my husband sits next to me at the Council meeting as he's taken Caspian's place.

I take his hand in mine. Wade smiles when he sees I've accepted his son into my life. Aquarius brings my hand to his lips and kisses me gently.

It's been two days since I released Cordelia in order to save Cascade. Search teams have been sent to find her. There has been chaos in the kingdom. Many of the citizens have moved from their caverns in seek of hiding. The citizens are seeking a safer environment for themselves and their young children. Although, I know the kingdom is now safer without Cordelia's presence, I don't blame them for feeling paranoid. We were all living with Cordelia right beneath our tails. How could our society trust Emperor Flotsam when he couldn't sense his sister was Cordelia in disguise? This incident has been a huge blow to his image. He'll be needing to do damage control.

"The good news is I no longer feel my sister's presence here," informs Cora. Her glowing violet gaze is gentle and calming.

"The bad news is I haven't an idea where she could be hiding. Cordelia has a new body and is more powerful in her youth."

"Marina, I think it'd be best for you and Aquarius to leave the kingdom," suggests Sam with heavy shoulders. "You're an easy target while living here. Cordelia may be in hiding now, but you could very well be the first person she will attempt to contact. I want you to find a safe haven."

"No!" I'm adamant. "What was the point of training me if your plan was to send me away when there's danger? You need me."

"Cascade and I can handle it," the emperor assures me.

Cascade sneers. "I want nothing to do with this family," she states. "None of you. I will marry the prince of the Northern High Seas and that's where I will remain."

"Cascade?" Sam's voice is thick with grief.

"All of you are strangers to me. Sam, I may have grown up with you, but our bond ended the day Oceane was turned and we were enslaved. Marina, you mean nothing to me. You're the one who caused my father to become powerless. His power runs through your veins and, in my opinion, you don't deserve it. You've done nothing but put this family in danger since the day you were born."

"I won't allow you to talk to my daughter that way," Jackson snaps.

"What're you going to do? You have no abilities. You're a lost human who has no place here." Her words are callous, as is the look in her golden eyes.

"You don't really mean all that," Sam interrupts from the other side of the stone slab.

"I've had years to think while trapped within my body. Hell, I've had time to think while I've hidden away in my cavern for the last two days. This family is a curse and I won't tolerate it for one more minute. I've made arrangements to travel to the Northern High Seas tonight. I'm gone."

Sam brings his fist down upon the stone slab. "You're a Kenryk. We don't give up on family."

"This isn't my family. I haven't been a Kenryk for eighteen years."

I won't lie, Cascade's words hurt. Her anger isn't unprecedented. If I were enslaved and trapped in my body for eighteen years, I wouldn't have the nicest things to say either.

"I'm sorry for everything," I tell Cascade, sincerely meaning my apology.

She glowers. "I'm only thankful I have the chance now to rid myself of this family."

The cavern falls silent for a moment before Sam gathers himself enough to speak once again. "If that's the way you truly feel, I won't stop you. I can manage the kingdom on my own."

"The only thing you care about is your precious kingdom," Cascade snarls. Slavery has taken away any ounce of love Cascade once had for this family.

"I have people to protect! I've lost my ability as an emperor. Cordelia has taken away the trust our society had for me. So no, I don't care if you want to leave. Marina allowed Cordelia to escape in order to save your life. Do you have no appreciation for her?"

"She could've let me die." Cascade glares in my direction, our golden gazes meet. "You should've killed me and saved yourself, and saved the trouble."

"If only," I scoff. "That's final. Aquarius and I will stay in City of Zale."

"Marina," intervenes Aquarius with a gentle smile, "your uncle is right. It's best if you're hidden away."

I'm bewildered by my husband's support of leaving. "I can't leave Sam alone to defend the kingdom."

"If I may speak," interjects Cora, "I'll be staying in the kingdom to assist Flotsam in City of Zale's defense."

"Oh." My shoulders fall. For so long I've wanted to be free of my royal duties. I should be happy to start a life with Aquarius somewhere no one will find us. Though I've learned to control my powers now with more accuracy. I have trust in my gifts to protect and now I'm being ordered to hide.

"This will be good for us," promises Aquarius.

Wade clears his throat. He's been listening and absorbing the conversation without interrupting the family drama. "With you and Aquarius in hiding, I will temporarily live in City of Zale to assist the emperor," the Australian king informs us. "Bay will take my place as leader of the Australian Border until everything can be sorted."

Cascade laughs before rising with a flick of her golden tail. "I'd say good luck, but I don't want to waste my breath."

I only shake my head. I don't regret saving my aunt's life, but we're her family. Zale was all about family. He didn't know me, yet he risked everything for me. In the end he died for me.

"Your father would be so proud," I remark with sarcasm.

Cascade thrusts her tail, shoots at me, and pins me against the cavern wall with a thud. Aquarius, Jackson, Sam, and Wade react quickly, swimming to my rescue. I hold up my hand in an act to stop them. I can handle myself against Cascade. Cora smirks behind the boys. She knows my strength.

"You knew nothing of my father." Cascade shows her resentment for me.

"I know he was loyal to his family. I know he'd do whatever it took to protect his children. He died for this family. You? You're pathetic."

"My father died because of Oceane's stupidity. He died because of you."

This time, her words cause pain. I hate to relive Zale's death. "I'm sorry."

"That's it? You had a hand in the deaths of our family, and that's all you have to say?" she asks, her voice raspy.

"There's nothing more I can say. Nothing I do will ever bring Lynn or Zale back."

"Cascade, you're more than welcome to leave the kingdom now," Sam intervenes.

Cascade loosens her grip on my shoulders and swims away from me, seemingly disgusted by what our family has become.

"When I say now, I mean this minute and not a second later," informs Sam with authority in his tone. "Or do I need guards to escort you out of the kingdom?"

Cascade glowers at her brother, hesitates for a moment, but ultimately decides to keep her mouth shut. With a quick flick of her tail, she swims from the cavern.

Aquarius pulls me into his arms, holds me tightly, and places a kiss on my forehead. I hug him just as securely as he holds me. "We need to leave," he reassures me. I nod my head against his chest.

Jackson approaches us and holds his arms out for me. Aquarius releases me so I can embrace my father.

"How am I expected to leave you? The only reason you're living in this world is because of me. If I leave, you should go home. You should be with your family."

Jackson lifts my chin to face me. "You're the only family I need. Once Aquarius ensures you're safe, he'll return for me. I'll visit you with every possible opportunity."

"You're confident you have a safe place for the two of you?" Cora asks my husband. "If Cordelia even gets a clue as to where you are, she could strike at any moment."

Before Aquarius can answer, Wade intervenes. "He knows how to keep her safe. Even I don't know where Aquarius disappears to for weeks at a time."

I know Aquarius will take me to his island.

"So it's settled then," announces Sam, "the prince and princess are taking a permanent honeymoon."

. . .

[BECK]

When I wake, Bandit is at the edge of my bed, jumping with excitement. The bright sun beams through the panes of my window. As I stretch my legs, I push Bandit, causing him to grow irritated. He grunts before jumping from the bed and making himself comfortable on the floor. I rub my sleepy eyes with a yawn.

From upstairs I can smell the wafting scents of eggs and bacon. My stomach grumbles at the thought of Annie's breakfast, so I crawl out of bed and give Bandit a pat before we head upstairs.

At the table is Aubrey—scarfing down her chocolate chip pancakes. Annie sits beside her. Above the rim of her steaming cup of coffee, her brown gaze watches me with a wariness.

"What?" I ask, amused at her show of uneasiness. I grab a plate and fill it with scrambled eggs, bacon, and toast.

"You feel all right today?" She sets down her cup on the table and warms her hands on the sides. I know she's referring to my absentness from the last few days.

On the way to the table I take a bite of the greasy strip of bacon. "Yeah... Sleep has been helping." I plop down next to Aubrey. "I think I've been dealing with the aftermath of the concussion from the accident."

Annie presses her lips together, silencing herself. I lean back in my chair, chewing the rest of my strip of bacon. I swallow before smiling. "I know I've been having a hard time at school, but I blame it on the anniversary of Ethan's death coming up so fast. And I have to admit, it hasn't been easy dealing with the fact that Nate, Brian, and Tyler died while I survived by some odd miracle."

"You don't remember how you got yourself to shore?"

I quirk my eyebrow. She knows I can't remember. "No," I answer it more as a question. "The waves got the best of us…I must've been pushed to shore where I passed out."

Annie nods and folds her hands under her chin while resting her elbows on the table. "Maybe it was a mermaid," she jokes.

A laugh rises from my chest and catches in my throat. "Yeah, and Santa Claus is real," I tease as I take a mouthful of eggs.

"Santa Claus is real!" argues Aubrey.

"Of course he is," I agree as I tickle her. She giggles loudly with pancakes falling from her mouth.

Annie chuckles, dropping her gaze to her coffee. "You better get ready for school. You're suspension has been lifted."

. . .

MR. REESE PLACES A PROJECT down in front of me. For a moment, I think he's made a mistake. I didn't do this.

The project is in comic strip form. The boxes portray a scene of friends surfing. One by one they drown. The last guy—who looks eerily like me—is saved by a beautiful girl. It's clear she's a mermaid with a golden tail.

"Mr. Reese, I think you—" I begin to say, but then I notice my name in the bottom, right corner. It's definitely my sloppy handwriting.

"One second, Beck," he says as he finishes handing out the last few projects.

This can't be right. I don't remember doing this project. How can I not remember? I had to have done it...*my name* is on the project. Attached to the comic book is an essay on water-breathers. Okay, I definitely don't remember doing this.

The bell rings, dismissing first hour. The rest of the class piles out of the room, but I'm left sitting at my table with no recollection of this assignment.

"What's wrong, Beck?" Mr. Reese picks up my assignment and smirks. "Is an A-minus not good enough for you?"

"It's not about the grade." I search my mind once again for any memory of doing this, but come up empty. "You're positive this is my work?"

Mr. Reese's brows furrow, creasing his forehead. "Of course." He exhales a quick amused chuckle, almost as if he doesn't believe I'm asking. "Do you not remember? You specifically asked me if you could do the topic of merfolk."

He sets the papers back down in front of me on the table. Shaking away any doubt, I decide to read the paper in an effort to remember. "I must just be confused," I tell Mr. Reese.

"It happens." He smiles with a hint of doubt. "Really, Beck, you did excellent work. I thoroughly enjoyed the story you had to tell."

Ella watches me curiously. She usually is one of the first people to bolt when the bell rings, but she remains in her seat next to me.

"I've missed my table buddy."

I smile. "You mean you missed a juvenile delinquent?"

Ella laughs; her dark eyes light up with amusement. "Honestly, I thought you were pretty badass. Zach needed a good punch to his pretty face."

"At least someone is taking my side." I rise from my spot.

Ella rises with me. "So Mr. Reese gave us the option to work solo or with a partner on the next project. After seeing your drawings, I know I'll be screwed without your help. Do you think, I don't know… say no if you want, but—" Ella's rambling is cute, but I have to stop her.

"Do you want to be my partner?" I boldly ask.

She exhales a sigh of relief. "I'm so glad you asked. Yes!" She clears her throat. "But only for the sake of getting an A."

"Right." I smile.

"Okay, well… I'll text you!" Ella collects her books and races from class with reddened cheeks.

I gather all my books and shove the project in my notebook before rushing to my next class. I wait until lunch to read the paper I wrote on merfolk.

Vampires. Werewolves. Fairies. Elves.

But what about water-breathers? Serpents of the seas. Mermaids. Sea nymphs. Whatever they may be referred to as, we can't rule them out.

With powerful tails, pruned fingertips, and gills, they're different from the human species. Their civilization is ruled by a higher power. There isn't such a thing as democracy, but instead dictation.

The world of merfolk have little freedom and remain in hiding from the humans, frightened of our relentless species. They live within the deepest trenches and the vastest caverns.

A select few even survive solely off the souls of humans while a rare few have the ability to walk among us.

I'd be wary the next time you go swimming or meet a new acquaintance. You never know who is lurking.

I have no memory of writing this paper. This can't be my work. Why would I write about mermaids?

My concussion might've been worse than I thought.

Chapter Thirty

[MARINA]

THE ISLAND HAS SERVED as my new home for nearly a week. For the first couple days I yearned for a bit of time alone, and chose to explore the island without my husband.

The extravagant private island—which Aquarius refers to as Sylvan Cove, after his grandfather— is shaped like a half-crescent moon, with a cove surrounded by lush greenery and a sandy beach. Our modest beach hut sits in the middle of the island, directly across from the beach, nearly hidden by the beautifully green, tall trees on either side of the house. Their large leaves shelter most of the island from the sun keeping it cooler beneath the shade.

This is my home. *My home*. The home I'll share with Aquarius—my *husband*. It still feels so strange to be married, although Aquarius has been a wonderful husband.

Our humble home matches its surroundings with siding made from the trees growing tall on Sylvan Cove. The roof is made from large leaves and brush, but indeed has a strong structure beneath. There's a massive deck attached to the front of the house, complete with a strange net hanging from the posts of the deck. I still need to ask Aquarius about this bizarre piece. The view from the deck is spectacular. I could sit for hours looking at the cove and watching the waves hit the beach.

The exterior of our beach hut is deceiving. The house is small, yet somehow spacious with a vaulted ceiling, and a large sliding glass door that leads out to the back deck, allowing a view of the backside of the island. The kitchen, dining room, and living area are open with hardwood flooring running through the floorplan. The white walls brighten the small space, and the light gray furniture with the aqua accents such as the pillows and large framed photos of sea creatures, makes it feel homey.

There's only one bedroom and bathroom. The bedroom Aquarius and I share is spectacular. It's by far the best room in the house. As soon as I walk in the door, I feel as though I'm standing outside. Two of the walls and the ceiling are solid clear, glass windows, allowing a view of the ocean and the crashing waves below, along with the trees surrounding the home. The bed rests on a platform of a few stairs, cornered at an angle to face the glass walls.

The bathroom follows the theme of the rest of the house with white tiles, a deep white tub for soaking, an enormous shower, along with gray countertops, and accents of blue to give everything a burst of color. Across from the shower is the closet. Aquarius, of course, had previously purchased dozens upon dozens of outfits for me. My husband has wasted no time attempting to prep me for the human life.

As much as I love the home, one of my favorite discoveries was the backyard cliff. Sylvan Cove has a slight hike up a hill behind the house. Once I reach the top of the hill, I can leap and shift midair in order to dive deep below the Pacific Ocean, leaving me feeling ecstatic at my ability. On my second day here I discovered underwater caves and tunnels winding beneath the island and leading out to the cove.

Floating in the cove on my back staring up at the setting sun, I consider the wonders of this island and the perfection of being able to live both as a human and a mermaid.

I'm lost in thought when Aquarius finds me in my water-breather form. He swims to me as a human. Flipping on his back, he drifts beside me.

We silently watch the sky for a few minutes before Aquarius speaks. "Shift," he says.

The request takes me by surprise. "No," I respond. Aquarius knows I can't swim while in my human form.

"You need to learn the human ways if we're going to live above the Surface."

I stare at him quizzically. "Why would I need to swim as a human if I could easily shift?"

"We need to separate our life forms. When we're human, we must commit fully to the human life."

"No one is watching us here," I dispute.

"Although Sylvan Cove is a place where we can be whichever form we desire, it's good practice to choose one form. Since we're hiding, we should commit to the human form for a while."

My human form is still unfamiliar and makes me feel awkward at times. Aquarius is right, though. I know I must commit to my human form and learn the air-breather ways.

"Fine," I grumble and close my eyes. With one flick of my tail, I will myself to shift. Quickly and effortlessly, my tail splits to form two legs with feet and toes, my gills close, and my fingertips smooth out leaving behind the wrinkles. As soon as I become a human, I sink below the water's edge. Aquarius is quick to pull me above the Surface. His laughter fills the cove as I find my feet and stand on the sandy bottom.

"You must balance yourself," he advises, chuckling. "First things first, you need to keep your body flat." Aquarius leaps and begins swimming around me in circles, alternating his arm and leg movement, and taking breaths before returning his face to the water. When he abruptly stops, he advises me to lie flat in the water and try.

With my cutest smile, I ask, "Can you show me one more time?"

He smirks and raises an eyebrow at me. I can tell he thinks I'm smart enough to figure this out. "Of course," he says.

When Aquarius leaps and begins to swim again, I wait until he's close enough to me so I can jump on him and push him underwater. There's a gurgle before bubbles travel to the Surface. Aquarius shoots up and shakes water all over me. Pulling me into his arms, he swings me around, laughing the entire time. His laugh causes me to grin.

"You think you're funny?" Aquarius comes to a halt, but still holds me. "I can be funny too."

I don't like his sassy tone behind the wicked smirk. "No!" I

Ashes of the Sea

protest as he swings me once more, and let's go. I fly through the air, but I refuse to shift to prove him a point. As I hit the water, I get an idea. Creating a force field around me, I float on the water's surface. The waves crash around my force, not penetrating the field.

"No, no, no." Aquarius shakes his index finger at me. "That's cheating!"

"I believe it's called a loophole." I release the field and sink below the water. When I hit the sandy ocean bottom, I push off with my feet, and shoot back above the Surface. I land on my feet and find my balance. "With that, I believe our swimming lesson is done for the day."

Aquarius and I return to the beach, wrap up in the towels he brought down from the house, and watch the sun set before dinner.

. . .

A COUPLE OF DAYS PASS, and I can admit I've had no motivation to do anything. Aquarius has offered many times to bring me to the mainland. Australia. He wants me to visit Sydney and explore the city a bit. I've done nothing but eat the meals Aquarius cooks for us and sit in this strange net chair on our front deck and watch the waves.

Aquarius steps out the front door and asks me if I'd like to tour the Sydney Opera House tomorrow. I'm confused, of course, since I have no idea why we would want to tour someone's house.

I tell him I'm content sitting right here. He nods, but seems a bit disappointed. I'm sure Aquarius would like to venture off this island with me for a day or two.

"What is this thing?" I point to the net I'm sitting in mostly for a subject change, but also because I truly would like to know what it's called.

"The hammock?" Aquarius asks.

"The hamWHAT?"

"Hammock," he repeats with a seriousness.

"What a strange word."

He cracks a smile. "But it's fun to say, eh?"

"Hammmmmock," I drag the word out and smirk. "Kinda."

"What do you want to do today? You can't just sit here all day again."

"How dare you. My days have been very fulfilling. Like today… I'm planning on sitting here for another hour or so, take a bubble bath, maybe take a nap, and then come back to this hammock to watch the evening waves."

"Just like yesterday how you woke up, sat in the hammock, ate breakfast, sat in the hammock, ate lunch, sat in the hammock, ate dinner, sat in the hammock, and then went to bed? It's very fulfilling."

"Don't sass me."

Aquarius closes in on me, and pulls the hammock around me, imprisoning me in the net. "I'll sass you whenever I please," he jokes before kissing me through the netting. "I made grilled cheese and tomato soup, if you're hungry."

I can't deny how hungry I am. I only ate a small bowl of cereal this morning. I follow Aquarius inside to find a grilled sandwich and a bowl of red waiting for me on the table. It smells tasty, so I'm eager to try a bite.

I dig in as soon as I'm seated. The bread is crispy and the cheese oozes out the sides. I'm a little more hesitant about the soup, but spoon it into my mouth, finding it to be rather delicious.

I finish before my husband. I've noticed he's a rather slow eater. He explains it as he enjoys being able to taste his food, unlike me. I don't understand this though because I definitely taste my food.

Aquarius notices my gloom. "Are you unhappy?" he asks as he spoons soup into his mouth.

"Yes," I admit. Aquarius slumps his shoulders and swallows his soup. He looks to be saddened. "No, not with you. I'm happy here with you. It's just—"

"What?" He sets his spoon down next to his soup bowl.

"I want to go home," I admit.

"You are home."

I shake my head. "I want to go back to the kingdom. My home is City of Zale. I miss my family," I confess with a frown.

"As they miss you, I'm sure. Marina, I miss my family, too. For now, we only have each other. Once it's safe, I will return to City of Zale for an update."

I lean back in my chair, filled with frustration. "I'm no help to them while I'm here. I have powers, but I can't use them to protect the kingdom."

"It doesn't mean you can't use your gift. We're alone on this island, you can practice all you want. You're growing stronger. It's probably safe to say you're only going to become more powerful. You should learn how to control the power."

I nod. Again, Aquarius is right. I shouldn't be wasting time by sitting around for days on end. I should teach myself to control my powers. Sam is no longer around to guide me. I'm all on my own.

For the remainder of the day I practice controlling the waves, ocean currents, and creating force fields, guiding them with my mind. There are a few mishaps... I take down a tree when I accidently thrust a force field its way. The tree is ripped from the ground, it rolls down a hill, nearly taking out the Marina James— the yacht Aquarius named in my honor. I'm able to catch it with my mind before it crashes into the yacht. From the deck, Aquarius slow claps as he teasingly praises me.

"I think that's enough practice for today," Aquarius recommends.

I have to say I agree.

Although I gave up on practicing for the night, I find myself wanting to challenge myself. I want to push my powers to the limit. A couple of months ago, the only gift I obtained was the capability of healing. Now I'm capable of manipulating force fields with my mind. I've killed with my powers. I will either control my gifts or they will consume me.

When Aquarius falls asleep beside me, I gently push back the blanket, and crawl from bed without disturbing him. My bare feet pad against the cool hardwood floor. I'm guided through the house by the light from the shining moon.

Once outside the night breeze gently blows against me. My nightgown clings to my skin against the light wind. The smell of salty ocean water is in the air, and I breathe it in. This is where I feel at ease.

I let my fingertips dance through the slight wind as I raise my arms out in front of me. I can conjure force fields below the Surface, but can I manipulate the ocean with them?

This is a power Sam possesses, but he hadn't taught me yet. He had promised I'd have the same capability one day. Sam only showed me this power once by creating a whirlpool around us and pushing the water out from us. He started by creating a dome around us, forcing us to sit on the ocean bottom as the dome formed a tunnel, pushing the water aside until we could see the bright sun above the Surface.

I start by enveloping myself with my power. It exudes from me with little effort on my part. As I walk into the waves, they're pushed away and out from my feet. The waves crash against the force field instead of my body.

Outstretching both my hands with palms face out, I conjure my force, and push it out from my fingertips. First, I push the water out in front of me, stretching the barrier around me to widen out from my sides. The water begins to rise above me as I force my power further around the cove. I can tell I'm growing stronger as I'm no longer trembling with using more of my force.

The wall of energy stretches all across the cove. It takes more effort for me to push against the ocean. The power within me is resilient and the water begins to quickly rise as my barrier expands higher and higher.

As I push against the barrier, my feet sink into the soft sand of the drained ocean bottom. The energy continues to flow from deep within me, helping me control the power and the ocean.

Once I'm at the end of the empty cove and the water is a couple hundred feet high, I stop. I've proven my gift to myself. I'm more powerful than ever and will only continue to grow fiercer.

The wall of water creates a mirrored effect. My reflection looks back at me. I smile at my accomplishment. I'm learning to manipulate the ocean. I've discovered this ability without Sam's help. Aquarius believed in me and he was right. I can teach myself. I can grow without my uncle's mentoring.

My smile turns into a sobbing laughter. I feel fantastic! I'm not drained from the usage of power. If only Sam could see me right now. He'd be so proud.

As I stare back at myself something strange begins to shift in my reflection. My golden eyes glow a burning fuchsia. My skin darkens. My blonde hair turns to tentacles. My human form shifts into the body of a homicnidarian. I'm no longer looking at myself. I'm looking into the reflection of Cordelia.

I blink, but the image of my mother remains.

I begin to tremble. I lose a bit of hold on the wall of water. The ocean begins to spill back into the cove behind me.

I'm frozen with fear. Did she find us?

The hold on my power is fading. My hands shake as I attempt to control the force.

"Marina!" I hear Aquarius scream from the beach.

I don't move.

Cordelia only stares from the other side of the barrier.

Slowly, I take a step backward against the wet sandy cove. The wall follows me as I move, but the image of Cordelia follows, too.

My heart beats faster beneath my chest. I can't breathe. My head spins. Cordelia found us.

In a split second, I've lost the hold on the wall.

The last thing I hear before the waves crash around me is my husband screaming my name.

Chapter Thirty-One

[MARINA]

THE WAVES SUBMERGE ME. I'm thrust every which way as the cove floods with water. I'm slammed against the ocean bottom, hitting my head during the impact. I can't see through the dark of the water, but there's no sign of Cordelia. She has disappeared.

Suddenly, arms wrap around me. I notice the glimmer of a tail before we shoot toward the Surface. Aquarius pulls me close as I inhale a deep breath of fresh night air. Once he has pulled me to the beach, he shifts back to his human form.

"Are you okay, love?" His gentle fingers caress my chin. "What the hell were you doing out there? Why didn't you shift when you lost control of the waves?"

The memory of Cordelia is burned in my mind. Was she real?

"She found us." My bottom lip trembles as I near tears. "I saw her."

Aquarius grabs hold of me forcing me to look him in the eyes, breaking me from my trance. "It's in your head. I promise you she hasn't found us."

I shake my head, disagreeing with him. "She was directly in front of me. She was staring into my soul."

"Do you think you could've created the image out of fear?"

"No—" I pause to think. Why would *I* create her image from myself? I faded into Cordelia. Am I afraid of becoming my mother?

"Come back to bed." Aquarius rises and helps me to my feet. I'm soaked and my nightgown clings to my skin.

The beach is soaked. I must've created a mini tsunami. I notice the Marina James has washed ashore. I hang my head. What have I done?

I suddenly halt. "The yacht," I sob. Did I destroy it?

"We'll fix it in the morning." Aquarius lifts me into his strong embrace and carries me back to the house. As we ascend the hill, I see the house was untouched by my mistake. At least I didn't flood our home.

Back in our room, Aquarius sets me down on one of the steps leading to our bed. He peels my wet pajamas off before heading to find me something new to wear. I don't care about clothes. I crawl back beneath the covers and pull them to my chin. When Aquarius returns, he smiles, and tosses the new night shirt on the floor. He crawls in bed next to me and cuddles close. I feel his lips against the back of my neck before he begins gently kissing me. A chill runs through my body at the gentle affection.

"Don't wander off this time," he says.

"I'm staying right here." I flip to my other side so I face my husband. "I promise." I kiss his soft lips.

I hold him close and shut my eyes. With the comfort of Aquarius, sleep finds me quickly tonight.

. . .

I WAKE TO THE SUN shining brightly through the windows and Aquarius holding me closely. He kisses me on the forehead and the tip of my nose before laying a kiss on my lips.

"Happy birthday, my love."

I'm baffled for a moment. Is it really my birthday already? I've lost track of time. I don't think about myself much. I find myself wondering about Beck a lot. I'm curious to know how he's been doing. I wonder about Lily and Dylan. I wish I could talk to her. A friend is something I need right now. I'd like to know about their relationship, too. Not only do I think about Beck, Lily, and Dylan, but I wonder about Annie, Malcolm, and Aubrey. Are the Hudson's a normal family without me in their lives?

What about my family below the Surface? I haven't seen my father or uncle in a week. Did Aunt Cora keep to her word and stay in City of Zale to assist the emperor?

I feel so distant.

Wafting into the bedroom, I smell a sweetness. My stomach grumbles at the scent.

"I made you waffles," Aquarius says before kissing me on the cheek.

I turn to lie on my back, so I can look into Aquarius' dark gaze. "Why are you perfect?"

"Because I have you." He kisses me softly, pulling me against him. I wrap my arms around his neck, holding him tightly. He nuzzles his face into my neck, leaving behind kisses. His hair smells of the salty sea.

"I have a surprise for you," he tells me.

I let go of Aquarius. "You do?"

"Yeah!" He jumps up from bed. "But I'm hungry, so let's eat first!"

"What's my surprise though?" I ask as I crawl from bed with a tired groan. I also realize I'm naked. The shirt from last night is laying on the floor, so I pick it up, and shrug it on before following Aquarius out of the bedroom.

"Can I have it now?" My bare feet pad against the floor as I make my way to the dining table.

Aquarius serves me a plate of waffles with fresh mangos and pineapple. "You're very impatient."

I shove a forkful of waffles in my mouth. As I chew, I say "Just let me eat so I can get my surprise."

Aquarius laughs as he cuts into his breakfast and slowly takes a bite.

I roll my eyes since he'll make me wait until he finishes every single bite.

It's an agonizing twenty-eight minutes before Aquarius is done and has finished his coffee.

Leading me out to the beach, he stops before the waves. "Wait here."

Aquarius wades into the waves. "Where are you going?" I ask, anxious to know what kind of gift he could've gotten me.

"Trust me." He smiles and shifts with an effortless leap. The

Samantha Seestrom

last thing I see is his large bronzed tail disappear beneath the Surface.

The suspense is eating at me. I twist my fingers together as I eagerly wait. I'm hoping my gift is a visit from my father. I miss him immensely. If I could just give him a hug, even for a minute, it would make my birthday that much more special.

As I wait for my husband to resurface, I notice how the Marina James is still washed ashore. Unless I can get it back afloat, we won't be getting off this island in our human forms.

Surrounding the yacht with my power, I force it back toward the water. It creates a deep groove in the sand as I drag it back to the dock. Once placed back in the waves, I realize it won't stay there on its own. I had watched Aquarius tie it to the dock and anchor it, so from memory, I do the same. I'll be sure to have Aquarius double check my work.

I'm walking back to my spot on the beach when Aquarius appears, although he doesn't shift back to his human form.

I freeze at the sight of him. "Where's my gift?"

He smirks.

"Why're you smil—"

Behind him, a massive dolphin breaks the Surface, leaping high above the water, clicking and whistling, before returning below the ocean.

I take a few steps closer to the waves. I've completely fallen silent with shock. The waves reach my feet, but I don't stop. I continue to make my way into the ocean.

The dolphin leaps once again, this time swimming closer to

me when he re-enters the ocean.

Happy tears form. "Is that?"

I'm fighting the waves as I'm racing to reach the dolphin. I don't bother to shift. I'm too excited to do anything but reach Finn.

"Finn!" I scream with my voice breaking.

I'm waist high in the ocean. Finn swims to me, forcing me beneath the water from excitement. Aquarius is by my side, helping me get back to my feet.

I begin to cry as I pet Finn's smooth body. He presses his cheek to mine.

My heart is overjoyed. The tears don't stop nor do I want them to quit. I'm overjoyed!

"How?" I ask Aquarius as I sob.

As I give Finn kisses on his melon, he clicks in admiration.

"Happy birthday, my love." Aquarius kisses me on the cheek.

"You brought my baby back." I kiss my husband hard on the lips. "How did you do it? How did you save Finn?"

"I was attending a meeting in Cordelia's Caverns when I overheard her speaking to a slave. She spoke of a dolphin you were keeping as a pet. I followed you that day. After you left Finn, I took him and hid him away."

"Cordelia served him as dinner…"

"Yes, she *thought* she had served him as an entrée."

"She wanted me to believe I ate my pet, even when she wasn't sure she had the correct dolphin."

I give Finn another loving peck on the snout. He clicks and

whistles before swimming off in the cove to swim and leap. Aquarius shifts and we wade through the water back to the beach. I sit in the soft, warm sand and watch Finn play. A smile is spread across my face. Aquarius has given me the most meaningful gift.

My happiness fades when I think of Cordelia. "Aquarius, what if she finds us?"

"I promise you she has no idea I'm a hybrid. As far as she thinks, we're somewhere below the Surface. She could have slaves searching for us day and night and she'd never locate us. The island is a secret. The only one who knows the location is my mother. She used to visit her father here before he passed away."

"What if our families are in danger?"

"Cora would never let anything happen to my family and your uncle is more than capable of protecting City of Zale." Aquarius pauses to hold my hand. "I promise, Cordelia will never hurt us again."

"I know her better than anyone. She won't stay in hiding for long."

"What's her motive? She escaped. She's free with her new body. You're gone and the kingdom belongs to Emperor Flotsam. Why would she dare come out from hiding?"

"She said she wanted me to join her. Maybe this hasn't been about revenge, maybe she really wants me by her side. I don't know if she'll ever stop until she gets what she desires."

"You're safe here. Finn is safe here. We're all safe here," my husband promises with confidence.

I lean into Aquarius as his arms surround me. "I hope you're right."

. . .

I PEACEFULLY WATCH FINN play all day, even joining him for a few hours in my merfolk form. When I grow hungry and tired, I give Finn a kiss and a pat on the melon, telling him to never leave me. His home is now the cove.

I shift back to my human self and return to the house where Aquarius has set the table for dinner. The smell of steak and potatoes fill the air and my stomach grumbles.

When Aquarius is living on the island, he has a shipment of food delivered once a week by boat, from a company that operates out of Sydney. I'm thankful, too, because it seems I'm always hungry while in my human form.

Without my husband, I'd be hopeless in this world.

"You know, you should really teach me how to cook so I can be helpful around the house." I take a seat in front of a heaping plate of food. The steak is grilled to perfection and the potatoes are cut in squares served with soft carrots. Warm dinner rolls sit in a basket in the middle of the table.

Aquarius shrugs my suggestion off. "I'm not going to rush the human things. I've had many years to perfect the human world."

"Your grandpa helped you?"

"He was my mentor up until the day he died. He gave me the necessities I needed to have a life here. Without him, I'd have nothing."

Cutting into the juicy steak, I find the meat cooked a perfect medium. My mouth waters at the sight. I slice off a piece of meat and pick up a potato along with it. My taste buds roar to life at the taste of the different flavorings.

I moan as I chew. It's involuntary. I'm hungry and this is delicious. Aquarius laughs.

"I love you," I say as I chew.

"You just want me for my food." Aquarius slices up his dinner as well and takes a bite.

We take our time eating, breaking from the food to tell each other more about our upbringings. Mine is simple to explain as I grew up with Cordelia and life was a bit repetitive until I learned I was a hybrid. Aquarius confides in me about how growing up with Bay was hard since his brother hadn't inherited the hybrid gene. Bay had always been a bit jealous of his older brother, especially knowing Aquarius would inherit the throne. Bay knows he could have the throne by simply exposing Aquarius' secret. Our people wouldn't want a half-human ruling them. Bay may be an arrogant fish, but at least he's loyal.

After dinner, I decide to take a bubble bath. I love the bathroom at this time of day because the massive round tub overlooks the back of the island where there's a beautiful view of the setting sun over the horizon of the ocean waves.

I've stripped down to nothing and sunken beneath the warm bubbles when Aquarius approaches me, wearing only jeans. He leans against the doorframe with his hands deep in his pockets and a smirk plastered on his face.

"You mind if I join you, love?"

I bite my lip and smile.

Slowly, Aquarius unzips his jeans. He slides them off revealing he wears nothing beneath. I feel my face warming as I stare. Although I can't see my own reflection, I'm confident I'm bright red.

Nakedness is natural in my community, but where we're from, men's... *genitalia* isn't exposed outside of their tails. I've never seen one before. I pictured them to be odd looking, and I wasn't expecting them to be so sizable.

His blonde hair just reaches the back of his neck in soft waves. He pushes his hair back and away from his eyes, revealing his dark hypnotizing gaze. His lips are rosy and soft. As he moves, I can see the muscles in his chest and abdomen ripple. Light tufts of hair spread from his chest down to his stomach and lower...

Aquarius steps in the opposite side of the tub and sinks down in the water, facing me. I study him, not believing he's real.

"Why do I feel like you're judging me?" he asks.

I laugh. "I'm not judging you. I'm admiring you." I slide my way over to him where Aquarius pulls me onto his lap. He kisses me and I don't hesitate to return his affections.

"I can't thank you enough for bringing Finn back to me. You risked your life so I could have my baby. You had told me you jeopardized your safety for me and I didn't believe you. Had Cordelia discovered you had assisted in deceiving her, she would've enslaved you."

"Most definitely, but it would've been worth it knowing your Finn would be safe from her malicious hands."

"I've been awful to you." The regret feels heavy. I hug him, resting my face against his chest. "I'm sorry for my behavior. You've done nothing but help me, and I wouldn't accept you."

"I understand." He kisses me on the top of my head. "Beck was your priority and I stood in your way."

This is the first time Aquarius has spoken his name since we arrived on Sylvan Cove. I've been trying to forget, but I can't help but wonder about Beck. Aquarius must know I still think of him.

"You didn't stand in my way. Without you I wouldn't have been able to save him. He's free to live the life he was meant to live. He doesn't need me."

"I do though."

As much as I'd like to say I can protect myself or that I don't need anyone, it'd be a lie. I know I need Aquarius. He's the only one who was capable of talking me down from becoming a murderer and killing my best friend. He's the one who is keeping me safe from Cordelia by hiding me away on his island. He's the one who will show me the human way. He's the man who will always fight for me.

"In all of my eighteen years, I haven't experienced a better birthday. This is the first year I can celebrate being alive. Thank you for a wonderful day."

Aquarius kisses me slowly but deeply. I hold him close, clawing at his back, as he pulls me tightly against his hard body.

"We still have tonight," he whispers in my ear, sending chills through me.

Tonight Aquarius and I will truly become husband and wife finding comfort and love with each other.

. . .

Nine Months Later

[BECK]

Lily, Dylan, and I have been accepted at University of South Carolina. Dylan and Lily bought a house together off campus—well, I should say Dylan's parents bought them a house. Lily begged for me to live with them. I was all set to live on campus, but decided it would be nice to be able to bring Bandit with me. So I packed Bandit and myself up and made the drive down to South Carolina. I hated leaving Aubrey behind, but I made her a promise I'd visit every chance I could.

In our new house there are three bedrooms. Lily and Dylan will be staying in one together—which I know our parents didn't agree upon—while I'm staying in another, leaving one empty. A couple of weeks ago, Dylan and Lily interviewed possible roommates wanting to live in our house. They chose one lucky student who I've yet to meet.

I'm in my room unpacking when Dylan finds me. "How was the drive?" he asks, taking a seat on the edge of my bare bed.

"Long," I reply. "I'm glad I had a buddy with me." I gesture to Bandit who is asleep on the floor.

"Lily is really happy you decided to live with us," comments

Dylan.

As I shove clothes into a dresser drawer, I look to Dylan quizzically. "And you?"

Dylan clears his throat as he looks to the ceiling, refusing to make eye contact with me. "It'll be cool, I guess."

As I pull out a pile of clothes, I nonchalantly say, "Thank you for extending the invite for me to live here. It's a pretty sweet house." I shrug.

"No problem. Like I said, it makes Lily happy to have you here."

I look to sleeping Bandit. "I'm sure she's more excited to have the dog here."

Dylan laughs. "Hey, our new roommate is moving in today. You should probably go introduce yourself."

"I don't see why we needed another person here." I shake my head.

"My dad isn't giving me any money since he just bought the house. This sucker can pay rent and I have an instant income."

"You're not making me pay rent though."

"Nah. Lily told me I couldn't scam you. All we need from you is to chip in for food and whatnot."

Dylan continues to speak, but I completely tune him out when I shake out a sweater and out falls a picture frame and silver ring; the ring clinks against the hardwood floor. Dylan reaches for the ring while I study the framed picture of me with a blonde girl. She looks around my age, and stunning with bright golden eyes to match her wavy hair. In the picture I have my arm wrapped around her and we're both grinning. Who is this? Why do I have this picture? Most importantly, how do I not remember her?

"What?" Dylan asks as he pulls the frame from my grip and breaks my trance. He studies the photo of me and the stranger. Suddenly, his eyes widen.

"Who is she? When did I take this picture?"

Dylan thinks for a moment, pressing his lips together. "Oh!" He snaps her fingers, waking Bandit. "This is my cousin. Yeah, you met her briefly at my house last summer."

"I did? I don't remember her at all."

"She was only there for a little while." Dylan tosses the picture down on the bed.

I pick it back up to study her face. "That doesn't make any sense. I would remember her."

Dylan shrugs. "You don't seem to always have the best memory."

"Why would I take a picture with her though?"

Dylan seems annoyed when he rolls his eyes. "I don't know! It's just a picture, bro."

Carefully, I place the framed photo on my desk. "You're right." I notice the ring he holds between his fingers. I have no clue why that was wrapped up in my sweater either.

Dylan brings it closer to examine the silver. "Do you think I could give this to Lily? She has a thing for dolphins."

I nod. I know my sister would love it.

Dylan expression lightens. "Cool. I'm gonna go play some video games. Lily is picking us up dinner. I can go for whatever, so text her what you want." He pauses for a moment. "On second thought, I do feel like tacos!"

"Tacos sound good to me."

I unpack for ten more minutes before I decide to go say a hello to the new guy. If we'll be living together, I'll have to make an effort.

Our roommate is in his room, unpacking his clothes from a cardboard box. With flip-flops, shorts, a T-shirt, and a beanie, he looks like he'll be an easy going guy.

"Hey," I say, startling him. Once he calms, he smiles. His skin is tan, from Latino descent. He has gauges about the size of dimes. Around his forearm is a tattoo of a jelly fish. The tentacles wrap around his wrist and extend to each of his knuckles. That way when he spreads his hands, it looks as if the jellyfish is fanning its tentacles. Cool.

"Oh, hey," he says with a laugh.

"I'm sorry to sneak up on you." I step inside his room and extend my hand. "I'm Beck."

He looks at my hand for a moment, looking as if he's never seen the gesture before. Finally, he takes my hand in his and squeezes. "Caspian," he says, "But you can call me Cas." I release his hand. For some odd reason, I feel as though I've heard his name before. That's preposterous. I'd remember if I had met someone named Caspian.

Cas' silver gaze almost sparkles beneath the lights. What strikes me as odd though is the pink ring around his gray iris. He must be wearing colored contacts.

"I have a feeling we're going to become really great friends," Cas admits with confidence.

"I could use one of those," I confess.

"Me too."

. . .

[MARINA]

FINN SWIMS OUT IN the cove as I watch him play and jump from the water's surface. I sit in the sand with a grin planted on my lips. I've never felt so at peace. Sylvan Cove has become my sanctuary. It is the one place I can be myself and breathe without worry.

The waves wash up on the shore, soaking my feet as I watch Finn. I'm in such a trance, I don't hear Aquarius approach me from behind. He takes a seat next to me in the sand and hands me an iced cold lemonade. The warm September days have been a relief compared to the heat of summer, but there's nothing better than sipping a cold freshly squeezed lemonade while sitting on the beach.

Aquarius gently presses his hand to my slightly round belly. "How's our little one?"

I press a kiss to his soft lips as I pat my stomach. "The baby is happy."

And so am I.

About the Author

Ashes of the Sea is the anticipated sequel to *Surrender Your Soul*, along with being Samantha Seestrom's second novel. When Samantha isn't writing, you can find her working with her preschoolers as she uses her imagination to help them learn. Samantha lives in Minnesota, but is always dreaming of the ocean. She's an avid lover of mermaids, pancakes, and a boy with a dog named Bandit.

Stay connected with her:
Facebook @SamanthaWritesBooks
Instagram @samanthawritesbooks
Twitter @SamWritesBooks

99449858R00211

Made in the USA
Lexington, KY
18 September 2018